THE POWER OF POISON

THE POWER OF POISON

A Dr. Lily Robinson Novel

BJ MAGNANI

Encircle Publications
Farmington, Maine, U.S.A.

Editor: Cynthia Brackett-Vincent
Book design: Eddie Vincent
Cover design by Deirdre Wait
Cover photographs © Getty Images

Published by:

Encircle Publications
PO Box 187
Farmington, ME 04938

info@encirclepub.com
http://encirclepub.com

Printed in U.S.A.

DEDICATION

To my mother—nurse, novelist, and educator—who did not
have the opportunity to read this book before her passing.
A unique, reserved copy is on its way—to heaven.

ACKNOWLEDGMENTS

Thank you to my colleagues who were my first readers—your comments, as always, help to enrich Lily's story, and my life.

CHAPTER 1

THE TUNDRA

Kallik felt the vibrations ripple under his feet. He could see the cracks beginning to form in the ice, and the hole for his fishing pole widen. The dogs started howling, and Miska, the lead, was pulling at the sled while the swing dogs were up on their feet whining and shaking. The thunder in the sky had a fiery red tail as it raced toward the earth. Kallik put his hand up to his face to block the light from above as the object burned its way to the ground. Pressure waves from the blast knocked him off his feet, and the dogs continued their barking after the boom ceased. Brushing the crust from his eyes, Kallik struggled to stand, conscious of the pain deep within his ears. When he regained his sense of awareness, he pushed the dogs forward toward the village, only sixteen kilometers away. Miska balked, but Kallik reassured his canine partner that going home was their safest option.

The disrupted ice sheet held onto the sled's runners making the escape difficult. Kallik steered the team away from newly formed crevasses and headed south. The tundra with a landscape of desolate snow-covered lichens and mosses, morphed to dwarf trees popping out above the frost. As he neared the village, downed evergreens blocked much of his path. Kallik jumped off the sled and grabbed hold of Miska's harness, the musher now working as the lead to get them home, weaving in and around the strewn brush, stone, and ice chunks. In the distance, he could see a large crater and debris—the remains of his small village.

Man and beasts slowed the pace as they felt their muscles stiffen in the deep snow. Miska and the other dogs started salivating. Kallik, too, felt his eyes

1

tearing, and he started drooling. The sounds from his breathing slowed. His pupils shrunk, diminishing the little bit of light remaining in the northern sky, but he could still see the dogs fall to the ground, one by one, twitching and choking. Fear overtook him, and the insides of his pants became sticky while a warm stream ran down his legs, wetting his socks. When his chest could no longer expand to bring in air, he dropped to his knees, embracing the uncontrolled electrical disturbance that engulfed his brain. Still warm, Miska's body covered in dense fur provided a soft landing for Kallik. The dog's blue eyes stared lifelessly into space, missing the stunning ribbon of purple and green sky in the closing darkness. Kallik blinked for the last time as a trickle of pink slipped from his mouth.

CHAPTER 2

BOSTON

Grigory Markovic is still out there. We thought we had him, and then like smoke, he just dissipated into the atmosphere without a trace. It's hard for me to accept that the Agency failed to capture the man behind the biggest terror threat to our country. The Russians distributed ricin-laced scratch-and-sniff cards along the Northeast Corridor, the epicenter being New York City, in an attempted mass poisoning. When the pad was scratched, the whiff of scent inhaled was not of exotic perfume and essential flower oils, but instead, weaponized toxin fine enough to work its way into the smallest alveolar spaces in a person's lungs.

And it didn't end there. We also discovered ricin embedded in the glue used in the souvenir program guides for the Super Bowl. But a flawed extraction process resulted in an unstable product, ultimately leading to the degradation of the ricin, inevitably saving many lives. The authorities chose to blame the deaths on a highly virulent strain of a novel virus. It would have been difficult to tell the American people that their safe world had been penetrated by Russian terrorism. Most likely, they would have felt betrayed that they weren't informed about the actual circumstances from the beginning, so the cover-up continues. At some point, the truth will come out when the right computer is hacked.

There's a knock at my office door. It must be Lisa. She's been with me for most of my career at the hospital. As an administrative assistant, she keeps my schedule, helps plan my days, and covers for my lengthy disappearances when the Agency pulls me away. Lisa knows that I'm a professor at the medical school and that I run a toxicology consultation service at the hospital. She understands just how many questions she can and cannot ask. Today she's got on her sneakers, so she must be running around the campus taking care of a lot of business.

"Hi, Dr. Lily. Just checking in with you to see if you have everything you need."

"Thanks, Lisa," I answer. "I'm working on those book chapters that were due months ago. I'm just way behind because I've had too many outside distractions."

"Dr. Lily, you have been traveling much more than usual. Is everything okay?" she says, eyeing my snakeskin stilettos. Her eyebrows are knitted together, and her lips are swollen with ointment. Those muscular legs of hers disapprove of high-heels.

She's concerned. Not just about my shoes, but by the fact I've had more unexplained absences than usual from the hospital these last few months. Oh, and the high-heels. They're staying put. They make me feel tall, and sexy. I can't say that for the travel.

"Do you want me to leave you your schedule for the week?" Lisa says. "You have some meetings, and Dr. Kelley was looking for you a little earlier."

Kelley is my fellow; he's training for two years in toxicology post his residency program. I'll go into the lab and check in with him. He's probably got a couple of consult cases that we need to work up.

When first-year medical students enter the clinical laboratory for the first time, they are amazed and overwhelmed. There is a dizzying array of tracks and instruments flooding the room with blood-filled tubes circling the perimeter. LCD screens on the walls hold dots of rolling averages of critical analytes, so if one moves outside the recommended range, it can quickly be brought back to baseline. Kelley is leaning over a large neutral gray analyzer with a blood tube in his hand. His white lab coat has his name neatly embroidered on the right breast pocket. He sees me, pokes his glasses back up the bridge of his nose, and heads over.

"Hey doc," Kelley says, "We have a few drug consults and, wait for it," he says with anticipation, "they pulled this big larva out of some guy's forehead and want you to ID it. Apparently, this patient was traveling along the Amazon in Brazil a few weeks ago, and when he got home he noticed a lump on his scalp. He let it go for a week or two, and it ballooned to the size of a ping pong ball. When the surgeon cut into it, out popped this mother. Techs want to know if it's poisonous. Can we see that first?"

Kelley is so eager, this plump little man with a brain that works with the same precision as his favorite analyzers.

When we reach the other lab section, we find the larva residing in a Petri dish waiting for me to place and poke it under my dissecting scope. This fat blob of tissue in the shape of an oval has mandibles at one end and slits for breathing at the other. The mandibles eat their way into your flesh, and the slits remain close to the surface of your skin so the larva can get oxygen to live. If the surgeon hadn't cut it out of the man's scalp, it would have eventually burst through the skin like the creature from the movie *Alien* and finished its life cycle on the ground.

"Kelley, this is nasty but not poisonous. It's a bot fly larva. The bot fly captures a mosquito on the wing, lays its eggs on its underside, and secures the package with a bit of organic glue. When the mosquito lands on its blood meal, the heat from the warm-blooded animal—in this case, our Amazon explorer—melts the glue, and the eggs fall onto the skin. Then the parasites burrow into the warm flesh to begin the next phase of their life cycle, feasting on the host's tissue. This patient will need some antibiotics, and several weeks with images of puppies and kittens to replace those of this creature found living beneath his skin."

Kelley laughs. "That's great, doc. I left a couple of folders by your door if you want to review the drug consults before we finalize. By the way, I really like those snakeskin stilettos."

*   *   *

When I get back to my office, I check for any messages from Chad, one of my contacts from the Agency. He usually brings me my assignments. Chad replaced Pixie Dust, an agent with a pink streak in her hair, who cornered me years ago after I suffered a traumatic event in the Colombian jungle. This woman, with charisma and cunning, snared my emotions and shepherded me into this undercover world. My daughter died while I was on a field trip in the jungle collecting poison dart frogs. This not-so-insignificant fact was buried deep within my limbic system until my therapist helped me regain the lost memories of that time—horrible memories of death and devastation. We never recovered my sweet baby's body, and the guilt of that loss has plagued me for most of my life. She was my gift, my flower, and I mourn her in every moment my brain is not swamped with facts. This is why I stay busy.

It's only been a few months since I returned from New York City. I killed a man, but only after he tried to kill me—and millions of others. I took a syringe filled with concentrated aconitine and unloaded the contents into his neck. Aconitine is an ancient poison and most reliable. It stops the heart. Derived from the plant monkshood or Wolfsbane, this beautiful hooded purple flower can grow right in your back yard. That's what I do.

Poisonous plants breach the boundaries of my secret garden. Twelve square feet hidden behind my coastal cottage is all I need to coax nature's miracles to assemble molecules in such an order as to make unique toxins. It's a summer pastime I enjoy. Digging in the soil, sowing seeds of death, and harvesting a bit of terror packaged in colorful petals. It's my first choice to use nature's gifts to protect my country and other democratic nations. We weed the garden of political threats, of undeniable evil, and hope that our actions will be undiscovered. My phone rings. It's Chad. The acid in my stomach swirls, unfiltered and potent, knowing Chad will want something that defies my inner core. I listen to his voice, and my ears select only the most painful words. He confirms what I had suspected. A new mission is being planned for overseas, and they need my help. Yes, Markovic is still out there... and he knows who I am.

Chapter 3

THE COTTAGE

The weather has been the worst. The winters never seem to end, and today it's snowing without any regard or respect for spring. Still, stormy days can be irresistible to watch as the trees blow horizontally in the wind, and ducks and geese struggle to stay aloft against the invisible force.

Without much sunshine, depression sets in, and life seems darker. Sunshine actually increases the chemical serotonin in your brain, which elevates your mood and gives you that feel-good feeling. What else can give you that feeling? MDMA: 3,4-methylenedioxymethamphetamine, known on the street as Ecstasy, stimulates the brain to release more serotonin and a little less dopamine and norepinephrine. It's not surprising that some people on the bleak edge of life choose to wrap themselves in neurochemicals that transport them to a warm, happy place. For most of us, it's that bright burning globe in the sky. We wish for sunshine, a single ray through the clouds, to highlight our path forward.

I'm up at the cottage to get my head in the right place. Still shaken by the events in New York, I can't let it go. Markovic identified me in front of the concession stand while we were at the Super Bowl. It all happened so fast. We were sitting in the Agency van scrutinizing monitors that looked everywhere around the stadium when this figure lurking by the main concession stand caught my eye. I have a memory for people—silhouettes and all. This stocky, balding man and I had had a previous encounter. My curiosity and my intuition kicked in when I noticed that he was wearing an N95 mask. Highly unusual. I ran out of the van and down to the concession stand before Agent Parker even realized I'd left. When I reached the booth, Markovic was just standing there, observing the football fanatics buying their souvenirs. And then, almost mechanically, he turned and looked directly at me with those hooded dark eyes. "Dr. Robinson," he said, "enjoy flipping through pages to satisfy your curiosity." He said my name. I couldn't believe it. He knows who I am.

Somehow, he managed to elude Agent Parker and the other men, who by that time had come out of the van and into the stadium to try and snare Markovic. That Russian moved through the air like a ghost on the wind, and the team just couldn't catch up to him. I hope they know where he is now, so they can chase him down like the vermin he is. When the hounds surround the den of this trapped fox, my hope is that the master of the hunt will easily cut off his head.

It's Sunday. I have time to think about what Chad told me the other day, and plan my course over the next few weeks. The light is spectacular this afternoon. It bounces off the water with such intensity that it appears like a hot flame reflected in a mirror.

Someone's at the door.

I look through the side glass panel and see that it's the dark-haired man— my Agency field operative, my savior, my lover, Jean Paul.

"JP, what are you doing here?" I say as I open the door. My face is alight with surprise.

"Lily, I know you spoke with Chad. We have a lot to discuss."

His thick French accent always places the emphasis on the second syllable of my name, like I'm Lil-lee. I adore it.

"Come in, come in," I say, pulling him by the front of his jacket as if I'm an impatient schoolgirl.

"JP, this is truly a surprise. Things must be worse than I thought if Chad has you coming up here. It's cold out there. Would you like some tea?"

"*Ma chérie*, I'm not sure anyone should have the tea that you brew. However, I would like a nice cup of *café, s'il vous plaît*." He kisses me gently on one cheek, then the other.

We retreat to the kitchen. I don't think JP has ever come up to my cottage before, at least not while I've been here. He's about to see the inside of the "oyster shell"—the luminous mother of pearl that lines the dusky exterior. I make him a cup of coffee, dark roast, black. What was he like as a young man, I wonder? It was only just recently that I learned his full name is Jean Paul and that he grew up in the Champagne region of France. Although JP and I had worked together for many years, the Agency revealed little about him, and the other full-on operatives, to shroud their existence. Of course, they know about my academic life and use me only as a "freelance consultant," you could say.

The government mines my brain regularly in its quest for new poisons or stealthy ways to conceal the true cause of death. My encyclopedic knowledge of toxins is the nectar they desire. Yet these assassinations leave a stain on my heart, and it's only the lives I save while keeping the Hippocratic Oath that provide an overriding iridescent light to blanch that darkness. I've been trained to handle myself as a field operative, just as I have been in the field of medicine; there have been many targets, and many clinical cases, over the years. No one other than the Agency knows what I do on my "away" time, and in all those years, only John Chi Leigh, the gifted chemist from Hong Kong, had discovered my true identity—that is, until Markovic.

"JP, how's the coffee? Come, let's sit down by the fire."

"Lily, the coffee is exquisite, and the view quite extraordinary. The wind sweeps across the water as if to pile it all into one corner," he says.

He looks around the room, eyeing the jewel-tone colors that pop against the winter white. Moving away from the window, he settles on the couch closest to the fire and places his coffee mug on the table. There's a candle burning brightly, its vanilla scent hanging in the air.

"Lily, I know you are worried about Markovic. We believe he has gone back to Russia. Alexis may be there too, and we do not know if they are together. But, we have an undercover operative in Russia, *eh* Scottie, who is well integrated into that world. So, we hope that he can locate Markovic's specific operation and uncover his next move. Like a chess game, *oui*?"

Jean Paul is trying to reassure me, knowing full well he is about to ask more of me.

"*Et*, there is a new concern that the U.S. mainland may be the target of a missile attack."

I let out a gasp, take a sip of my coffee, and focus on JP's craggy face.

"We have reason to believe that the warhead of this missile will carry a devastating poison, not a thermonuclear bomb. Of course, a nuclear attack kills people and then contaminates the environment. Remember the Chernobyl disaster? The radioactive plumes showered the area making more than 2,600 km^2—*eh*, 1,000 square miles—uninhabitable. Now it's called the Zone of Alienation. That area will be contaminated for the next 300 years. But, if the missile delivers poison instead, it kills the target and then allows the attacker to inhabit the land much sooner. It is a much cleaner plan."

"JP, that's terrifying." I squirm on the couch as this thought registers in my brain—mass poisoning delivered by a warhead.

"Where do I fit in?" I ask.

"There is going to be a scientific conference in Seoul, South Korea. We believe that a Chinese scientist—a Dr. Wei Guan—may use this conference to feed the North Koreans, posing as South Koreans, information on a new, highly intricate missile design. He will be attending the conference and so will you. You are to assassinate him."

"Where? In Seoul? How's that going to happen?" I ask.

I feel uncomfortable. The room is suddenly hot. It's much harder for me to blend into Asian countries, and being inconspicuous is one of my strengths. The assassination I did in Hong Kong years ago was an international affair, so I was not out of place. I put my coffee cup on the table next to his. Mine says, "Sweetie" in bright, bold letters, while his cup says, "Lover."

"Lily, non-Asians will attend this conference, too. We will make sure that you blend in and fade out. As usual," he says.

"I know, I know, JP," I say, my voice rising, sounding hurried. "Chad did indicate a mission overseas, details to come later, but I... I guess I didn't realize I would be traveling to Asia. And so soon after New York."

I stare out the large window overlooking the water. The sky is still bright and cloudless, and a chevron of Canada geese stream by, honking their plans as they fly. They are a united front. Their formation conserves energy, reduces wind resistance, and allows the leader to fall back and let another lead until the fatigue has passed. I feel the strain.

"Lily, *ma chérie*! Are you okay? You are quiet. No doubt lost in thought."

"I'm fine, JP. Just fine." My fingers touch the stubble on his chin and then the furrows at the outer edges of his eyes. Those beautiful blue-green eyes. To me, they are hypnotic. I do love this man.

"Lily," he says as he takes my hand in his and kisses my palm, "Do not worry, I will be there. *Et*, so much information in the Asian countries is kept in silos, *eh*, no pun intended, and with this scientist eliminated, the missile program will slow down, giving the United States a chance to work on negotiations. The assassination must look absolutely natural, of course; there can be no suspicion. This is critical, *n'est pas*? Too much is at stake to have it known that the Western world made this happen."

"Got it. I understand now where the North Koreans fit in."

Here we are talking about a new mission when we haven't had closure on the previous one. Too much, too fast.

"By the way, JP, I meant to ask you earlier, what have they found out at the Hillview Reservoir in New York? We know the Russians tampered with it. I heard drilling when I was trapped in that closet with the two dead guards. It's been on the news that the New York authorities have asked most New Yorkers to use bottled water."

"We have our chemists working on it. I believe they know what the problem is. Yet they are going through every drop methodically, *eh*, so as not to miss a thing."

He has a silly smile on his face to reduce the tension in the room. So perceptive of my feelings.

"Well, I got a call from Francis Becker. You remember Becker, don't you? He's the tall pathologist from Mercy Hospital with the western drawl. We trained together in Boston. He helped sort out some of the cases from the start, having performed the autopsy on one of his staff, as well as several of the patients that died from ricin poisoning. Anyway, he's got a case he wants me to take a look at. A twelve-year-old came into his Emergency Department this morning. She's in intensive care now and not doing very well."

"What are her symptoms?" JP asks, shifting his body on the couch as if to embed himself into the cushions like a rabbit burrowing into a nest.

"Not sure. Becker was kind of vague but said he was initially called by the ED doc because there was something odd about the lab results. He wasn't quite sure what to make of it, so he wanted to run a few things by me. I have to go to New York on Monday anyway, so I'll swing by his place. Are there any other loose ends, um, other than Markovic and Alexis, that we need to discuss?"

"Lily, we had a long debriefing with your curator friend, Eric Vandermeer. It seems that Alexis had worked for the catering company for maybe twelve months. She had done several large events in Manhattan and several for the museum. It was not unusual for her to be there, and she was well known by the museum staff. Her credentials were impeccable. Eric also said that there have been sponsors of previous events that provided cash donations to the museum and had advertising literature or other information about their companies or products, so according to the staff, there was nothing out of the ordinary for the dinner that you attended at the museum that night. This was obviously a very professional, well-planned attack. And well-rehearsed."

"Do we know anything else about her? Where she came from, who else she may have been associated with, and most importantly, how did she know I am deathly allergic to lilies?"

"That I cannot answer, my Lily. We do know she is from Russia, and we do not believe she went back with Markovic. In the end, Markovic seemed on his own, and as you know, she was not able to connect with her other contact, Maxim Petrikov, either, because you killed him at the reservoir. And we believe that when she heard Maxim was dead, she may have also assumed that Markovic was dead, too. Chad has got Scottie on this. Our asset—Jackson Scott—has lived in Russia for years, speaks fluent Russian, and lives as one of them. I do not know when he will contact the Agency, or how we will contact him. All I know is that he is looking for Alexis, Markovic, or both."

"I don't understand how Markovic or even Alexis could just leave the country without a trace."

"That is because you are thinking of conventional transportation. For the right price, certain people can be hidden within cargo ships and their merchandise, and be smuggled across oceans and borders."

Out the window, there's a darkening in the sky.

"Did you see that?" I'm on my feet like a teetering Jill-out-of-the-box, and race to the window dragging the spotting scope up to the pane. I focus on the huge beast who has flown in like a dragon from the sky and lands on a small remaining triangular ice floe. The sizeable white-feathered head and tail, with talons sunk deep into a duck's back, are his hallmarks. The large menacing bill begins to rip into the lifeless fowl.

"Lily, what is going on? What have you got there?"

"JP, come have a look through the scope. It's a bald eagle about to have duck for dinner. Gorgeous creatures; that wingspan is almost seven feet."

"*Eh*, truly majestic. No wonder the founders of this nation chose such a formidable symbol for the United States of America. Such a bird of prey represents world dominance," he says.

I can see his brow scrunching up the way it does when he thinks deeply. In my heart, I know this man. Jean Paul is my soul mate, my strength, my "*raison d'être*." We spark each other's eyes.

"JP, why don't you stay for dinner. I'll make something simple. How about some *fromager d'affinois*, a warm baguette, some grapes, a veggie omelet, and a bottle of champagne."

"*Eh*, Lily. You have an amazing kitchen. This, too, is why I love you."

The atmosphere carries the afternoon shimmer as it reflects off the water. Pink and turquoise fill the sky as the light extinguishes. JP takes my hand and leads me from the window to the large fur rug in front of the fireplace. He unbuttons my blouse to reveal a black lacy treasure, and then kneels on the rug while unzipping my jeans. He kisses me, there. My black stilettos, snug on my feet, dare to balance on the dense rug. When I do fall to his level, our lips meet, and we embrace like intertwined swans. He has a masterful touch, a gentle and empowered with experience, guided by passion.

Making love with Jean Paul is like nothing I have ever known. I have spent years blocking every emotion, every human connection. One loss after another sewed my heart closed until it was almost impenetrable. Yet, JP, like a gifted surgeon, was able to remove stitch after stitch until a small trickle of love could flow from my heart again. Without me even realizing what had happened, he tapped into me with the skill of an archer, cementing our bond for life. I am forever grateful to love again, to hope again, to one day forgive myself for losing my precious daughter. My eyes shut tight at this prospect.

"My Lily," he says while kissing my eyelids, "You are not in the moment. Your body is here, but I do not have your mind. Let go, *mon amour*, be here, be with me."

I feel him wrap himself around me, and I let go. It's a beautiful free fall.

* * *

Venetian glass pendants shed soft light throughout the kitchen, stretching the fading sunlight. Thoroughly satisfied, our hearts filled, we now look to feed our stomachs.

"Lily, that omelet smells good." He bends his head over the frying pan to inhale the scent of the flavors.

"I used a little fresh spinach, chopped tomato, and some Herbs de Provence. Would you like more champagne?" I ask.

"*Mais oui*. This is wonderful. Cheese, bread, fruit, and now an omelet. Nothing could be better for a Frenchman. Lily, have you thought about this next assassination?"

"You mean, what am I going to use?"

"*Oui*, what do you think might work?" he says.

"We'll be in South Korea, right? You said the conference was in Seoul. So, I was thinking about poisoning kimchi," I say.

14

"Isn't food rather obvious?" he says. There's a funny look on his face; his eyebrows dip in question.

"I could make several people sick to produce similar symptoms, just not poison them to death. Actually, not sure what I'll do. I need to know a little more about my victim. Specifically, if he has any well-established medical conditions," I say.

"I'll make sure you have the dossier on the lead scientist, *tout de suite,*" he says.

I take half of the omelet and place it on a small turquoise blue dish—the crackles in the glaze sparkle.

"Thank you, Lily. The strawberries and orange slices on the side are a nice touch. You think of everything." He kisses me on the cheek and then places a forkful of egg in his mouth.

While Jean Paul is dining on my entrée, I'm thinking about using a potential poison that Dr. Leigh and I worked on last summer. After spending hours in the lab, we synthesized a rudimentary derivative toxin, a novel toxin, that is completely undetectable. Undetectable because no one knows it exists yet, and if we can get the toxin to be stable, it will be deadly. John Chi Leigh, my brilliant chemist friend, is capable of synthesizing and detecting any poison no matter how obscure. I've said it before—chemistry runs in John Chi's DNA. He's pure genius. Years ago, he was paid to kill me in retribution for an assassination I carried out in Hong Kong. He needed the big money they gave him to pay off his gambling debts. Yes, he's an addictive gambler. But he crossed back over the line and saved my life, rather than take it when he realized that I was the one "who fought on the side of angels." John Chi has been flying with me ever since.

I can see JP watching me as he eats his meal. Is he reading my thoughts? The dark-haired man with the blue-green eyes finishes the last nibbles, pushes himself away from the counter, and walks back to the couch to pick up a small case he brought with him. I hadn't noticed it when he came in earlier. There is no sound accompanying his movement, only silence. I can see him take out some large manila envelopes from the brief as he walks back into the kitchen.

"Lily, there is something else," JP utters almost under his breath, his eyes now looking toward space and not at me.

I shift my weight on the counter stool and regain my balance. Where is Jean Paul going with this?

"JP, what is it?" I say this with angst in my voice.

"Lily, take a look at these photographs. What do you see?" he asks.

"Okay," I say, dragging out the pause. "Where were these taken?" I pick up the photos and make an initial shuffle through the deck.

"Syria. I do not want to be too specific," he says and waits for me to review the photographs in more depth.

"It looks like some of these people have pink-tinged foam coming out of their mouths," I say as I turn one of the pictures sideways and close one eye, trying to get a closer look at the victims in the photos. "Do we have any reports from medical personnel from the field?"

"*Oui*, a few reports. Most of these victims had difficulty breathing, corneal burns, pinpoint pupils, decreased heart rate, and an odor of chlorine about them," says JP.

"It sounds like a possible mixture of an organophosphate compound and maybe chlorine gas. Organophosphates produce those kinds of symptoms, and pesticide poisonings have been reported in farmers, particularly in more rural areas. Of course, we know that sarin is one organophosphate that is much more toxic than ones used in farming and has been used previously during terrorist attacks. Now chlorine gas is a whole other story. Were there any deaths?" I ask JP. I assume that there were.

At this point, I'm curious if these photos were from the presumed chemical attacks that I had heard about a few years ago.

"*Et oui.* There were, but more importantly, I want you to look at this next set of photographs, and then I will share with you the autopsy reports."

JP hands me another packet of photographs, and this time the backdrop looks different, definitely not from a desert region of the world. There are bodies strewn about. Some are intact, others not so much. Animals, too.

16

What I can see is that they're all dead. In the distance, it looks like there was a blast or explosion. Houses look more like piles of wood and rubble.

"My God, JP. This is complete devastation. Where are these from?" I ask, worried that this is similar to the event I just viewed in the previous set of pictures. But much, much worse.

"These photographs were taken in Alaska," he says and stops as I let out a guttural sound. My eyes widen, and I can taste the acid in my mouth.

"JP, I don't understand. If these pictures are from Alaska, why wouldn't it have been all over the news?" Even I hear the pitch in my voice elevate. The implications are scary, more than scary.

"*Ma chérie,* this was a remote part of Alaska with not many inhabitants. The entire village was wiped out. We only recently discovered what happened when a government team went north to investigate the cause of some inexplicable seismic activity. That small earthquake turned out to be an explosion caused by a missile."

"Do you know where the missile come from?"

"We believe from North Korea."

My mind is racing. He hasn't shown me the autopsy reports, but having seen the photographs, I can imagine the findings.

"Lily, the missile used in this case, in Alaska, did not contain the technology that we believe Wei Guan has developed. This missile is one currently stockpiled by the North Koreans. *Et,* there is more. Our chemists found evidence of chemical weapon residue which we believe to be sarin," he says.

There is no softness to his face. I feel his concern. He hands me the autopsy reports. Scanning the title page, it's obvious that this document has been prepared by those that work in the government. A very secretive group, no doubt. There are several pages of description of the findings, and some reports contain more information than others. In addition to what's clearly described as blunt force trauma from the explosion (bits and pieces of body parts), those individuals that were intact showed evidence of severe respiratory distress leading to extensive lung congestion. I assume these patients convulsed, lost consciousness, became paralyzed, thus shutting down the muscles that helped them breathe, and then died.

"Jean Paul, I still don't understand why the American people never heard of this? Shouldn't there have been some kind of retaliatory response?" I ask.

"*Écoute*, this missile literally flew under the radar, Lily. Initially, the blast was attributed to a meteor. It was the government geologic survey team that discovered otherwise. And when they became sick—*eh*, this information is highly sensitive, and I have probably told you more than I should."

Now that I think back, I have heard of meteors from outer space striking remote regions in Siberia. Not many people pay attention to this anymore. Unless, of course, it's big enough to shift the planet out of orbit. But right now, the world is overfilled with problems that have serious consequences compared to meteors—war, political upheaval, epidemics.

"So, what you're telling me is that a rocket that contained warheads with chemical agents was fired toward the U.S.—maybe inadvertently, maybe not. And it probably came from North Korea. But no one is admitting anything."

"*Oui, ma chérie*, as you say, you have got it. You see, the new technology created by Wei Guan would allow a missile to fly lower, farther, and go undetected compared to anything on the market today. Missiles could reach further inland, and by the time they are detected, it would be too late. This technology threatens all democratic nations. With failed arms talks between the North Koreans and the U.S., the decision has been made to kill this operation at the source. We can always hope for negotiations and sanctions, but this is critical."

I'm spinning now and need some antacids. This is much scarier than I imagined. Yes, I know. I've been here before, but for some reason, it seemed less complicated. I look at JP straight on and tell him, "I'll focus on assassinating the scientist. But I would really like to know where Markovic is, JP. We haven't closed the loop on the Russians in New York, and now we're chasing a North Korea–China alliance. Oh, and please, when you do find Markovic, just shoot him. Don't wait for a poison solution."

My face feels hot, and my brain is full of new information.

"*Eh*, Lily," he says with a laugh, "I predict all roads will lead to Seoul. I am sure of it." JP has perked up, now that the hard part of his job is out of the way—letting me know what ledge I'm about to go over. His eyes are brighter.

"You do know I need time to prepare for a mission mentally. Chad didn't share a whole lot of details with me. And there's a lot here, JP."

In reality, all I have been able to do is think about Markovic since New York. Markovic is like a tick stuck under my skin. It's been there long enough to be engorged with blood, and now it's ready to explode.

"*Eh*, Lily. We will see." He moves toward me and places his hands atop each of my shoulders. "You are a complicated woman. Let us spend this night in each other's arms and worry about the world when the sun rises."

And here I am, at the intersection of obligation and conscience. One night to pretend otherwise. This night, I'm someone else, someone whose life path is so straight that the future is always there, in plain sight. I look out the window and see the moon, full in the sky, round and bright, with a ribbon of dark clouds rippled across its face like the mask of the Lone Ranger.

* * *

Morning brings me back to the path that I'm traveling—the one with sharp turns and hidden destinations.

Track 1. On time. I drag myself onto the train at the Boston station and find the quiet car. Exhausted from a frightening yet exhilarating evening, I brace myself for what's to come. Horn rims frame my eyes, and the coffee—light, no sugar—attempts to ignite my engine. It sputters. There's a hypnotic blur outside the window. Hay bales curled in snug balls lay in fields, and coastal edges trimmed with remaining ice remind me that the Northeast will hold onto winter with the grip of a New England quarterback.

I close my eyes just for a second. It's dark. I'm on the brink of a precipice, my back to the inevitable fall to my death, and in my face, the man about to drive me over that edge. Maxim. Markovic's right-hand man. My poison-filled syringe is clutched tightly in my hand. I grab his shoulder as I'm about to fall. We tangle like birds of prey, talons hooked to talons, spinning uncontrollably toward earth. Then an abrupt stop. A bump. Silence. The compartment fans above me have ceased, and the train wheels glide along the track without a sound as we slip into the station. I must have dozed off. I'm in New York.

CHAPTER 4

NEW YORK CITY

Francis Becker's quiet and predictable life had been turned upside down. His days were usually consumed with making diagnoses from small pieces of tissue or conducting an autopsy. He shared the work with few colleagues, and after his junior pathologist, Dr. Avy Bajian, died from ricin poisoning during the winter chaos, many more cases were assigned during Becker's service weeks to alleviate the staff shortage. Days were long, and by the time he reached his irrelevant apartment downtown, his fluffy cat and bottle of bourbon exhausted his remaining energy. The interjection of Lily Robinson into his neat life created feelings that stirred up his past, a past he kept trying to convince himself had long ago been buried.

Lily, Marie Washington, and Francis Becker had all trained together in Boston. Marie, a vivacious curly-haired blonde, envisioned herself one day as a prominent Chief Medical Examiner (ME) and had hoped that Francis would choose a life and career path with her. Although they dated for some years and almost became engaged, their relationship suffered from her relentless control, which Becker barely tolerated, and the ever-present Lily Robinson. Marie's ambition alienated those around her—including Becker—and her jealousy of Lily Robinson created a chasm that could not be bridged. Marie resented Lily's smoldering green eyes and sleek dark hair, her exhaustive knowledge of medicine, and the obvious feelings her man, Becker, had for Lily.

Yet, Becker understood that Lily was emotionally unavailable and focused all her energy and interest in her work. She never led Becker to think otherwise, and he never declared his feelings for her. Marie had been a satisfactory second. When Marie's career took her to New York for her fellowship, Becker reconsidered and chose not to follow, making peace over the breakup with a sigh of relief. Ultimately, he settled on a job as Chief at a New York City hospital and knew his tracks would one day cross again with Marie's. By that time, she had achieved her dream of becoming the ultimate in command at the Office of the Chief Medical Examiner (OCME). Her controlling nature, now legendary with the OCME staff, confirmed with Becker that he had made the right decision. There were no lingering doubts. Lily Robinson, however, was another story.

The sheer numbers of autopsies conducted over the winter as a result of the ricin poisoning burdened medical examiners throughout the city. These deaths added to the growing number of opioid deaths due to heroin, fentanyl, and prescription opioids that already overwhelmed all pathologists in the five boroughs who answered the call for help. Most of these hospital physicians, now deputy MEs, spent their careers autopsying the elderly dying of age-related illnesses, and not victims of drugs or poisons.

All of these pathologists, except Francis Becker, were unaware that their patients had died of an exotic toxin released on the unsuspecting masses. The Agency never fully disclosed to health officials at the various organizations, or to the OCME, the true nature of the illnesses. Health authorities attributed most of the respiratory deaths to a mutant strain of flu, a lethal novel virus, and now also warned the public to buy bottled water, suspecting that some related organism may have taken refuge in the reservoirs. Hospitals were put on notice to alert officials of any unusual sicknesses.

Francis Becker had been called by the medical staff to review the laboratory values on a child brought into the ED with abdominal pain of undetermined origin. He couldn't fully explain the results, and the opportunity, the excuse, to appeal to Lily Robinson for her input on the case was compelling. The last time he had asked for her help was with the identification of the contents of a vial of white powder found in the handbag of a dead woman. It had set forth a cascade of unexpected excitement that stimulated his intellect and awakened his dormant feelings. Francis Becker didn't know at the time Lily had already been propelled to unravel the New York mystery. Still, her involvement in his life once again seemed like a gift. The gift that might keep on giving, if he only asked. Lily Robinson would be coming by the hospital this afternoon to review his case and scrutinize the laboratory results. For one brief moment, he entertained the thought of inviting her to have dinner with him.

* * *

Had the Russians poisoned the drinking water of New Yorkers? I thought so. And there may have been two opportunities. While hiding in the bushes near the Metropolitan Art Museum, I observed an interaction between the driver of a water tanker truck and Markovic. Certain that Markovic had my ampoule filled with saxitoxin—the one John Chi and I had prepared in Hong Kong—I thought he spilled the contents into the tank staged to deliver water to the art museum. I had planned to use that toxin for an assassination. But as I was about to dial for help, Maxim enveloped me from behind, squeezing the air from my lungs, and transported an unconscious me to the Hillview Reservoir.

Later, after I was rescued from the reservoir and got the chance to tell my story, the Agency officials were directed to collect water from the storage tank suspended high above the museum roof for analysis. But there was nothing in the museum's storage tank or the water truck that caused any alarm during testing by the chemists. And, my ampoule of poison was never recovered. I always suspected that it had been taken out of my Delgado handbag by Alexis during my anaphylactic attack at the science museum a few days before and then later given to Markovic.

Once at the Hillview Reservoir, Markovic's thugs locked me inside a utility closet with the two dead security guards. When I regained consciousness, I could hear drilling outside the door. I'm convinced that Maxim and his men had tampered with something in the pump house, and although the

Russians had cleared the area so it appeared pristine, the Agency had been able to detect small metal filings beneath one of the large pipes. They focused their investigation there. The conduit above the metal filings did not look any different from the others. It was the same size, color, and consistency. But where it was threaded into the next pipe showed signs of recent wear as if it had been removed and rejoined.

* * *

At 8:06 on Sunday night, a twelve-year-old girl named Evy Chandler who had been admitted through the Emergency Department the Friday before, died. This child had been a known sickler; that is, she carried both mutant genes for sickle cell disease. She had been doing well, living at home with her mother and younger sister, but frequently experienced bouts of sickle cell crisis.

During these episodes, the pain was unbearable, and no matter how many opioids she was given, the pain just wouldn't subside. Evy's laboratory results showed that her red cells were smaller than normal size, and this was attributed to her bone marrow turning out new red cells at a faster rate than usual. When the blood sample was viewed under the microscope, there were many red cells that, instead of being round with a concave center, were folded in the shape of a sickle. These were the telltale signs of sickle cell anemia. The young girl's body was transported to the morgue after the doctors caring for her urged the mother to have her daughter autopsied. They explained that the autopsy could help answer open questions that couldn't be satisfied solely by the diagnosis of sickle cell disease.

Francis Becker was on service. He had already been contacted by one of the ED doctors when the patient was initially admitted, so he had some familiarity with the case. On Monday morning, Becker reviewed Evy's medical record, and then mentally and physically prepared himself for the autopsy. He donned a white zippered jumpsuit over his hospital scrubs, added his shoe covers, and put on his mask and goggles.

The autopsy suite was lifeless and stark, fitting for the dissection of a human body. Francis Becker closed his eyes for a moment and then focused on the corpse in front of him. A lovely dark-skinned child lay on the stainless tabletop while the diener, an autopsy assistant named Billy, waited silently. Dr. Becker nodded his head to indicate he was ready. The pathologist created a deliberate Y incision from shoulder joint to shoulder joint and down through the chest and abdomen. Billy, rib cutter in hand, knew the routine, and he and Francis Becker tangoed through their procedure as they had done hundreds of times before.

Evy Chandler's autopsy was remarkable for widespread infection and a large congested spleen. Becker took a small sample of bone marrow by puncturing the lower thoracic vertebrae using a syringe connected to a bone marrow needle. This would be important for the microscopic analysis. Several large vials of peripheral blood, heart blood, and urine were also collected for toxicology testing.

* * *

The office seemed quiet. Becker pondered the autopsy he had just completed as he reviewed his notes and tried to make sense of the case. The microscopics would be out tomorrow, and there would be ample time to preview the slides before Lily Robinson arrived in New York. Feeling concerned that he may have overreacted by contacting her for what she might dismiss as a routine case, Becker inwardly denied any selfish motives and justified the call, thinking that this death was somehow related to the poisonings last winter. What he didn't know was that he had inadvertently discovered the index case of the Hillview Reservoir's contamination, and that his feelings about both Lily Robinson and Marie Washington were about to resurface.

CHAPTER 5

NEW YORK CITY

It's hard to get your breath here. The city is so big, so crowded, sometimes just walking down the street is a challenge. No room to move, shoulder to shoulder as the masses weave like flocks of pigeons through the air over the sidewalk. Coming or going, it's tough to get around. When I leave, I always end up walking the last few blocks to Penn station on my way back to Boston. The taxis stall in traffic foiled by huge trucks, vendors' carts, and pedestrians, and never seem to get over the finish line. It's like trying to squeeze the last bit out of the toothpaste tube. Frustrating. I'm on my way to see Becker and review his case. He let me know the young girl died, and that he's already performed the autopsy. All we are waiting for now are the tissue sample slides. However, the initial blood work was done before her death, so there is some material for me to evaluate when I arrive.

I haven't been back to Becker's office since the night of the Super Bowl. Funny thing about Becker. I remember now, when we were training in Boston years ago, it was obvious he had a bit of a crush on me. Marie Washington knew it, too. And she did everything she could to make my life miserable because of it. Nasty bitch. She and Becker became a couple. It didn't last, and I didn't see any love sparks reignited over all the dead bodies last winter. It's curious that neither one of them married or had children. When your first love is unrequited, it's hard for some people to move on. Love is such a complex emotion. Disguised as neurochemicals that flood your brain, these molecules of love bind you to your mate and can make you a little crazy.

Walking into Becker's hospital feels natural. I like the buzz you get when doctors and nurses, looking crisp in their white coats or scrubs, badges dangling around their necks, scurry in and out of elevators and whisper about the patients they are on their way to see. I reach the pathology department in the lower level of the building and make my way to Becker's office. The receptionist is expecting me and leads me to his door.

"Knock, knock. Hey, Francis, good to see you," I say, kissing him on the cheek and giving him a hug.

"Lily," he says brightly, "how was ya trip comin' down?" Squeezing me a little more than my comfort level enjoys.

His eyes land on my black stiletto knee-high boots and then reel back to absorb my gray tweed suit, belted around the jacket to cinch in my waist. He's wearing black calfskin cowboy boots with fine tooling around the vamp. I can see the narrow toe peek out from under his trouser leg.

"Fine, thank you," I say.

"Lily, can I ask you about the ricin cases? What happened after New York?"

"Francis, I don't have too much to add. What I do know is that the authorities are tracking down the perpetrators and are still trying to unravel the details."

Becker doesn't know the extent of my involvement, and I have to keep it that way. It's safer for both of us. He is a colleague, but this is not *his* game. I'll break this chain now.

"So, Francis, tell me about your case. What do you think is going on?"

His eyes catch mine, and in his mind, he's thinking deeply. I feel it. He relinquishes, and we move on.

"Well, Lily, this is a twelve-year-old girl named Evy Chandler. Had a history of sickle cell disease, as you know, and spent many days in this hospital in a pain crisis. Always been severely anemic and had required multiple blood transfusions over the years. Autopsy showed enlarged spleen, and evidence of joint damage from years of hemarthrosis. I have microscopics cookin' in histology."

"Sounds like she had a tough life. Bleeding in her joints, anemia, and lots of pain undoubtedly requiring narcotics. Do you have the peripheral smear so I can look at the red cell morphology and all the other parameters?"

"I do. Why don't ya have a seat and we can look together under the double-headed microscope. The reason I want your input is that somethin' just doesn't click for me. Looks more than a sickle cell smear, but I couldn't quite put my finger on it."

"Francis, you know sickle cell disease is an inherited blood disorder where the patient has two abnormal hemoglobin genes, and as a result, the bone marrow makes hemoglobin S rather than the normal hemoglobin A."

"Right, and jess one small change, bein' the replacement of the amino acid glutamine by valine at the 6th position on the beta chain from the N terminal creates hemoglobin S," he says.

Francis was always smart—there were no flies on that boy.

"You got it. Unlike normal hemoglobin, these mutant genes produce a sickle-shaped cell in the presence of oxygen, which gets trapped in blood vessels and blocks blood flow. The resulting lack of oxygen to the tissues produces a pain crisis while damaging the body's spleen, brain, heart, kidneys, and joints."

He puts the glass slide of Evy Chandler's blood under the microscope. I can see many red blood cells stained with pink eosin that are small, and some are in the form of a crescent. Classic sickle cell disease. Then there are larger red cells, with a dusky blue hue, in the field with large blue dots inside the cytoplasm. Basophilic stippling. The concentration of these cells is more than I would expect and suggests a toxic injury to the bone marrow.

"Francis, what laboratory tests were ordered on this patient before her death?"

"I have the chart here, Lily, if you'd like ta breeze through it. Mostly tests to manage her medically through her crisis, ya know, CBC, electrolytes. Why, what are ya thinkin'?"

"Did you collect any blood at autopsy?" I ask, flipping through the paper medical record, looking for the most recent admission.

This child suffered greatly. Her paper chart is thick and bursting at the manila edges for someone who was only twelve years old. Old people have large medical files that mirror their long lives and acquired illnesses. A child's record should be thin and represent the heights and weights of the normal milestones that parents enjoy as they watch their child grow.

"Lily, I have some heart blood and peripheral blood," he says.

"Let's get a lead level. My guess is this child died of lead poisoning. I think the fact that she already had sickle cell complicated the findings because you were already dealing with a microcytic anemia. Small red cells are found in sickle cell disease, as well as in lead poisoning. But this amount of basophilic stippling is more than I would expect for simple sickle cell."

"Lead poisoning? Dang, how'd I miss that one? I'll have the lab send out the blood right away. How would she get lead poisoning?" he asks.

"That's a good question. Have you had any other patients present with similar findings?"

My mind is clicking back through time. What if this is connected to the Hillview Reservoir? All along, we've been thinking that the Russians used biologicals, but it's possible they used a heavy metal instead. Lead poisoning.

"Francis, please let me know when the results are in and when you get the bone marrow slides. Right now, I need to run. I'll check back with you later."

Becker stands up from the scope with a slight stumble, as if his leg has dropped out from under him, grabs the microscope table, and then limps to the door. His face is flush like he's embarrassed.

"Ah, Lily, it's always a pleasure to see ya," he says, recovering from his wobble and regaining composure.

"I'll send the blood downtown and have it run right quick. I'll give ya a holler when I get an answer. Um, Lily, ah, any time for a cup a coffee before ya race out the door?"

I look at his face, and his brown eyes are wide open and asking me to say yes. Is it possible that Becker still has a thing for me after all these years?

There's just something in his look and body language, the way his head is tilted forward that signals an open track. But my path is not his path, and we part ways.

"Sorry, Francis, I really do have to run. Please give me a call when you have the info."

*   *   *

I'm back at my favorite hotel in the city, The Rosewood. You know, the one with the grand lobby lined in marble, gold leaf everywhere, and lavish chandeliers hanging from the hand-carved ceiling above. Beautiful vases of roses and baby's breath surrounded by lacy ferns sit on a mahogany table in the central foyer. This is an old-fashioned hotel and what I like most is the room key. It's not a plastic card loaded with my information; it's just an old-fashioned skeleton key with an elaborate bow. Simple and elegant.

JP said I was to meet a contact here who will give me the next coordinates. The plan is straightforward enough. After New York, I'll go back to Boston for a quick go at the med school, then pack up for Hong Kong. There I will meet John Chi, and he and I will finalize the new toxin. We started working on it last year, but had some difficulty keeping it stable. With so many drugs, toxins—well, poisons—it's hard to imagine why we would need to create a new one. I have always favored the natural toxins, ones that are assembled by Mother Nature and embedded in one of her chosen creatures. These toxins are usually there for a good reason, mostly for the natural defense of the organism.

Yet, humankind has found a way to exploit many of these poisons and has used them in the art of medicine: paralyzing agents during surgery, regulators for heart rhythm, anticancer agents, and powerful pain medications. Synthesizing a new compound isn't original. Illicit chemists have been creating novel opioids, benzodiazepines, and cannabinoids for years for the black market. We did them one better. John and I have taken a natural toxin from a rare cone snail, tweaked a molecule or two, and created a completely untraceable poison. I don't want to be more specific because I don't want to give away our design. Not that we're going to patent it, but the fewer people who know about this novel toxin, the better.

As I said, we had difficulty stabilizing the compound, but now John Chi tells me it works like an assassin's dream. Instant kill, with complete heart block in fifteen seconds (that's if you get it directly into a vein). Not reversible with any of our current meds, and it has a half-life of two minutes. That means that within five minutes, most of the drug clears from the blood of the victim. We just need to get in and get out.

There's a knock at my door. Through the peephole, I see a tall man in a blue suit holding up an ID with his name and badge number. I know this man. Why didn't JP just tell me who was coming? I hear my cell phone notify me of a text on the secure line. It's JP with a message: *Jones should be at your door.* I open the door.

"Dr. Robinson, good to see you again. I'm Agent Jones," he says, knowing that this is a way to rattle me.

"So you are. Chad, I had no idea you had a last name. I've never seen you outside of Boston. Come in, come in."

The door closes behind him, and only emptiness occupies the outer hall. I wave my hand toward the small table by the window where we can sit and talk quietly.

"So, Agent Jones—or should I just stick with Chad?—I assume you're here to give me more details."

The wisps of brown hair remaining on his head have been deliberately combed to cover the emerging baldness. He looks around the room, and I see him making mental notes of his surroundings. Then he takes a seat.

"In a few weeks, there's going to be a conference of about two to three hundred scientists discussing emerging engineering technologies. The conference will be held in Seoul, South Korea, and we have word that a Chinese missile scientist, Dr. Wei Guan—you should already have his file—wants to connect with the North Koreans to sell his new technology. We think he will be at the conference posing as someone coming from one of the Hong Kong programs. He plans to pass this information to the North Koreans. We're working on the specifics of the connection now."

"Yes, JP told me as much. But why wait until he goes to Seoul? Why not get to him while he's in China?"

I use my toes to pull off each of my shoes while sitting at the table and settle in.

"It's been hard to get one of our men into China. We think it'll be a lot easier in South Korea. Also, Dr. Robinson, you and I both know that you are not known in espionage circles. You work under deep cover. The Agency thought it would be easier to slip you into the conference without much notice. I understand you are going to Hong Kong first to gather a few things. Is that correct?

"Yes. I need to pick up my new toxin," I tell him.

"Do you have a plan for its delivery?"

"I do, Chad. It'll be subtle yet effective. I have to devise a way to deliver the toxin so there will be a time delay between administration and death. I've read the dossier on Dr. Guan. I'm not sure how you get this stuff. Does the government employ unscrupulous computer hackers or undercover agents in hospitals to steal personal medical information?" I ask.

Chad looks down at the table, moves his forefinger around in a circle, lifts his forefinger, and taps the surface. Then he moves his hands to the knot on his blue striped tie and gives it a wiggle—his white shirt beams from underneath the jacket. I'm surprised he's not wearing khakis.

"Doctor, you don't need those details. Tell me more about your strategy."

"Well, in the file, I saw that Dr. Guan suffered an MI—you know, a heart attack—about two years ago. He's on a calcium channel blocker and some antiplatelet therapy."

"So, what does that mean?" asks Chad.

"Well, antiplatelet therapy helps prevent clotting if he has another heart attack or even an ischemic stroke."

"Ischemic?"

"Sorry, by ischemic, I mean reduced blood flow and, in this case, either

32

to the heart or the brain. But it's the calcium channel blocker that's going to be the key," I say.

"Ok, you lost me again. Explain."

"The heart works because it gets certain small molecules like sodium, potassium, and calcium moving in or out of certain channels in the heart muscle. Calcium channel blockers affect the way calcium moves into the heart cells and therefore decreases the heart's pumping strength. I think exploiting his heart disease makes a good cover. Foul play will not be suspected. It'll appear as a natural death."

"Okay, so, your toxin will affect the heart. You do like those heart poisons; not the first time you've used one of those," Agent Jones says as he raises his eyebrows.

"Not this one. It's a derivative of a toxin I haven't used before with an LD50 of 0.001ng/kg."

"Doctor, come on. Is that good, that LD50? I'm just an operations guy."

It's so much easier just talking to JP. At least he knows some science.

"Yes, very good, Chad. The LD50 is the lethal dose which kills 50% of the test animals. Obviously, the lower the lethal dose, the more lethal the toxin. And since it has such a short half-life, it will be cleared from the body quickly, it won't be detectable."

"But how will you deliver the poison? This is critical. You'll have to get close," he says.

"I know, I know. But I have an idea that I think will work. It better work, because if it doesn't, Dr. Guan won't be the only casualty."

This is the scary part because I haven't quite figured out all the finer details, and playing with this powerful toxin could be my undoing. I don't want to share any specifics at this point.

"You understand that if you don't kill this guy, we could have an apocalyptic war on our hands," Chad Jones says. His words are blunt.

I cringe when he says 'kill.' The goosebumps on my arms start to pierce through my blouse. My stomach churns. I get it. They need this hit, but it cannot, under any circumstances, look like an assassination. Talk about pressure. How did I get myself into this? I always ask myself this question. I just want to save patients. But the good of the many… I won't register any emotion; I just give Chad the blank stare, my woman-of-steel look. But behind my mask, I'm wishing I had my baby, my Rose. Someone to save the world for.

"I get it, Chad. I'll work on getting the toxin in Hong Kong, and then I'll head to Seoul. But first, I need to go back to Boston and take care of my students and my patients."

The table is buzzing. It's my cell phone.

"Will you please excuse me?"

I press the green icon on the phone and say, "Hello, yes, this is Dr. Robinson. Oh, hi, Francis. What's the news?"

He answers with a "howdy Lily" and then tells me that the young girl's blood results showed that she had sky-high levels of lead. I pull the phone away from my ear, and Chad and I can both hear Becker say, "Just like ya thought. Probably pushed her over the edge seein' that she was already in sickle cell crisis."

"Thanks, Francis. Could you please email me the report, too?"

I remind him that it's also important to let her family know the results right away so that her parents and any siblings can be tested for lead poisoning.

"Francis, I'll contact State officials since I've got some connections there. I really appreciate your calling me about the case. It's made a huge difference."

Then I pause, and he says, "Will do, Lily. Are ya coming back to the hospital?"

"Not today Francis. I need to take care of some other business. I'll touch base with you later."

The truth is that I don't know when I'll see Francis again. Once I let the authorities know that that child died of lead poisoning, New York City will be focused on filtering their water and sending out emergency notifications from the health department. I'll be going overseas, uncertain about the outcome.

I'm about to hang up when Francis asks me if we need to alert Marie. Marie, Marie. Probably. I'm thinking we can get public health or some other agency to work with her. Unless… Out of the corner of my eye, I can see Chad rolling his hands, indicating for me to wrap it up.

"Francis, unless you feel like talking with Marie, you could just leave it to public health to inform her office. What do you think? Since the winter, you two have been… have been… communicating regularly," I tell him, pushing the envelope.

I think he knows where I'm going with this. There is a thoughtful pause. He agrees to send me the reports, including the bone marrow follow-up, and let me contact the government.

And then he says, "Lily, next time, stay awhile."

I can hear his tone flatten as we end the call.

"Goodbye, Francis, and thank you again."

I turn and look at Chad. I've been walking around the room, talking on my phone in my bare feet. He's watching me.

"Robinson, what was that about?"

"I need to call JP right away. I think the Russians found a way to get lead into the Hillview Reservoir. It may take a while to harm healthy people, but children and compromised adults are at risk for lead poisoning."

"Why don't you let me handle that," Chad says as I work on wiggling back into my black snakeskin stilettos.

"That'll work. I have a lecture at the medical school anyway, so I've got to get back to Boston. Will you be going back, too? I guess you and I will meet once more before I leave for Hong Kong. Correct?"

"Don't worry, Robinson. You just pick your poison. The war is getting closer."

CHAPTER 6

BOSTON

Rose Moreau was excited to begin her journey in medicine. Since high school, it had been her dream when she had heard an inspirational talk about Lily Robinson's own academic medical career. Rose chose the very university where Dr. Robinson worked, and had already attended one of her lectures when the school year started. She decided at that point that she, too, would become a pathologist, the doctors' doctor.

Rose's early childhood had been marred by uncertainty and tragedy. Her presence in Colombia, South America, had never been explained, and other than her horses and her books, Rose's sister and their mother were her only companions. Adrienne Moreau was the mother Rose knew and loved, and Rose had been grateful to have such a parent in her life. In spite of the difficult life on the coffee plantation, Adrienne embodied selfless love and proved a model of strength and courage. A true dragonfly. Rose recalled her mother's encouragement to pursue her science interests even as a young girl and motivated her to continue her studies after the fateful move to the United States. Rose and her sister Bella had once been near prisoners of her mother's uncle Alberto while at the Compound, but those days were long behind her.

The coffee plantation was her great uncle Alberto's responsibility, having inherited the operation after his father-in-law, the original owner, passed away. Coffee beans were big business, but not as profitable as the hidden production in the background. High in the mountains grew the real cash crop, the coca plant, and making and selling cocaine brought both earthly riches and underworld perils. Casualties could be tallied along with the spoils, and there were many over the years. Young Bella was just one of them.

At thirteen, Bella and Rose had finally earned a trip outside the Compound for their birthdays. At the end of that remarkable day, their car was ambushed, their driver killed with a single shot to the head, and their mother Adrienne knocked unconscious. Rose had watched the nightmare unfold and her sister disappear forever.

Now, as a young woman living in Boston, Rose still thought of her sister, Bella, and her mother, Adrienne, every single day. Most often, it was when she dressed and could see the rose tattoo just below her right hip. It was that same auspicious day when she and Bella were visiting the small village outside the Compound—a tourist spot with charming cafés and novelty shops, and an unexpected tattoo parlor. The time spent there determining the design of choice for each of them ultimately defined their future and bonded them by the stroke of the pen—Rose chose her namesake flower, and Bella chose a spider.

Rose found medical school stimulating and challenging. She spent hours studying in the library, always searching for just the right book that would have all the answers to the next exam. When she wasn't reading in the library, she could be found in a small room in an apartment on Commonwealth Avenue, sharing space with two other medical students. One of her roommates came from the middle of Nebraska, cow country, while the other was from sunny Florida. Living in Boston was exciting for both of them, and when all three needed a break from their studies, there was always Haymarket Square, Faneuil Hall, or shopping at Copley.

Rose and her classmates took the Greenline branch of the T to the medical school to absorb another day of flipped classroom teaching, small group learning, and an endless bewildering medical vocabulary that they thought they would never learn. They would, of course, in time.

*   *   *

The medical students sat about midway in the lecture hall and waited for their professor to arrive. Lily Robinson entered the room, and the students quieted down. Their computers were open with the requisite case studies they had prepared the night before. Rose and her classmates took notes and tried to understand the complexities of the cases, both the clinical and pathophysiologic aspects. After the session, one of Rose's roommates pointed out the resemblance of Rose to Lily Robinson.

"Rose," she ventured forth, "you know, you look a little like Dr. Robinson. Do you see that?"

Rose had noticed the similarity between her physical attributes—raven-colored hair, fair skin, emerald-green eyes—and Lily Robinson's. This thought had not escaped Rose's keen mind.

"Yes, I see it, Claudia, but I'm sure lots of people resemble others. I think it's just one of those things."

They headed back to the library to review their work for the next day.

* * *

I enjoy teaching, although I don't know a single medical student. It's one big class with many faces. Sometimes they write to me with questions to clarify a teaching point but rarely do I ever get involved in a face-to-face conversation. Currently, I have more important things on my mind. My bags are packed for Hong Kong and parts unknown. My documents have been secured in an RFID blocking purse. Radio Frequency Identification skimming is rampant, and most of my bags contain a shield that blocks the RF signal. This prevents my personal information embedded in RFID chips from being accessed by cyber thieves, and God knows I will be heading into cyber-thievery territory.

I'm anxious to connect with Dr. Leigh. The toxin we have been working on is fully synthesized and ready for me. My job is to figure out a way to deliver it and make the circumstances of the scientist's death seem natural. It was Robert Christison who once wrote that "the crime of poisoning, from its nature, must always be a secret one." He recognized that not only did the art of secret poisoning require a dexterous toxicologist, but also a skillful physician.

CHAPTER 7

SOUTH KOREA

The link between Russia and North Korea is poison. North Korea never signed the Chemical Weapons Convention, posing a threat to global security, while Russia has been accused of its continued use of chemical weapons—even to the extent that it backed the Syrian government in its use of chemical warfare.

After New York, Markovic found a way to leave the United States in the pit of a Russian tanker. He escaped, but just barely. The Americans had identified him, and now he would be hunted across all borders. While in New York, Markovic and his team had used poison on a local scale to provoke chaos, fear, and death to the American way of life. Given his broadening knowledge of chemical warfare, he hoped to connect with those in the North Korean military and, at the same time, find a way to alter his looks to avoid capture. Markovic could pull favors to get him into South Korea, and once there, his old war comrade could solve both his other problems.

Aaron Stone had once been a dedicated United States citizen. Discharged from the army at the rank of Colonel, his leadership qualities and medical knowledge had been his strengths. Short in stature, but nonetheless sculpted, he was known for his prowess in Tae kwon do, the Korean martial art, and had achieved the designation of grandmaster. He held the 9th *dan* or black belt, and was a formidable opponent to anyone who questioned his authority. Trained as a trauma surgeon, Dr. Stone had provided medical support for the troops in places like Iran and Afghanistan. At some point during his military service, his brain suffered irrevocable psychological damage that produced a profound change in his view of the world. This transformation propelled him into a life that would undermine his own country, as he followed the path of corruption and aggrandizement. He had turned into a traitor.

Markovic was introduced to Stone in Afghanistan. The premier producer of the opium poppy, Afghanistan is also the world's leading manufacturer of illicit opium, making almost 90% of the world's supply of heroin. Back in the early days when the Soviets were in bed with the Afghans, agents from the U.S. intelligence service were known to smuggle opium out of Afghanistan to western Europe to raise money for the resistance movement swelling inside the country. There were also reports of drugs trafficked into the Soviet Union with a single objective—to weaken the country by producing a flood of drug addiction.

The Soviet Union, now Russia, wounded by the U.S. during that period, had adopted the same strategy in its current plan to compromise the U.S.—diminish the enemy with an influx of drugs creating a burgeoning opioid crisis. Markovic and Stone had crossed paths while Stone had been in Afghanistan stitching soldiers back together in the late 1980s. He had needed opiates for his surgical patients, and sometimes the only ready supply was the local crop. The troops also needed salve for wounds that were not easily sutured but required the chemical euphoria provided by heroin.

Afghanistan and the army were difficult pills to swallow. Dr. Stone, on the other hand, had developed a taste for power and used his rank and his brawn to make men cower. Even before the change in his allegiance, his first love had always been himself. Everything he did, or accomplished, was to earn the adoration of those around him. Miraculous surgeries knitting impossible pieces of flesh together, demonstrations of his head-high kicks during sparring competitions, or marksman class shooting of an enemy target were all ways to garner kudos. He didn't care about any of it. Dr. Stone was the black hole from which nothing could escape, and Markovic knew it.

After his discharge from the army, Stone moved to South Korea. He had been stationed there for a short time before Afghanistan, and he embraced an Asian culture influenced by Confucianism and profound respect for authority. Food was to his liking, and Stone's women were compliant. At one point, he married a Korean woman but left her so he could have free reign during his travels.

Dr. Stone had an impressive cover while living in Asia. Ever diligent, he obtained additional medical credentials from South Korea, allowing him to practice his trade. His growing business in plastic surgery kept him flush with cash and in contact with many Asian government officials throughout the Southeast who required his services. Rhinoplasties, commonly called nose jobs, double-eyelid surgery, and glutathione injections to slow pigmentation in the skin were his bread and butter procedures. Seoul, the plastic surgery hub of the world, had the highest rate of cosmetic surgeries per capita, and Stone was the surgeon in most demand. Markovic had kept the lines of communication open with the successful surgeon and now, years later, required his services.

*   *   *

"Dr. Stone, good to connect with you again. How is business?" said Markovic while sitting in an exam room in the clinic.

The medical clinic located in Seoul's *Apgujeong* area was attached to a small ambulatory surgical center and had two entrances. One entrance in front of the clinic was for patients with no political motives. These individuals wanted to keep their skin pale, create visually larger eyes, and change the bridge of their nose. However, there was another entrance reached by the underground from a building next door.

"Markovic, it's been years. To what do I owe the pleasure?" Stone was suspicious. Markovic had used the more secretive entrance to gain access to the clinic, indicating he was here on some surreptitious business.

"Stone, I assume you have sufficient opioids for your procedures," said Markovic in an unconvincing way.

"Markovic, don't bullshit me. What is it you want? I have patients to see."

Markovic stood up, and his eyes burrowed into Dr. Stone's face.

Stone stood his ground.

"What I want is to change my face. Can you help me or not?"

Dr. Stone took a hard look at Markovic and then cupped his hands around Markovic's chin.

"I could give you a narrower jawbone," he said, turning Markovic's head to one side, then the other, "and I could take a little off the nose. Is that what you had in mind?"

Markovic took his hands, grabbed both of Stone's wrists, and led them down to the doctor's sides.

"Something like that," said Markovic, "but I have another proposition for you involving the North Koreans."

"Not here. We're not going to talk about any other business here," Stone said. "If you want plastic surgery, then I can accommodate you, but for anything else, I will have to see you outside the office. Do you understand?"

Markovic did not appreciate the tone in Stone's voice. He looked around the sparse consultation room. Dr. Stone moved behind a small wooden desk with a computer monitor on the surface, and was boxed in by a single flat brown painted wall and three walls tiled in a brown and tan mosaic. Markovic sat down on one of the two squat leather stools placed in front of the wooden desk.

"Perhaps a change in the contour of my nose," Markovic said, now settled to the task. "And then tonight, I meet with you elsewhere."

"All right. I'll meet you tonight at 21:00 hours. There's a little American café off *Nonhyeon-ro*. Now, how soon do you want the rhinoplasty? I assume this is something you would like sooner rather than later. Concerning recovery, you'll need at least five to seven days before I can remove the splint, and then you can travel again. Your physical activity will be limited for a few weeks. Overall, let's say six weeks before you feel up to normal."

"*Da.* The sooner, the better. Fit me into your OR schedule. I will see you at 21:00 at the café," said Markovic as he stood up.

Markovic left the same way he had come while Stone sat quietly in the consultation office. The visit from the Russian had surprised him. It had been many years since the two were together in Afghanistan. Markovic's ability to move drugs across continents was well known, and the illicit narcotics had helped Stone quell the pain in his troops. At a cost. Now the "favor" was to be returned.

Some time ago, a North Korean Army General who required "delicate" surgery had traveled to South Korea using an alias. Stone had been the General's obvious choice, and the operation was a success. Now Stone required a service in return. Information did not readily travel between North and South Korea divided as they are by the Demilitarized Zone or DMZ—a 160-mile long, 2.5 miles wide border separating the peninsula near the 38th parallel. Curious as to what Markovic wanted, Stone would reach out to his contact to find out what political and military games were at play. Dr. Stone looked at his watch that dominated his right wrist, opened the drawer to the consultation table to remove the small recording device, and left the consultation room. He had patients to see.

*   *   *

The small café was brighter than Markovic had wanted. A large neon sign loomed over the counter displaying the café's name in blue and white light. Countertops, interspersed with glass displays of colorful desserts, sandwiches, and gelato lined the café's walls. Belgian waffles were on the menu along with espresso and *misugaru*, a traditional Korean drink consisting of barley, brown rice, sesame seeds, and black bean. Markovic searched the room and picked the quietest table in the darkest corner of the coffee shop. Stone was nowhere in sight.

A young man opened the café door and went directly to the counter. Markovic watched as the Korean ordered blueberry and cream cheese waffles with dark roast coffee. Out of the corner of his eye, he saw a short, muscular man with a military presence enter through the door and step behind the young man in line. When the young man stepped aside, Dr. Stone ordered two espressos, some chocolate covered almonds, and paid in cash. He brought the coffee and almonds to the table and sat next to Markovic.

"So, what is it that you need?" asked Stone. He popped a chocolate-covered almond into his mouth.

"As I told you earlier, I need to disguise my face. Interpol and the Americans are looking for me."

"And why is that?" said Stone, shifting his weight in the chair.

"We released deadly toxin in New York City last winter. And played with their drinking water, too. There was some effect, but we hoped for more. Disruption, yes. Defeat, no. *Da*, the Americans, and the North Koreans have failed talks over missile disarmament. My Chinese sources believe that arming Korean missiles with toxin rather than plutonium would be more interesting. I am happy to supply chemicals." Markovic paused, lifted the espresso to his lips, and took a sip.

"I'm listening. But first, you should have your surgery." Stone had no love for America. His patriotic days were history.

"Can you arrange for this in two days?" asked Markovic.

"I'll see what I can do. Oh, and if you want to heal faster post-surgery, I suggest you stop smoking. I can smell it on you."

Markovic's right hand instinctively dropped to his jacket pocket and felt for the pack of cigarettes.

"*Da*. I will wait for your call."

Picking up his empty coffee cup, Dr. Stone stood up from the table and walked toward the exit, stopping at the trash bin. He crushed the cup in his hand and dumped it. With a last look at Markovic before he left the café, he thought, *the Russian won't have to wait long for the call. It doesn't matter. They already know he's here.*

CHAPTER 8

HONG KONG

A dizzying skyline bursts through the billowy clouds, pink and gray over the mountain tops. Hong Kong International Airport at Chek Lap Kok dead ahead. I'm meeting with John Chi Leigh in a few hours. First stop is my hotel in the buzzy Tsim Sha Tsui district. Although touristy, I like to stay in an area surrounded by designer shops, so if there's any free time for a diversion, I can check out one of my favorite shoe stores off Canton Road and buy a pair. I've had my eye on a beautiful rainbow printed multicolor suede stiletto. These shoes will make my sheath dress with the front zipper and birds of paradise stamped on the black fabric look fabulous. I need something to fill my mind that is not associated with death.

My brain is consumed with thoughts of Leigh's new toxin, and I'm eager to go to his laboratory. Synthetic designer drugs are all the rage, yet I still have great respect for the naturally derived ones. Mother Nature was the first and most ingenious of all chemists. That's why I've brought with me a vial or two of one of her creations from my natural plant collection. Over the years, my poison garden has been one of my sources of inspiration for lethal compounds. You can live, or die, off the land. I feel the bump when the plane touches the runway, then another bump, the breaking thrust driving me into my seat. I take a deep breath.

Arriving at the hotel, I'm traveling light, for me. Just a four-wheeled roller with everything I need. Hong Kong is so cosmopolitan that I can always buy something if I need to. Walking into the lobby, I'm mesmerized by the vaulted ceiling, opulent glass chandeliers, and patterned floor tile. The clerk at the reception desk takes my passport and double-checks my reservation. The Agency has provided me with a counterfeit identity. I've used this alias before when I've had to travel for government work.

"Madame, do you want one or two keys for your room?" the clerk asks in Hong Kong English.

"I'll take one, thank you."

There's no need for a second key. I don't expect that JP will show up in Hong Kong. But then again, he doesn't seem to ever need a key to get into my space.

Simple but elegant. *More than satisfactory*, I think as I open the door to my room. John Chi should be calling me at any moment—there's the phone now.

"Hello, hello, my friend. Yes, I'm in the room now. It's great with a fabulous marble bathroom. The shower alone could fit two or three people. What? I can be ready in thirty minutes if that works. Okay. See you soon."

Leigh will pick me up in half an hour, and we'll go to the lab. The new toxin is ready.

*   *   *

"John Chi, so good to see you," I say to him as he exits his black sedan. His dark hair is cut short, and black eyeglass frames outline his eyes. Hmm, there's more gray in his hair than I remember.

Leigh is looking a little strained. I can see it in his eyes, and in his hands; his fingers are curled into the palms.

"Lily Robinson. We meet on my ground once again."

He leans toward me to deliver a hug.

"This way," he says.

47

His right arm moves away from his body into the air, indicating my place in the passenger seat of his vehicle. Of course, it's on the left and not the right side of the car. Vestiges of the British Empire.

"So, are we going straight to the lab?" I ask.

"Yes. It's Sunday, and there will only be a skeleton crew. The toxin is ready. Lily, you have not said much about how you are going to use this toxin. What are you doing?"

"Oh, I'm hoping we can develop this into a new heart drug," I tell him.

His eyes narrow, and he downshifts around the curve in the road.

"Dr. Robinson. You surprise me. I killed a man with your tea not too long ago. I know you better," he says as he shifts into fourth and shoots down the road now unfolding after the curve.

Out my window, the landscape blurs into a mixture of brown and green. There is a quiet pause between us. We are both guilty of breaking the sixth commandment. My inner demons begin to surface, and, in my mind, I see the bodies on the jungle floor. The smell of the blood-soaked steam fills my nostrils. I killed my baby. She should never have come with me to Colombia on that expedition so many years ago. Why didn't I just leave her home, safe in the U.S. with my... with my... who? I cannot escape a past that propelled me into the life I lead now. I have to save the world. My baby's already gone.

"John, the University is looking to partner with big pharma for new cardiac drugs. This novel design of the cone snail toxin would be perfect. I promise you that if it works, you will get credit on the patent and share in the research with me."

He pulls the car into a parking spot painted with Chinese characters. His name? A number? I don't know.

"We are here," he says.

The building has a light brick, perhaps a sandstone façade. A large arch graces the main entrance, and columns fan out from each side, completing a semicircle. In the center of the grounds is an artificial pond filled with koi, and wrapped with a stone walkway. We go in through a side entrance.

It leads down a long corridor, and we arrive at an office at the back of the building. I've been here before. My eye catches the tea kettle balanced on the back sideboard. Books are stacked on the floor, and wooden shelves contain older chemistry journals. Even though most literature is now online, some scientists like to have a paper journal they can hold in their hands—something tangible. There are no recent photographs of family or even any pets on his desk, a desk that looks like a piece of art. The ebonized wood, elegantly and intricately carved with serpents, acacia trees, and pagodas, contains such fine detail, a master craftsman must have created it.

I've never asked Dr. Leigh if he has any children, and he's never talked about his personal life with me. Only the shelving beyond the desk displays one old photograph of an English couple, perhaps some distant relatives on his father's side. I've not seen that before. The seat in front of his bureau beckons me to sit while Dr. Leigh assumes his chair with a lumbar cushion fashioned across the backrest. Does he experience pain when sitting? I watch him open his desk drawer and pull out a red folder, placing it on the surface.

"Here, Lily Robinson, are the details on the toxin. You will need only a small amount to make this lethal. Take protection for yourself. Now, let us go to my lab where the poison is stored. It is stable at room temperature. I have a small vial hidden in a transport thermos. I suggest that you use my laboratory and all its safeguards to prepare whatever it is you need. Follow me."

Always one step ahead. Always—one—step—ahead. Damn it! I walk out of his office without saying a word. I just happen to have everything I need with me.

CHAPTER 9

CHINA AND SOUTH KOREA

Wei Guan would be well prepared for his meeting with the North Koreans. The country just south of the northeastern provinces of China was looking for a new missile prototype that he was more than willing to provide. Russia had been playing with their own warheads, but their latest mishap did not bode well for their next deal with North Korea.

After the explosion at the Nonoksa missile testing facility that left several dead, the Russians were quietly spinning their story. No need to evacuate; the government attributed the problem to a malfunctioning nuclear reactor. In reality, a new nuclear-propelled cruise missile test had gone wrong, and calming the fears of the outside world was more difficult than it had been years ago during previous accidents like the sinking of the Kursk submarine in the year 2000. Evidence of radiation more than ten times the normal background levels had driven residents of the little village of Nonoksa in the Arkhangelsk region of northern Russia to scramble for iodine pills to save their thyroid glands. Even the port city of Severodvinsk, just twelve miles from the military testing range, showed evidence of elevated radiation levels.

Intelligence reports recognized that this Russian missile was capable of traveling any distance because it used nuclear propulsion rather than traditional fuel and could fly low to the ground, going undetected. It could also move in such a way that made it more difficult to track its end target. Known as the SSC-X-9 Skyfall by NATO or the Burevestnik (Storm Petrel) by Russia, this missile could be an incredible game-changer with Dr. Guan's modifications, and he knew it.

Wei Guan's original technology would enhance a missile's flying capabilities like the Storm Petrel, allowing it to fly further, and so far below the radar that it could not be detected until it was too late. It would also allow for chemical weapons to be harbored in the warhead. As a secretive scientist, Wei Guan had not shared his technical blueprints for the modified missile with his colleagues in China, choosing instead to store them in his genius brain and on a tiny computer chip he then had embedded in his arm. However, he let it be known that he was going to attend an engineering conference in Seoul, South Korea. His true intent was to sell the technology to the North Koreans. They had tried a Russian Storm Petrel loaded with sarin and aimed for the North Pacific Ocean as a test run, but it ended up in Northern Alaska. With Chinese technology, it could hit dead center in the heartland of America.

Wei Guan believed his homeland would be more than pleased to undermine the United States. The American White House has been deemed unstable, the U.S. government luffing in the wind, and any newly created turmoil such as a missile launch with chemical weapons from North Korea would create enough chaos to change the world power rankings. China, eager to be the top superpower, could intercede and negotiate terms. This overriding objective convinced Guan to work in isolation with the hope that his design would be a means to move his country to the peak of global politics. His government was unaware of his plan, and Guan liked it just that way.

The Chinese scientist prepared his luggage and checked his ticket for his flight to Hong Kong.

*   *   *

Markovic was all-too-prepared not only for an exchange of information but for a sale of chemical weapons. Engaging Dr. Stone as an intermediary between North Korea and South Korea would be an asset since the colonel's reputation preceded him. The great equalizer was money—poison for cash.

Markovic recalled that the ricin used in the New York assault had been created in Hong Kong by an eminent chemist and was now almost exhausted. However, Novichok agents were not. These binary chemical weapons were developed in the Soviet Union as far back as the early 1970s. He knew where he could get his hands on A-232 (Novichok-5). His colleagues had recently used this to poison Sergei and Yulia Skripal in Wiltshire, England. Markovic liked this plan because precursors for the nerve agents could be put in a munition just prior to its use, thus making the transport of the weapon much safer.

Arrangements were made to ship the Novichok agents to an address in South Korea. The ultimate destination had not yet been passed on to Markovic. When the shipment occurred, the Russian would negotiate a deal with North Korea.

Finalizing his plans, Markovic noticed his hands shaking while he made some notes. He pushed away from the wooden desk, got up, and went into the small bathroom. Looking at his reflection, he could see his raccoon eyes staring back at him and the bandage still covering his nose. Dr. Stone had chiseled just enough bone and cartilage to change his profile. Would this be sufficient to confound facial recognition programs? Markovic wasn't sure. He assumed that international authorities remained in pursuit of him, the terrorist behind the attack in New York City and beyond. He looked down from the mirror. In his hand, the pen wobbled, and a drop of sweat fell from his forehead, hitting the edge of the sink. Startled by a knock coming from outside his room, he left his image behind.

"What, what is it?" he said as he stood behind the door. "Go away; you bother me."

"Delivery for you," said the voice on the other side of the door.

Markovic didn't recognize the voice other than it sounded Korean.

"I have a package for you," said the voice.

"Leave it, leave it and go," said Markovic.

He heard the footfalls move away, waited a few more minutes, and then opened the door. On the floor was a plain brown package tied with some white string. Markovic looked around the hall and saw no one. With shaking hands, he quickly brought the box inside.

"Fuck this, where are my cigarettes?" he said and slammed the door.

CHAPTER 10

RUSSIA

Jackson Scott looked at his reflection in the mirror and approved. He tweaked his blue striped tie, pulled down the edges of his waistcoat, and slipped his suit jacket over his shoulder holster. His left hand checked that his Glock 19 was secure and reassured him that his close shave just below his high cheekbones had succeeded. Scottie, as he was known in the Agency, had been living in Russia under deep cover for many years. He had always been able to gather intelligence as needed, and tonight would be no different. A mutual acquaintance had arranged a blind date—drinks and dinner in a small café—for Scottie and a woman friend.

When Scottie arrived at the café, the woman with the long blonde hair was already waiting for him. Her bright red lipstick and scarf wrapped around her long neck indicated an elegance that Scottie rarely encountered. He was intrigued. They spoke to each other in Russian.

"*Dobryy vecher*, my name is Sasha, but I'm called by my nickname Scottie since I was a schoolboy. I'm delighted that Pavel was able to introduce us. Were you waiting long?"

"*Dobryy vecher*, Sasha, Scottie. I'm Alexis, and very pleased to meet you, too. I've been here for just a few minutes. Do you speak English? I would like a chance to use English if you do. It's good to practice."

"Of course," Scottie replied, still holding on to a Russian accent for authenticity.

"Great," Alexis said, using an American accent.

"I hear that you have no accent when you speak English. Did you go to

54

school in America?" Scottie pressed.

Alexis gave a small laugh under her breath, like a whisper.

"No, not at all; I was schooled at home, mostly. My family was multilingual, and I had the opportunity to learn many languages."

The Agency was not clear on how Alexis came to be in Russia but was certain that she had not been born there. More information was needed about her, and from her, to track down Markovic.

Scottie took his fingers and inserted them under the cuff on his shirt sleeve and pulled on it. His skin felt damp. This date—a setup from his contact Pavel with a woman that could have critical information about Markovic—felt different. Scottie didn't anticipate that he would find her alluring, even compelling, and he let his mind wander.

"Would you like a drink?" he asked.

"No, no. I don't drink."

When she thought of alcohol, she thought of Markovic and could still smell the odor of vodka from his breath. She felt a queasiness in her stomach that lingered. Markovic had deserted her, but Alexis had found a way to survive, and sitting here with this man provided proof of her independence.

"How do you know Pavel?" she asked.

"Oh, he and I work together at Global Software near the Moscow International Business Center."

"*Da*, I mean yes, the MIBC. I'm familiar with it," she said.

She felt a small drip emerging from her right nostril. Using the napkin in her lap, she patted her nose to soak up the wet. Alexis found the man opposite her attractive. His blond hair and blue eyes were almost a match for hers, and she let her body relax as she took him in. The conversation continued longer into the evening than either had anticipated, and despite its superficial nature, it was clear they had enjoyed each other's company.

A spark had been ignited between the two that night, and while Alexis chose to welcome it, Scottie chose to push it to the back of his mind. This was business. Alexis could provide a path to Markovic. The Agency's expectation included the delivery of hard evidence and required Jackson Scott to come through with something tangible. Alexis had left the dinner date with a feeling of having experienced a sense of comfort with the man she had just met. His easy-going manner drew her in and threw her slightly off-center. Although still wary of a relative stranger, she had agreed to go out with him again. With Markovic now behind her, she would fully engage with the world.

The next few dates were casual, with several lunches near the MIBC, which was Scottie's reported workplace. Alexis always managed to arrive early. Scottie would sometimes watch her through the window before entering the restaurant and admire her style, her blonde hair in a long ponytail with a twist of her own hair wrapped around the base. Scottie liked the way she threw her head back when she laughed, and he imagined kissing her long swan-like neck. She drew him in like a mermaid's siren song, and his focus started to blur. Alexis would sit and wait for Scottie to arrive at the designated spot with anticipation and all the excitement of a new connection. She laughed at the formality of his three-piece suits and the way he gently pushed his wire-rim glasses into place. She wondered what it would be like to kiss him.

Alexis' relationship shyness retreated as she spent more time with Scottie, and she opened up little by little talking about her work in a bookstore in Moscow that had floor-to-ceiling English-language books. Recent fiction, hardcovers, and paperbacks, many of the books were about art or travel to exotic places. As they walked along the Moskva River, taking in the smells of the crisp fresh air, they discovered they both shared an appreciation for art and music.

"Sasha," said Alexis using Scottie's Russian name, "have you always loved living in Moscow, or would you like to travel and see the world?"

Scottie paused for a moment. She had called him Sasha. Another lie. He was beginning to care about this woman but knew that, like him, her life was not all it appeared to be. He took her hand in his and said, "Yes, I would like to travel, with you."

Scottie had used each date to gain her confidence, but now he found himself falling for her.

*   *   *

After dinner at a trendy restaurant in an old building with high ceilings, rustic brick walls, and delicious croquettes, they swayed in unison when the lounge bar turned into a dance floor. When the bar closed, Alexis invited Scottie back to her flat. She led the way up the stairs that spiraled to the 3rd floor. Scottie held onto the banister as he followed her. He noted her shapely silhouette filling her black sheath dress, and felt the sweat beneath his collar. Stopping at flat 303, Alexis unlocked the door, thick metal with several locks, and turned, motioning to Scottie to enter.

As soon as he shut the door behind him, he could no longer contain himself. He pushed Alexis up against the living room wall, his hands on her shoulders, and kissed her. She responded and peeled off his jacket as his hand slipped beneath her skirt.

"Where's the bedroom?" Scottie asked.

Alexis took his hand and led him to a small room at the end of the flat. A brass lamp sat on the nightstand by the bed, and she switched it on. Scottie had already unbuttoned his shirt, and while removing his pants, he saw his date frozen in place.

"Alexis, what's wrong?" he said in Russian. "I thought you wanted this."

Alexis realized she had only been with one man in her short life, and that man was Markovic. It had never been a love story; it had been an assault. But Markovic deserted her, and she had feelings for Scottie that she had never experienced before. With Markovic, it had been pain and disgust. But with Scottie? She wasn't sure how to react, so she let her instincts guide her.

"I do. I do want this," she said.

Emboldened, Jackson Scott pushed Alexis onto the bed and removed her lacy bra and panties. Just below her right hip, he noticed the tattoo of a spider and wondered what kind of web he was about to enter. He kissed her breasts and stomach before he moved into her and let his powerful thrusts take over. At first, Alexis lay still underneath his large frame but soon began to move her body in rhythm with his. *So, this is what it's like?* she thought. When they both reached climax, each released a breath and clung to each other, satisfied but unsure of what had just happened.

Scottie rolled over with eyes wide open and caught a view of the room. It was small, not unlike his. On the dresser across from the bed was a single worn picture of a woman and two small girls in the photograph. It looked like something one would carry in their wallet.

"Alexis, you wouldn't happen to have a cigarette, would you?" Scottie asked. He had given up smoking, but now and then craved some nicotine.

"I do, but I have something better."

Alexis pushed the sheets from around her and went to the dresser opening the top drawer. Scottie couldn't help but notice her delicate frame and her lovely roundness.

"What have you got there?" he asked.

"It's cocaine."

Scottie was not into drugs, and clearly, the Agency would not endorse this, no matter how much they needed the intelligence. But he had already crossed the line and thought one hit couldn't hurt.

"Here," said Alexis, "just take a little and put it under your tongue and rub it on your gums."

Scottie dipped his finger into the white powder and placed it under his tongue and around his gums, as she suggested. Within minutes he could feel his heart racing and a renewed source of energy. His usually pale skin turned red, and the heat coming from his body radiated across the room. No longer a means of escape, Alexis enjoyed the cocaine high, and the two of them rekindled their sexual encounter with a greater sense of excitement.

"I can feel your heart racing," Scottie said. "Shit, it's really fast."

"*Da,* I feel yours, too. Your skin is on fire," Alexis said.

She could see that his pupils were dilated, and his eyes were wobbling uncontrollably.

After an hour or more, complete exhaustion overcame them, and they laid in their sweat and spent emotions. They were quiet, perhaps wondering if this encounter had all been a mistake. Then Scottie stirred, trying to focus on his assignment.

"Alexis, when did you start using cocaine?"

Alexis hesitated but then thought that maybe secrecy didn't matter anymore. After all, Markovic was dead. Maxim was dead. Without them, she had returned to Russia from the U.S. with only the soldiers. Not the leader or his right-hand man, just the soldiers. And then they, too, abandoned her, and she disappeared into the vastness of Russia. She was alone.

"I lived on a coffee plantation in Colombia," she blurted out. "However, my great-uncle ran a back-room cocaine operation. My mother may have been aware, I'm not sure, but I discovered the set-up when I was a child."

"Did you use cocaine at that time?"

"No, but after the kidnapping..."

"Kidnapping? You were kidnapped?" Scottie said with some alarm, now rolling over to stroke her hair in a gesture of reassurance.

"Yes, a Russian man ripped me from my home, and I spent the remainder of my teenage years growing up in Russia."

"Where is this man now?" Scottie asked.

"He's dead."

"Shit, what a nightmare. How did this *svolach* die?"

"I don't want to talk about it," she said and then got up from the bed abruptly. "I'm going to take a shower. You're welcome to join me."

Scottie had made a breakthrough but was confused about the information. *Who was the man who kidnapped Alexis? It couldn't have been Markovic because we know he is alive*, Scottie thought.

"I'll be there in a minute," he said. The torn picture atop the dresser summoned him. He found his phone in his suit jacket and photographed the image of the woman with the two little girls. *Could this be a clue to Alexis's origins?* He wondered. Jackson Scott would contact the Agency in the morning.

CHAPTER 11

SOUTH KOREA

My wig is bothering me. I'm trying not to keep pulling it down around my ears so I don't look too obvious. I picked a curly honey brown one to compliment the hazel contacts I'm wearing. I think the problem is my hair is too long, and I didn't do a great job of getting it tucked under the wig cap. I'm also nervous. I had an idea of how I would carry out this assassination, and then changed my mind. Sometimes you just have to fly and hope the wings do their job.

The banquet room for the conference luncheon is enormous, and there are dishes set out on the tables. On this one, there is Korean style marinated beef stir-fried with vegetables, stir-fried sweet potato starch noodle, oh, and I see spicy raw flying fish and squid. Maybe they're lightly steamed and not wholly raw. There's more as I survey the other tables and look around the room for my target.

I think the man I want is sitting in the corner at a small round table with a pale pink table cloth over the top set with several water glasses. He's chatting with other men, presumably scientists. I don't see many women here when I survey the room. Two large men are standing around him and appear to be wearing surveillance headsets. Is it possible these are bodyguards? I can barely make out a clear coiled wire down the back of one chunky neck. I'll need to get close so I can deliver my poison. As I'm watching, I can't help but notice that these men are deflecting any waiter with food and drink away from their man. I guess that they're concerned that the contents could be tainted. How many others in the room notice this, or is it just the poisoners?

"Would you like Eomuk?" says the server in English, but with a strong Korean accent.

"I'm sorry, what?" I say using a British accent. My attention is now focused on my immediate surroundings.

"It's a Korean fish cake ball," he says.

"No, thank you," I respond.

Food for eating is the last thing on my mind. My stomach is already on edge. Now to me, it looks like some American scientists are gathering at the far side of the room. A thicker crowd will provide cover and distraction, and I walk toward them for a closer look. Where is JP? He said he would meet me here.

Everyone is dressed in business attire, but I can see the various cultural influences in individual choices. I'm wearing a plain black suit, pencil skirt, with a long sleeve peplum top, and black stilettos with a peep toe. My small handbag has a long strap so it can cross my body from shoulder to waist. Nothing too flashy. Ah, finally, Jean Paul is here wearing attractive horn-rim glasses. Copy cat. I can see him talking to some of the non-Asian scientists. I visually scan back to the other side of the room, to that small round corner table. Where is my Chinese scientist? I look around, and someone else catches my eye. He's a stocky fellow, talking with the Koreans, but he has a definite American look to him. And he looks familiar.

I walk closer to the other side of the room to get a better look. Oh, my God. I know this man. Our paths crossed in college, and I remember he went on to become a surgeon. I'm not sure where he ultimately landed, but what in God's name is he doing here? Will he recognize me? I'm wearing a modest disguise and also sporting large tortoise framed glasses. Is it enough? Sure, it's been a long time, but then I have an excellent memory for shapes, faces, and detail—does he? Years ago, he was a martial arts fanatic and fitness guru. I heard that he had joined the army, and then I lost track of him. What was his name? It's on the tip of my tongue. His body, hard as a rock. That's it. Stone, Aaron Stone.

Lily, I tell myself, *deep breath; remain focused. Get in, get out.* Stone is not

61

near my target, so I can discreetly move around. The Chinese scientist is by himself now, and I should be able to do this. Out of the corner of my eye, I see JP move toward me, but I don't want him anywhere near me when I deliver the poison drop. His eyes try and signal me as I move closer to my mark, but I'm focused dead ahead. I'm almost there when I feel a bump, and someone grabs my arm.

"What the h—?" I blurt out.

Are they on to me? My heart starts the familiar thump. My head whips around, and I instinctively close my purse.

"Come with me now and don't say a word," he says, adding, "Let's step out into the hallway."

"My God, Jean Paul. Do you know what you've done?" I razz. "I was almost there; that was my window of opportunity. What the hell, JP?"

"We have a problem, *chérie*. Dr. Wei Guan is not at the conference," he says, now sitting in one of the two overstuffed chairs upholstered with chintz.

"What do you mean?" I say. "I thought the Chinese fellow talking with the other scientists was Dr. Guan."

"*Eh*, no. That man is a decoy who normally lives in Hong Kong. He has the same name, Wei Guan, but he is not the scientist we want. We believe he may have been asked to attend this meeting for the Chinese scientist who we are looking for," says JP.

"Jesus, JP. Are you telling me I was about to assassinate the wrong scientist? I feel sick. We should get out of here."

"Lily, right now there are protests in Hong Kong in response to the proposed extradition bill. The Hong Kong airport has been closed for two days due to the pro-democracy demonstrators blocking access. Flights have been canceled, and now there is, *eh*, much turmoil in the city. You left just before this problem interfered with travel. And we don't know if the Wei Guan we want is even in Hong Kong. We need more information."

"So, now what do we do? Do we think our Wei Guan will come to Seoul, or do we go to Hong Kong and assassinate him there?"

I hate this. We had a plan.

"We are looking at all the possibilities. You are ready nevertheless, *oui*?"

"JP, I've prepared for the delivery of this poison to be up close and personal. Either way, Seoul, Hong Kong, or wherever. And I was just in Hong Kong." My voice has that edge to it. "This doesn't seem like a very tight plan at the moment," I say.

"Lily, you know the drill. Sometimes you must *improvisez, et,* how do you say it? Fly by the seat of your pants. *Oui?*"

"Yes, I get it, but do you really think taking this one guy down will change anything?"

"Lily, Sergei Korolev was the director of the Soviet space program in the late 1950s, early 1960s."

"So, what does that have to do with our mission?" I ask him.

His blue-green eyes light up and become animated as he speaks.

"*Chérie*, at that time, the Soviets were ahead of the United States in the race for space. Sputnik was launched in 1957 as an earth-orbiting satellite. This incredible feat caught the attention of the United States. Then in April of 1961, cosmonaut Yuri Gagarin orbited the earth. The U.S. realized that they were woefully behind in rocketry, satellites, and technology. President Kennedy decided that the United States needed to demonstrate America's space superiority, and thus the race to the moon began. But remember, *eh,* they were so far behind the Russians at that time."

"I still don't see where you're going with this," I say to JP.

"Sometimes, there is one person who drives a mission. For the Soviet space program, it had been Korolev. But when he died unexpectedly in 1966, the Soviets lost their momentum—their strategic plan for the moon. You know the rest, my Lily. The Americans put a man on the moon in 1969. They beat the Soviets."

"So, what you're saying, JP, is that if we eliminate the driver of this mission, Dr. Guan, the wind will fall from the sails, and the missile attack will fail."

"Or at least lose momentum. *Oui, chérie,* you have got it. And it must, under any circumstances, look like a natural death. There can be no suspicion, no speculation of any foul play."

Yes, yes, I think to myself. *I know. I must save the world.* Then I say, "JP, we may have another problem."

"*Et,* Lily, what is it?" he asks.

"I saw a man that I think I know talking with the Koreans. He was maybe 5' 8," muscular, and looks like military. I'm sure that's Aaron Stone."

"You are correct, Lily," he says. "We were alerted a short time ago that he was here at this conference. I am surprised you know such a man. Aaron Stone has been a thorn in the side of the U.S. government ever since he retired from the army. He has been living in South Korea for many years now. We know him to be a plastic surgeon with rather, *eh,* questionable clientele. *Oui,* he could be trouble. You say you know him?"

"Yes, from my college days," I say. "Stone and I took some courses together and were part of a study group. The man is brilliant but very controlling. What's he doing here?"

"*Eh,* my best guess is that he is using his influence to make something happen. What that is, I do not know, but we will find out."

I don't dare go back into the conference hall now. The wrong Dr. Guan sits in the room, and I don't want to get anywhere near Stone. Recognizing people is not just about the color of their hair or their eyes, but it's small things like hand gestures, the way someone walks, or the cadence to their voice. In a situation like this, I try and use different accents since I'm a good mimic, and I'm conscious of my gestures.

But Stone. There he is in all his glory, just older. He's not hiding anything, and why would he? He's in South Korea at a scientific conference and the odds that he would recognize someone from his college days are pretty slim. JP is on his cell phone in the hall. I wait, my foot pumping the rug until he is finished. He looks up at me with his right forefinger raised and moving to the rhythm of my shoe tapping. Finally, he pays attention to me.

"Lily, this meeting has only just begun, and we need to locate the right Wei Guan. We cannot risk you being seen by Aaron Stone. And I need to find out what he is doing here. I have alerted the Agency, so we will see."

JP looks at me directly, and I see the crow's feet etched around his eyes grow deeper. Then he says, "*Ma chérie,* did you sleep with him?"

I feel my face getting flush. My cheeks are on fire, and I take a deep breath.

"JP, why would you ask me such a thing. What's the difference?"

"I remember every woman I have ever made love to in my life. Some men do. I believe that Stone is one of those men who remembers, I am sure. No wig or dark contacts will make him forget you, my Lily. You have a way of getting under a man's skin."

Oh shit, now what? "Well, we have to find a way around Stone. And we need the real Dr. Wei Guan. But that's your department, not mine," I say.

I know JP can feel the point of the dagger honed by the tone in my voice in his chest.

"JP, I'm going to go back to my room. I need to rework the problem if our venue changes."

I also need to blow off a little steam.

*   *   *

The retired American colonel across the room watched as Lily Robinson exited from the banquet hall. There was something familiar about her, yet intangible. It would come to him. It always did.

CHAPTER 12

FRANCE

Adrienne Rosario Moreau cherished her family chateau in Reims and felt eager to keep this part of her heritage intact. Bathed by the subtle fruity fragrance of grape blossoms, she found comfort walking in between the rows of vines planted by her ancestors. The house, too, remained surrounded by the rose bushes she knew as a little girl, and released a perfume that lingered over the house long into the cooler months. She was grateful to be home again. But by the time she returned to France from Colombia, her mother's health had significantly deteriorated. There had barely been time left to share, and Adrienne, her faith strong, prayed for her mother's wellbeing. As the dutiful daughter, she continued in the role of compassionate caregiver until finally, the aging matriarch passed away after a long illness. Adrienne once again felt abandoned and clung to what little family remained. Her daughter Rose, safe in the United States and going to medical school in Boston, brought joy to her life. Bella, dear Bella, was another story.

After Bella had been taken from her, Adrienne never heard a word about her again. She felt the loss of her natural child deeply, and although Rose provided comfort and love, Adrienne recognized she was not her flesh and blood. Unlike Bella. Presumed dead, Adrienne kept Bella in her daily prayers and hoped her daughter had not been tortured before her death. *No child could have survived that Russian monster*, she thought.

The man who stole her daughter had raped Adrienne one night more than twenty years ago on the plantation. Bella, the offspring of that violence, arrived nine months later. Even so, Adrienne loved her daughter with her whole mind and body and still grieved her absence. Her uncle Alberto had been the cause of all of this. A deal gone bad, and Bella had paid the price. Only later did Adrienne learn the Russian's name—Grigory Markovic.

Adrienne's uncle remained in Colombia in poor health, and she had not heard from him in quite some time. A few times a year, however, he did continue to send some of his men to work at the vineyard so they could help make a profit, although modest. Drug trafficking made the real money— cocaine shipped with the wines from Reims, just as it was shipped with the coffee beans from Colombia.

Adrienne needed more time to sift through her mother's belongings after her passing. She had already taken some of the clothes to a thrift shop in town and planned on donating more items to the church once she had a chance to survey the multiple rooms in the home. It was daunting seeing all of her mother's photographs, knick-knacks, treasures, and books still in drawers, on tabletops or shelves. Decisions would need to be made about what to keep and what to let go. The silver baby rattle in one drawer brought tears to Adrienne's eyes. It had been hers. Although the house had been modernized over the years, there were still many places that Adrienne had never fully explored. The buildings at the vineyard were old, drafty, and large. Looking almost like a stone cathedral, the main house roof reflected gothic architecture, and the windows appeared almost church-like; it loomed like a historical artifact in the modern world.

When her mother married into the Moreau family, she moved to the Reims estate, where her husband and his brother resided with their parents. Adrienne recalled that her mother told her that the younger brother moved from Reims to pursue a career in government. They lost touch, and at the time of Adrienne's birth, both her grandparents were deceased. Looking out one of the two attic windows, Adrienne remembered how she loved the vineyard and played among the rows and rows of vines. The only child of two loving parents, she kept herself busy with imagination and hard work. Now a mature woman, she longed again for the family she desired in her youth. The room surrounding her smelled musty and old, and a cool draft blew in through the walls. Adrienne pulled her sweater around her shoulders. There were boxes everywhere.

Not knowing where to start, she settled on one of the boxes labeled "photos." Tossing the dusty lid aside, she sifted through the black and white photographs. There were many pictures of her grandfather and grandmother, and presumably their two sons. Adrienne looked more closely at one of the photographs. She assumed the taller boy on the right in the picture was her father. Her eyes flooded with tears, her emotions anchored her to her seat—the images of the past sinking her heart. Adrienne's father died when she was only twelve, and she still missed him. To her, he had been a tower of strength—tall and handsome with his dark hair and blue-green eyes. He was striking even as a young man. She looked closer at the photograph and saw that her grandmother was wearing the ring. A family heirloom, the ring had been handed down for generations among Moreau women. It was the ring Adrienne had wanted to give Bella, but had in fact, given to Rose. A circle of gold with a red heart-shaped diamond center stone crafted by hand. Inside the ring was an engraving of a cluster of grapes and the word *amour*.

Adrienne continued looking through the box and found more photographs that intrigued her. One showed a picture of her father, now grown up, standing with his brother in the vineyard with big smiles on their faces. Nestled in his brother's arms was a small boy, perhaps two years old. Another showed her uncle and his wife holding hands with the same boy only now a little older. On the back of the picture, a faint script read *avec JP*. Curious, she kept the pictures out of the box to review later. By this time, Adrienne was thirsty and wound back down the stairs, intent on going into the kitchen for a cup of tea. When she reached the landing on the second floor, she decided instead to go into her mother's bedroom. She sat on the bed and placed her hand on the pale green silk comforter. Once again, her eyes filled with tears. She opened the drawer in the bedside table and saw her mother's Bible.

Removing the book from its resting place, she started leafing through the pages. Several Mass cards of people who had passed away over the years dropped from the spine onto the floor; one card noted her father's death. Page by page, she worked her way through the book until she reached the center of the Bible. There rested the family pedigree, and Adrienne realized that this book had been here long before her mother's time. She moved her finger along the family tree, stopping at her name, and then at the corresponding branch with another name. A boy named Jean Paul had been born before Adrienne and was the son of her father's brother. A cousin. She wondered if he was still alive and, if so, where he lived. She made a promise to herself that she would find the remnants of her Moreau family and unite them all. As for her mother's side of the family, Adrienne had already had enough of her uncle to last a lifetime.

CHAPTER 13

SOUTH KOREA

Okay, I'm fuming. Fuming, pissed off, whatever you want to call it. Yes, I slept with that bastard Stone. How dare JP ask me that. I wonder how many women he's slept with? "I remember every woman I have made love to," he said. Great. I thought we were soul mates—are we not? Trust is not easily earned. Maybe I'm overreacting. I feel the pressure. I know what I need to do. Lily, work on your fine focus, just like it's a microscope. Focus on the details of this mission.

First and foremost, I need to be in the same country as Dr. Wei Guan. Then we must meet—close range. Yes, I know what you're thinking. Why do I do this? Why can't I just give my toxins to the guys that do the killing every day? Why? Because they will screw it up. I know how to handle poisons, and they don't. It's not like the bomb squad. I'm also not on anybody's radar, well, except possibly Markovic's.

The conference is at least a week long. We're not sure if the Wei Guan we want will show up here in Seoul or somewhere else. What's predictable is that nothing is predictable. And why is Stone here? If I get back into the conference, I'll carefully study the faces of the attendees and look for any signs of plastic surgery. It's easier to see the scars if you're a physician. We know the tissue folds and where they hide the incisions.

Right now, a hot cappuccino would work for me. And, if I need a bit more distraction, there's a large shopping mall popular with foreign travelers and shoppers adjacent to my hotel near the small café just around the corner. I could use a walk.

* * *

I leave my room and stroll through the lobby. Brown and brown. Darkly stained wooden floors in herringbone waves with brown wooden columns enclosing mirrored panels. The high bright arches overhead have recessed lighting to help fight the darkness. I see they also have a spa here and an in-house café. I'll skip the walk for the sake of time and dart in here instead. The pungent smell of coffee and vanilla fills the air.

I go up to the counter to order a cappuccino with low-fat milk, and then stand to the side and wait for it to come out steaming.

"Excuse me. Do I know you?" says a voice directly behind me.

I turn, and there in front of me is Aaron Stone. I take a quiet breath.

"I don't think so," I answer in my very British accent.

My passport's under the name of MaryBeth Chadwick, address most assuredly England. I'm covering the conference for the scientific journal *Experimental Missile Science.* I have press credentials; I should be just fine. Why, then, do I feel a little scared?

"I'm sorry to have bothered you. You remind me of someone I used to know, although she had dark hair and green eyes," Stone responds.

"Not a problem at all," I answer, feeling him searching my face for a telltale clue.

Stone is cunning. As a plastic surgeon, of course he also knows how and where to look behind the mask. I step aside and turn toward the counter, ready to pick up my coffee.

"I'm having a coffee, too. Mind if I join you?" he asks.

"I'm sorry, but I do have to run. It's getting late. Good day," I say and make my way back to my room as quickly as I can.

* * *

Aaron Stone watched the woman retreat from him, holding her cappuccino in hand. He was confident that they had met before. A feeling, so familiar.

71

Yet, he just couldn't place her—for now. He decided that he would do a little detective work later and review the symposium's attendance list. This diversion would not steer him off his primary objective.

After Stone had met with Markovic and then spoke with his North Korean contact, he learned that a Chinese aeronautic engineer planned to deliver a blueprint for a new missile design to the North Koreans. The involved parties set the exchange of information for money in Hong Kong, not Seoul. The decoy attending the Seoul conference via a generous travel grant was an engineer in his own right sharing only a name: Wei Guan, a name some thought, was as common as John Jones.

Back in Russia, Markovic had heard rumors of a particular meeting in Seoul, where a Chinese scientist planned to meet with the North Koreans. He smelled an opportunity and came to South Korea, seeking help from his old associate Dr. Aaron Stone.

Markovic told him that he had chemical weapons to sell and reminded Stone that he owed him. Afghanistan lingered between them, and Stone was asked to repay his debt to the Russian. Thinking it all through while sitting in the café, he drank his latte, his biceps bulging each time he brought the cup to his lips.

When he finished, he went into the conference registration area and asked for a list of attendees. With the booklet in hand, he quickly scanned the names. Nothing stood out. Then he looked through the short vendor list and found nothing familiar there either. Not a man to give up easily, Stone felt sure he could smoke her out. It was just a matter of time.

* * *

I just got back to my room. Stone is going to be a problem, so I get out my secure phone to call JP.

"JP, yes, it's me. I need to speak with you right away. Can you come to my room?"

He lets me know he'll be right over after he finishes with some other business. I mentally review what toxins I have with me, thinking about what would be best. The collection looks benign to the uninformed, but the liquid extracts in the vials contain some different poisons that I have at my disposal. There's a knock at the door that separates our adjoining rooms.

"Come in," I say, as he quickly brushes past me and moves toward the chairs near the desk.

"Lily, what is it? What is going on?" he asks.

"It's Stone. I'm pretty sure he's on to me. He may not have my name just yet, but he will get there. That man is cold, clever, and cunning. This could really mess things up, but I have a plan."

"*Mais oui.* Of course, you do. And what poison would that be?"

"Poison, yes—death, no. I think I might be able to doctor his food so that he gets sick, very sick. Perhaps enough to take him out of the game."

"You have such a poison with you?" JP asks.

"*Mais oui, mon cher.* I have just the thing," I tell him.

I walk over to the closet, slide the door open to reveal the rack of clothes and shoes in a row on the floor, and the hotel safe nestled tightly in the corner. Punching in the code on the keypad, the door springs open, and I remove a small ampule from a black zippered bag. One of my many "medicines".

"This is what I will use," I say as I hold the vial up to the light. "This should do the trick."

"*Ma chérie*, how will you titrate the dose? If you overshoot and start killing people, you will surely blow our cover. We must be extremely careful."

"I know, trust me. I know what I'm doing," I reply. "Look, JP, I've done the calculations. I know the LD50 for this poison, too. I just need access to the food that Stone will eat. I'm sure he likes Korean food, but I recall he also likes a good breakfast and a late-night snack."

JP is thinking, an eyebrow shoots up. Before he can answer, I ask, "Do we have someone on our side in the kitchen?"

"We do, but hotel security can sometimes set up camp there," he says.

I wonder if that's routine, or if there is some concern with this recent meeting of scientists.

"Let me see the room service menu," I ask JP.

The booklet with the lists of hotel services, including the menu, sits on the desk, and he takes it to hand it over. I'm about to go through it when he wraps his arms around me.

"You know we are alone, *ma chérie*," he says as he kisses the length of my neck.

It's been said that when the concentration of adrenaline increases in the body, there is an increased level of attraction. The sense of danger produces fear, and fear produces adrenaline. The stimulation of emotional arousal creates this connection between willing partners. We indeed share this bond. However, I must stay focused. My main concern now is to get Stone off my trail.

"Jean Paul, you know I adore you. More than anything, I wish we could be back at my cottage, away from all of this, and be together. However, ummm… however, your breath on my neck is distracting me. You, you hardened operative, should know better," I say, trying to stop him. Sort of.

There is gentle sarcasm in my voice, and it's so hard to say no to this man. Then it hits me.

"Wait a minute; you're not worried about Aaron Stone and our history, are you?"

No, I can't believe that for one second this seasoned soul, this man who always operates with confidence and precision, whose connection to me is an unbreakable bond, could be jealous.

"*Ma chérie*, you, I trust. Stone, not so much. I cannot act like a jealous lover, or I will jeopardize our mission and our relationship. I do not want to add any more danger to what we already have, and my Lily, it is considerable. My feelings for you have made me rethink how the Agency uses you, and perhaps we should take you out of any future equations."

"No, JP. We're not having this discussion now. Once you cross the line, there's no going back. You know that. My God, you know that! Don't tell me that I will be written out of the future of my country. Yes, I have bitched about this for a long time. And I've thought about it for a long time. I just want to save lives; I want to heal people. But I have been brainwashed by your superiors into thinking I will save many more lives if some of these missions are successful. Let's not second guess this now," I bark with an impassioned voice.

And with my last word, we topple onto the bed. Like tangled vines, our beginnings and ends cannot be distinguished. He is the love of my life.

*   *   *

"I'm looking at the menu, and if Stone is anything like he was in college, I see a few items here that he may like," I say.

JP is washing up in the bathroom. I can hear the water running, so I know he doesn't hear me.

"JP," I say just a little louder, "can you find out what room he's in and if he's ordered a room service breakfast? Even though we're in South Korea, if he's ordered breakfast, he will order the American style, you know, eggs, toast, coffee."

JP emerges from the bathroom drying his face with a hand towel. I can see the wrinkle that runs just outside the top of his cheekbone to the middle of his cheek. It's the wear and tear of age and burden.

"*Eh*, Lily, what is it?"

"Can you find out what room Stone is in and whether or not he's ordered breakfast for the morning?" I repeat.

"He is in room 12-258 in the north tower. I believe he has ordered two eggs over easy, white toast with butter, and black coffee for 7:00 a.m.," he says without blinking.

I just stare at him and say, "Did you know that before you came into my room?"

"*Eh*, Lily, ever since we saw Stone at this meeting, we have been watching him while at the hotel. Your plan for breakfast?"

I shake my head and continue, "Just get me near the food before he opens the door for room service."

* * *

Early the next morning, I'm up and ready. Just in case, I'm wearing a blonde wig and blue contacts. I don't intend to have Stone see me, but you can always count on the unexpected.

JP has worked out the logistics. I leave my room and take the elevator down to the floor that links the north and south towers of the hotel. When I get to the north tower elevators, I find elevator 6. At exactly 6:55 a.m., I get on to the elevator. The woman with the breakfast cart makes room for me. A pink hibiscus is pinned onto her uniform, the signal for our prearranged verbal exchange.

"Is that a Korean rose?" I ask.

"Yes, mugunghwa," she replies.

"Eternity," I say.

I remove the top from the coffee pot and empty a carefully measured dropper of poison into the dark liquid below. The aroma of the Colombian brew is strong. I have been assured that the camera in elevator number 6 has had a glitch. This encounter never happened. The elevator stops, and the woman with the breakfast cart exits. I press the button and go back down to the bridge and cross over to the south tower.

Back in my room, I remove the blonde wig and contacts and change into the brown curly wig with hazel contacts. The image in the mirror stares back at me. "Do I know you?" I ask her. It's not the wigs or the contacts; it's my soul I question. I truly have become the destroying angel. Maybe JP is right. Perhaps I should be factored out of future equations.

* * *

Aaron Stone emerged from the shower feeling fresh when he heard a knock on his door. He wrapped a towel around his toned body and peered out the peephole, eyeing a woman with the breakfast cart at the entrance. He let her in. She placed the breakfast tray on the desk with barely a glance at his partially naked body. She then removed the plastic wrap from the butter and poured the coffee into the cup.

"Is there anything else I can get you, sir?" she asked.

Stone surveyed his breakfast. He picked up the metal cover off the plate and eyed the two eggs nestled in parsley. They looked ordinary enough, although he would not touch the parsley. The coffee smelled strong. Brewed the way he liked it, and it had a pleasing parsnip-like aroma. Stone signed for the room service and escorted the delivery lady to the door.

He pulled a chair up to the desk, sat down, and began to butter his toast. An old fashion breakfast reminding him of his American past provided an indulgence to his normal routine. Needing to feel the jolt of caffeine to start his day, he downed the first cup of coffee quickly. It tasted good. Smooth with a strong aroma. Then he began to eat the eggs. Within fifteen minutes of sitting down, he felt nauseous, and his head hung over the plate where he imagined that the yolk of the egg was bouncing like a yellow ball. The room began to spin, and his view of the bed became fuzzy.

Focusing on a familiar face in the mirror over the dresser, he saw what he presumed were his pupils, only large like a bat's. *Mydriasis*, he thought, and then he doubled over gripping his belly. It was the pain in his stomach that was unbearable. He was going to throw up. Stone crashed to the floor, shaking uncontrollably. After a momentary pause, blood dripped out of the corner of his mouth, his teeth sinking into his tongue again and again. Agony overwhelmed him, and he could feel another, more violent seizure about to explode, and there, teetering on the precipice of consciousness, he remembered. Lily Robinson.

CHAPTER 14

SOUTH KOREA

Markovic couldn't understand why Stone hadn't gotten back to him. For one thing, he wanted the surgeon to check his healing. Much of the swelling had subsided, and only bruising remained around his eyes and the folds around his mouth. Nothing that couldn't be covered with a little make-up. More importantly, he had asked Dr. Stone to orchestrate a meeting with Stone's North Korean contact. He was waiting to hear about a designated time and place. Russian chemical warfare united with the best in missile technology. The Novichok agents, available for the right price, were Markovic's choice for this marriage. Not exactly novel nerve agents but certainly successful in previous trials. Intrigued by A-232, he imagined it would be the perfect weapon.

The parcel that had been left outside his door earlier contained information on where the Novichok agents would be delivered in South Korea. He carefully unwrapped the brown paper surrounding the box and opened the top. Inside was a key fob, two small silver-colored keys, and a letter with instructions. Carefully scripted in Russian, and partially in code, the paper told Markovic that the two reagents could be found at a shipyard near the coast. Reading further down the lines, he discovered that they had not sent him A-232, but rather a new derivative of A-234. Markovic was impressed.

A-234 is at least five to eight times more potent than the original VX, or venomous agent X. He imagined that a novel derivative of A-234 would be even more deadly; smaller quantities of the chemicals would be needed to deliver a massive lethal dose. He knew that VX was a potent type of nerve agent. These substances—thiophosphonates—originated from the pesticide research that occurred during the creation of certain organophosphate compounds. It was first discovered in England at Porton Down in Wiltshire. Porton Down houses the United Kingdom's military research facilities, which are now known as Dstl, or Defense Science and Technology Laboratory.

Markovic peered deep inside the box, checking that nothing remained. Under a thin layer of cardboard, another set of instructions was found that specified how to "launch" the non-toxic precursors. Markovic, aware that South Korea once possessed a chemical weapons arsenal that contained sarin, assumed that they probably carried older binary agents as well. No one could, or would, say what happened to those chemicals over time. As a military man, Colonel Stone would have contacts not only in North Korea but in the South Korean Army as well.

Stone's lack of communication irritated Markovic. The Russian paced his room, popping the last of the pain killers, and decided to hunt him down. Vacating his space wearing a hat, dark glasses, and some beige concealer to tone down the remnants of his surgery, he managed to find a taxi on the street below. Stone's medical office in the *Apgujeong* district would be the first stop.

Having reached the front desk of Dr. Stone's clinic, he told the receptionist that he wanted to see the surgeon. She informed Markovic that Dr. Stone was unavailable and away attending a conference for several days. As a member of Stone's office, she easily recognized the concealed bruises of facial surgery and asked Markovic if he needed the surgeon on-call. Markovic told her no, but he was perplexed.

What conference could Stone be attending? He wondered. Stone never mentioned he would be away, and Markovic had been waiting for the promised introduction to the North Korean General. Something didn't feel right. Rather than ask the receptionist for more information and calling too much attention to himself, he sat in the waiting area reviewing his options.

He needed to get to Stone. While his mission in Seoul flew beneath the radar, Markovic didn't want to take any further chances of being seen in public. He would go back to his room and try again to contact Stone.

Markovic reached into his pocket to pull out his cigarettes, but stopped, reminded that he was still in a medical office. Heat filled his face, and his fingers started to twitch. The absence of personal contact and Stone's silence was annoying. As Markovic lingered before exiting, he overheard the receptionist on the phone.

"Oh, no, no. What happened? That's terrible. I don't think so. Thank you for letting me know."

Markovic's curiosity buoyed. "Everything all right?"

"Oh, sorry. I didn't realize you were still here. It appears Dr. Stone has had an accident."

"An accident?" Markovic said, his attention now focused solely on the office worker. *At least someone knows where I can reach Stone*, he thought.

CHAPTER 15

SOUTH KOREA

The patient lay in his hospital bed, intubated, and connected to various monitors checking his heart and breathing. After the maid found him unconscious in his hotel room, the muscular man had been brought into the Emergency Department. Barely alive, the medical staff stabilized him in the ED and then transferred Dr. Aaron Stone to the Medical Intensive Care Unit. Some of the physicians recognized him immediately. He was not held in high regard by the South Korean medical community. They knew he had a surgical practice of dubious design, but were obligated by oath to care for all patients despite their feelings.

The etiology of Stone's seizures was unclear, and the results from the toxicology screen were pending. No previous medical history could be found, so he was treated empirically with intravenous benzodiazepines after an initial course of barbiturates to control the seizures. Brain activity per the electroencephalogram began to approach normal, and the MICU doctors hoped they could extubate him by the next day. The staff found Stone's resilience and progress both remarkable. Unable to locate any next of kin or emergency contact, the nurse called Stone's office to let them know his whereabouts. There were no visitors and no calls. Stone would remain in the hospital until he was able to fend for himself.

* * *

A few hours ago, I heard a siren outside my hotel window that overlooked the street below. I could see someone being transported by stretcher to an awaiting ambulance. I imagined it was Aaron Stone.

Another knock at the adjoining door to my room. Yes, it's JP.

"Lily, you no doubt watched the commotion outside a little earlier," he says as he carefully peers out the window to the street below to see that it's all clear. "It was Stone. We have one of our men on it at the hospital."

"Yes, I could see that. I mean about Stone," I reply.

"*Ma chérie*, what did you use? How did you poison him?"

"Cicutoxin. Water hemlock."

"You mean poison hemlock, *oui*?"

"No, poison hemlock is *Conium maculatum*. True, it's very poisonous and a member of the carrot family, Apiaceae, but that's not water hemlock. Poison hemlock leaves look like parsley or carrot leaves. This is the poison of Socrates and other condemned prisoners of ancient Greece," I say.

"So, what is water hemlock?" JP asks with one eyebrow up and his lips pursed.

He's snuggling up close to me now.

"Water hemlock is *Cicuta maculata* also of the Apiaceae family. This plant has been referred to as cowbane or poison parsnip by those who keep livestock. Just like with poison hemlock, grazing animals get into trouble when they eat this vegetation. Same as people."

"*Eh*, Lily, you just happened to have this with you?"

"I told you that I brought a few things with me—just in case."

"So, explain why this toxin, *eh*, cicutoxin, *oui*?"

"I remember that back in college when I knew Stone, he had a history of a seizure disorder. It was very minor I recall, but it did come up once in conversation. I do have a memory for such detail, you know," I say, patting myself on the back. "Variety, my Frenchman, is the spice of life, and I came to Asia with several different toxins," I add with a slight laugh.

"*Oui, tellement vrai*, so true."

"Cicutoxin is known to work at the $GABA_A$ receptor in the central nervous system," I tell him.

"Gabby? Please explain, Lily."

"GABA$_A$ is gamma-aminobutyric acid antagonist," I answer, and I see JP's hand flying up.

"In English Lily, *si'l vous plait.*"

"Yes, yes, just give me a minute here. You see, the cicutoxin binds at the same receptor in the brain that GABA binds. When GABA binds at its receptor, it activates it so that chloride ions can't move across the cell membrane."

"Now, you have lost me, *ma chérie.*"

"Okay, I'll just skip to the finish. Sometimes, you can be so difficult, JP. I don't know if you do this on purpose, just to annoy me."

He takes my wrists in his hands and gently pulls me toward him for a hug.

I continue, "If the toxin binds at the same place that GABA would bind, then the nerve cells don't work, and it leads to seizures. Is that simple enough for you?"

He lets out a laugh. I know he knows his chemistry, but perhaps not in the same detail as I do. He's just pulling my chain. Love this man.

"*Ma chérie*, you are too good. Stone was unconscious when they found him. I thought you said you were going to titrate the dose."

"Look, I did the best I could under the circumstances. We haven't heard that he died yet, have we?"

"No. Stone is on a respirator in the intensive care unit," he says.

"Damn, we better get this done before he wakes up, JP. This man scares me."

Jean Paul takes my hand and squeezes it, and I rest my head on his shoulder. What is it about Stone that I find so unnerving?

* * *

The high-intensity buzz continued in the intensive care unit. Stone was a unique patient—one of their own. After receiving the information that their boss remained unconscious, his office staff canceled all his surgeries.

The following day, Stone's assistant decided to go to the hospital. When she arrived, she was initially denied entry since she wasn't next of kin, but after checking, the day staff couldn't find any family, or even a health care proxy, on file for Stone. He had alienated his ex-wife, had no children, and few friends. Yet his assistant was devoted to him since he had transformed her eyes to make them look rounder, and had repaired her son's cleft palate soon after his birth.

The ICU intimidated her. Unaccustomed to seeing her boss in a bed hooked up to various monitors and IV lines snaking from his arms, she backed out of the room. A feeling of light-headedness overcame her, seeing her man of strength unable to move to her aid. Once outside Stone's room, she sought the company of the nurse.

"How long will he be here?" the assistant asked the nurse.

"I'm sorry, who did you say you were?" the nurse replied.

"I'm Dr. Aaron Stone's assistant. He doesn't have any family that I know of. We canceled his surgeries for the week, but I'm not sure if that's realistic. Do you think he needs more time in the hospital? What's wrong with him anyway?"

"We know he suffered a seizure. Beyond that, we're not sure," said the nurse.

Behind the nurse's station, a young man in scrubs emptied the waste bins. His ears focused on the conversation between the two women. He noticed the physician in his white lab coat, hands in pockets, approach the pair, and shifted his task into slow motion.

"I've got the results of the toxicology report," the physician said to the nurse while fiddling with the stethoscope around his neck. "Nothing really out of the ordinary except a therapeutic amount of lamotrigine."

"What's that?" asked Stone's assistant.

"And who are you?" said the doctor turning to face her.

"She's the closest thing Stone's got to family," said the nurse conveying sarcasm in her voice. "She works in his office."

The roll of her eyes messaged her feelings to the doctor.

"Oh, I see. Do you know if Dr. Stone suffers from seizures, epilepsy, or bipolar disorder?" asked the physician.

"Um, I'm not sure if I know the answers to your questions. He seemed fine to the office staff," replied the assistant.

"Well, lamotrigine is a drug used to treat those medical conditions. When we extubate him this afternoon, I'm sure we'll be able to get more medical history. Thank you for stopping by," said the physician closing the conversation down, eager to get back to his patient.

The young man in scrubs finished emptying the waste bins and made his way outside the ICU into the hallway. He picked up his phone and sent a text: *Stone to be extubated this afternoon. Tox=Lamotrigine.*

* * *

After traveling to Stone's office the day before, Markovic sought refuge in his scanty room, debating his next steps. He called the hospital in the *Gangnam* district to check on Stone's condition. Stone was still there, but the hospital would not disclose his status. Markovic deliberated whether to venture out again. Anxious to collect his chemical compounds, have his meeting with the North Koreans, and get back to Russia, he found this delay with Stone unacceptable. Markovic kicked the chair that was next to the desk and watched it fly across the room. His fists slammed on the wooden surface, and pain traveled up his arms, through the elbow joints, and then through the shoulders, finally settling into his eye sockets. He reluctantly touched the bandage on his nose, not wanting to yield, and walked over to the small refrigerator located beneath the dresser. Inside he found a cold bottle of vodka stored in the freezer, ready to be consumed at a frightening pace. He welcomed the anesthesia.

* * *

Extubation had been considered then stopped, but finally, when the intensivists felt that Stone could breathe on his own, they pulled the tube. He was still unconscious, but his breaths were powered now only by his lungs, and the fluids pouring into his veins would help speed his recovery. Stone's most recent EEG showed normal activity, and yet he still had not opened his eyes. This puzzled his care team, who, to date, had been unable to obtain any past medical history on their patient. As long as he was breathing on his own, they would wait for him to wake up.

Arrangements were made to have Stone transferred from the ICU to a medical floor. The nurses in that unit, surprised to see the name of their new admission, remarked on Stone's history of harassment and their dislike for the doctor, and noted that he had been known to do good and charitable deeds but only when forced to by peer pressure.

Later in the evening, Markovic finally decided to go to the hospital and make contact with Stone. He entered the building after the sky went black, wearing a long coat, dark glasses, and copious amounts of make-up to camouflage his bruises. It had been hard to determine what to do about the bandage on his nose. He chose to peel it off on his own, splint and all, and replace it with a common nude-colored band-aid. Less than satisfactory, but the less attention he called to himself, the safer he felt.

Markovic found his way to Stone's room 256 after checking the patient/ room location board without further intervention of the hospital staff. There he found Stone, lying in bed, eyes closed, seemingly so vulnerable. Markovic pulled up a chair next to him and reviewed the situation.

He stared at Stone, willing him to awake. *Was there a way to make all the contacts without Stone?* He thought. When the nurse entered the room, Markovic tried to cover his face with his hands, as if to scratch an eye. She asked if he was a friend of Stone's, and Markovic nodded. Assured by his answer, she took Stone's vital signs and assessed his IV. Satisfied, she turned to Markovic and requested that he notify her if he saw any change in her patient. Her shift was busy, and they were short-staffed. The nurse left the room to check on her other patients, making for a long evening of rounds. Markovic sat quietly and watched her go, still undecided about his next move. There was no guarantee that Stone would wake up tonight. After a few hours, he saw Stone rousing but chose not to alert the nurse.

"Stone, Stone. Wake up, you bastard," Markovic said, coming close to the bed. He was careful not to raise his voice. "Wake up, wake up."

Stone was groggy, disoriented, and felt dizzy. There was pain in his arm. He opened his eyes and saw a cast on his left wrist, an IV line in his right hand, and Markovic nearly on top of him.

"Where am I?" he asked. "What happened?"

"*Da*, you are in hospital. Some kind of accident. Where were you?" Markovic responded.

"I, I was in my hotel room. Yes, that was it. Having breakfast. The room started to spin, I felt nauseous, and the abdominal pain was unrelenting. Shit. I felt myself having a seizure; then, I must have passed out. Where am I?"

"This is main hospital in the *Gangnam* district. Not too far from your medical office. No time for small talk. I need to meet with that contact. I will take you out of here."

Markovic moved to where the IV line attached to the bag of fluid and started manipulating the connections.

"What the fuck are you doing?" Stone said.

His voice was weak, unable to muster the deep annoyance he felt. He could hear his pulse rate increase on the heart monitor. *Why is this Russian here*, he thought.

"I am getting you out of here," Markovic responded, unmoved by Stone's reluctance. "We go now."

"No, you idiot. I'm not going anywhere. Not just yet. I have some unfinished business at my hotel. I need my strength and to know what the fuck is going on," said Stone.

He could feel his mind clearing.

"We don't have that kind of time," said Markovic, his hand rolling the clamp on the IV line.

"Maybe you don't, but I do. I need to find out what happened to me. I don't believe for one fucking minute that I just happened to fall sick. There was a woman at this conference. Her hair color was wrong, even her eye color, but some intangibles made me think I know her," said Stone.

"Stone, we go way back to Afghanistan, enough of this shit. This is war, and I have a payload to deliver. *We* are getting out of here."

Markovic's voice had an urgency and power that blanketed Stone.

"And I want more details on this conference. That wasn't part of the deal," said Markovic.

Aaron Stone worked to open his mind. He felt Markovic's voice urge him, but he couldn't let go of the image of the woman he saw at the conference.

"Lily Robinson, Lily Robinson," Stone whispered.

"What are you talking about, Stone? I can't hear you. Speak up, you bastard."

"Nothing, it's nothing to concern you. It's that woman," said Stone.

"Fuck the woman. We need to stick with our plan."

Markovic took his thumb and forefinger and wrapped them around the middle of his nose. The pain was real. Loud vibrations from his voice climbed up into his nostrils.

A figure dressed in scrubs and wearing latex gloves stood at the door. Neither Markovic nor Stone heard him when he entered the patient's room.

"Oh, excuse me. I'm here to empty the trash and sweep the floor. I didn't realize the patient was awake," he said, dragging his broom behind him.

Markovic said nothing, and Stone closed his eyes as if he were asleep, fully knowing it was too late.

"I'll get the nurse," said the man, leaving his housekeeping chores until later.

Once outside the room, he removed his gloves, threw them into the trash, and moved to the end of the hallway. There he took out his cell phone and sent a text: *Stone awake with unknown visitor. Review surveillance when available.* The response consisted of, *Come in,* and nothing more. Back at the charting area, he notified the nurse that her patient in room 256 had regained consciousness, and also let her know he was going on break.

*   *   *

Too many patients and too few nurses presented a challenge, and when the night nurse entered the room half an hour later, she found an empty bed. She knocked on the bathroom door but heard no response prompting her to look inside. The washroom was empty. Alarmed, her eyes scanned the entire room in detail, seeing the monitors and then noticing the bare IV pole. Running back to the nurse's station, she alerted hospital security, calling the officer in charge.

"Yes, yes, I have a missing patient. Dr. Aaron Stone. Yes, I know he's a surgeon here, but he's also a patient. He's not in his room. He had a visitor an hour ago, but they're both gone."

*   *   *

In the taxi, Markovic held onto Stone as he sat in the backseat wrapped in the Russian's coat with the IV bag tucked underneath. Stone still had on his anti-slip socks, brown with white sticky treads on the bottoms. *This is crazy*, Stone thought. *They know who I am, where I have my medical practice, where I live. How will I explain this?*

"Driver, use the side roads, not the main road," said Stone in Korean, still having difficulty speaking in his normal voice.

He struggled at projecting volume, and his throat was sore from the intubation. Then he turned to Markovic and said, "We'll go to my office; I have recliner chairs for minor surgical procedures, for recovery, you know. I'll spend the night there, with my IV. I don't know the full extent of my injuries yet. Let's hope they're not already there waiting for us."

He did know that his office had a good supply of narcotics. Opioids would dull the pain in his wrist and the other body parts injured when he crashed onto the hotel room floor. He could feel the bruising on the left side of his chest.

"What is today? What day is it?" asked Stone. "How long was I out?"

"A few days, maybe," responded Markovic.

"Is the engineering conference over? I need to get back to the conference," said Stone.

"Why were you there? Not in the plans. And I need that meeting with the North Koreans. I want that contact information now," said the Russian.

"Markovic, I make my own plans. Who knows you're here in South Korea?" Stone asked.

"No one."

"At the conference, I saw a woman. I'm sure I know her. But she looked like she could have been wearing a disguise."

"Stop, Stone, with this woman. You are delirious," said Markovic, checking once again that the window separating the driver from its back-seat passengers was tightly closed and that the music was turned up. His hands tapped the plexiglass, and he could see the driver-focused straight ahead.

"I'm sure it was Lily Robinson," said Stone in a whisper.

"What did you say?" asked Markovic.

"Nothing, just that the woman at the conference reminded me of someone I knew from college. An American with a photographic memory and a love of botany. Then went on to graduate school after college to study toxicology."

"You say you saw this woman at the conference? Someone you knew from university?" asked Markovic.

"Yes, a clever bitch. And what would she be doing at an engineering conference? I could be wrong, but my gut says differently."

Looking out the window, Stone recognized the location and said, "We're almost there. My pulse is quickening, I can feel it, and some of the dizziness has returned. I've got to lie down. Pain killers, Markovic. I need those pain killers."

"What did you say was her name, this woman?" asked Markovic.

Stone's consciousness clouded. His head hurt, and his mind started spinning. Creeping pain challenged him, but war had been far worse. With his strength fading, he returned to the evening's events. How would he explain his bolting in the middle of the night? His colleagues would find it irrational and inconceivable that he would leave against medical advice, but he had done it. Could he make a case for kidnapping? He could hear the Russian's voice driving into his ears and shaking his brain.

"What Markovic? Shut the fuck up. Get me into my office so I can get some meds."

"Her name, Stone. What is her name?"

"The beautiful flower. Lily Robinson."

Chapter 16

SOUTH KOREA

"What do you mean that Stone's not in the hospital? I thought he was unconscious and in the ICU." I ask JP.

Jean Paul notices my pressured speech and the tapping of my foot. I'm worried that this maniac Stone, now out of his cage, might come after me.

We had a pretty straightforward plan. While undercover attending the engineering conference, I assassinate the Chinese scientist before he can pass on his novel technology, and boom: we go home. But somehow, it all got screwed up. Aaron Stone appeared, I was sure I poisoned him enough to slow him down and knock him out of the game, but now the hospital has somehow misplaced him.

"Lily, our sources have confirmed that only lamotrigine was found in Stone's urine. There is no suspicion that Stone was poisoned, much less by you, *ma chérie*. More importantly, he had a visitor last evening."

"A visitor in the ICU?" I ask, then add, "Lamotrigine is used to treat seizures, so I guess I had a good cover for my toxin."

"*Eh*, you continue to amaze me, my Lily. *Mais*, he was extubated yesterday late afternoon and transferred to a medical floor with general neurology and medical surgery patients. That is where he had his visitor, and now, they have both disappeared. We believe they slipped out of the hospital unnoticed while the nurse was caring for other patients."

"JP," I start to say while I pace the hotel room in bare feet, noticing that the rug doesn't feel soft when I knead my toes into the nap. It's a thin commercial grade with a swirl pattern in gold and forest green.

Focusing my clinical mind, I ignore the part about Stone's disappearance from the hospital and my angst about him, and continue with my questions.

"JP, we're just going to change the venue for the assassination once we find out for sure where Dr. Guan is. Right?"

"*Oui*. We recently learned that the exchange will take place in Hong Kong, not Seoul. So, it is a little more complicated, Lily," he answers.

"Well, once your men know where to find him in Hong Kong, let's just get on a plane and go. It doesn't matter where we stop him, does it?"

The crows' feet around his eyes deepen.

"There is more, Lily. Jackson Scott uncovered some crucial information."

"Oh, did he ID the woman and the girls in the photo?" I ask, remembering that Scottie had found a small worn photograph in Alexis' flat.

"No, not yet. Let me finish, *si'l vous plait*," he says with a mildly agitated voice. I see the corners of his mouth turn down, and I stop talking.

"There is an elite Russian intelligence system known as Unit 29155. Markovic may be one of their agents. Or he may have gone rogue from the G.R.U.," says JP.

"I don't understand. I've never heard of Unit 29155," I tell Jean Paul.

"Up until recently, no one had, *chérie*. This is a special faction of Russian Intelligence that is used to destabilize countries using assassination, sabotage, and other tactics."

"You mean like our specialized elite unit," I point out.

"*Oui, c'est vrai*. While we only recently discovered this, it became clear that this unit has been in operation for over a decade. We knew Markovic had roots in the Russian military intelligence agency."

"What does this mean for us? We still don't know where Markovic is, right?"

"Lily, Markovic was associated with Stone back in the day, in Afghanistan. They worked together on drug and munition deals. *Et... et*, Lily, we believe that Markovic is in Seoul, with Stone."

I can feel my heart thumping in my chest. A drop of acid, titrated just so, swirls in my stomach and leaps up that long tube leading to my throat. And there it stays, etching my teeth and bathing the back of my tongue. There is a buzz in my ears, so that sounds seem muffled. I take a deep breath and a hard swallow.

All I can say is, "More complications. Now what?"

"We assumed Markovic fled to Russia after he escaped from New York. He must have come to Seoul to meet Stone, and I can think of several reasons why, Lily. We know they connected at the hospital. Surveillance tapes that were reviewed this morning showed a man who looked similar to Markovic on the footage."

"What do you mean by 'similar' to Markovic? It's either him or not," I say.

"His facial features did not match what we have on file."

"Well, if it is him, just hunt the bastard down and end this, please JP."

He can hear the pitch in my voice, and I'm sure he knows that I am trembling inside.

"As you said earlier, a bullet would work, *chérie*, just as easily as your poison."

"Does it matter how you take down Markovic? He poisoned so many Americans; he should be brought in for justice."

"Ah, Lily. Not everyone knows what happened in New York. It is not common knowledge. Only certain areas of the intelligence community are aware. *Rappelle-tois*, it is buried on that particular covert server. The United States does not want to alarm the American people. We have discussed this. The U.S. government is already destabilized given the erratic leadership; this would only create more chaos."

"Listen, JP, didn't you tell me that the Russians had used nerve agents in the past?" I ask, now regaining my composure and trying to think through the problem. I feel my heart rate and rhythm returning to normal. I'm focusing.

"*Oui*, we believe they gave chemical weapons to Syria. *Pourquoi*, why?" he asks.

"Why else would Markovic be here if not to meet with Stone and Guan? He assumed they would form the perfect triangle, don't you see? Guan has the missile technology, and Markovic must have the chemical weapons. The North Koreans want both. Stone was probably there to help broker the deal.

There are several chemical warfare options, but I wouldn't be surprised if Markovic is considering nerve agents."

"At this point, it is our best guess. Still, the Agency is looking at all the possibilities and will feed us the intelligence when they get it."

"I know, I know. But it would be what I would choose," I say.

Without even realizing it, the words fall out of my mouth.

"If you find out where Dr. Wei Guan is hiding in Hong Kong, I'll go there and finish what we came here to do. That will leave the rest of the team in Seoul to find both Markovic and his friend Stone. Let them meet their fate."

"*Ralentis*, slow down, Lily. I am not so sure about you going to Hong Kong by yourself."

I can see the wrinkles in his forehead grow.

"I can do this, JP. You have to trust me. And you can join me as soon as you can. Look, you told me that the decoy here in Seoul is a real bioengineer at the university in Hong Kong. Maybe that's where our Wei Guan will be. Remember, I can use Dr. John Chi Leigh as my cover. He has an academic appointment at the same university. And, and, I truly hate this wig," I add as I rip it off my head and throw it on the bed.

JP takes me in his arms and holds me close. It won't be the first time that we part not knowing if we will ever see each other again.

CHAPTER 17

BOSTON

Rose Moreau worked diligently in her gross anatomy lab. Dissection of a human cadaver was conducted carefully and with great reverence. Noble citizens had willingly donated their bodies to science so medical students could explore the human form, seeing and feeling for themselves, organs, nerves, and blood vessels. Rose had decided early on that she wanted to become a pathologist and planned to visit the pathology and laboratory medicine department to arrange to shadow her idol, Dr. Robinson, one afternoon a week, if she could swing it.

Rose found Lily Robinson's assistant Lisa in the hospital and put forth her case.

"Hi, I'm Rose, one of the first-year medical students, and I wonder if it's possible to make an appointment to see Dr. Robinson."

"Hi Rose," said Lisa, "I'm sorry; you just missed her. Dr. Robinson is away for several weeks. Would you like to meet with her fellow, Dr. Kelley? Is there something he can help you with?"

"Um, I don't know. I guess I could talk to him. But I still want to make an appointment to meet with Dr. Robinson."

"That's fine. I just don't know exactly when she will be back, so as long as you can be flexible, I can set something up, but we'll probably have to change it," said Lisa shifting in her chair and looking at her computer screen.

This was the part of keeping Dr. Robinson's schedule that she hated. How could she book appointments with such an unpredictable boss? Lately, it had gotten worse. She pushed her dark hair behind her ears and folded her lips one on top of the other.

"Lisa, good morning," burst in Dr. Kelley, "excuse me, but I need to have you set up a con-call for me for this afternoon."

Kelley looked at the young woman standing in front of Lisa's desk. He was a little taken aback to see that she looked a lot like Lily Robinson, his mentor. Then he turned to Rose and said, "Sorry to barge in, but I need to get this call set up right away."

"Dr. Kelley, this is Rose," said Lisa, "She's a first-year med student and looking to shadow Dr. Robinson. Do you have any time to talk with her this morning?"

"Sure," Kelley answered. Then turning to Rose, he said, "Why don't you give me ten minutes, and then we'll meet in my office. It's just around the corner."

"Great!" said Rose with enthusiasm. "Can I just sit here and wait until you're ready?"

"If it's okay with Lisa, it's okay with me," answered Kelley. "I'll be back in ten."

Kelley dropped off the information for the conference call with Lisa and turned to walk back to his office.

Rose watched the man dressed in a neat white lab coat jog down the hall. He seemed energetic and even a little exciting. The outer administrative office was a modest waiting area with wooden-framed chairs with blue cushions, a sparse philodendron hanging in the window, and printers churning out articles of note.

Rose twirled the gold ring around her finger and thought about her mother. Adrienne Moreau had given the family heirloom to Rose one Christmas day. She had hoped to give it to her daughter Bella, but since Bella had disappeared from their lives, Adrienne was more than happy to give the ring to her adopted child. Rose recalled how she had lost the priceless gift while she and Adrienne were on Christmas vacation in a picturesque New England coastal town but were blessed with good luck when the owner of a charming flower shop recovered the ring. Rose hoped that she and her mother would again be together for Christmas.

Kelley finished his business at his desk and walked back to the administrative office to collect the first-year medical student. He found it interesting that she not only resembled Dr. Robinson but that she also wanted to be a pathologist. There she was, brunette hair and green eyes, dressed in dark blue jeans and a bright pink cotton blouse, waiting for him, by Lisa's desk.

"Hi Rose, are you ready for a little tour first?" he asked.

"Hey, that would be great, thanks so much," she replied.

Rose asked Lisa if she could leave her backpack with her rather than carry it around the lab. Lisa nodded her head, slid the pack under her desk, and refocused her eyes on the computer screen.

"Okay, let's start in my office, where I can give you an overview of our sub-speciality," said Kelley.

On the walk over, he asked Rose why she was interested in pathology and lab medicine, and Rose told him about the career night experience she had when she was in high school. Dr. Robinson had made quite an impression.

"Here's the thing about pathology," Kelley started when they reached his office, "there's something for everyone. So, if you go through med school and like pediatrics, you can be a pediatric pathologist, or if you like GYN, you can do gynecological pathology. You get it, right?"

"Yes, I've looked over the brochures on pathology. Do you have a pathology interest group here?" Rose inquired.

"You mean PIG meetings? Yes, we do. Make sure you sign up for the more extensive tour. Before we go into the lab, do you want to review a case with me? I'm doing a toxicology fellowship, so that's the kind of case I usually work up. Um, Dr. Robinson is a toxicologist also. Do you know if you want to do AP, CP, or both?"

"Wait, could you just review that again?" said Rose, settling in a chair inside Kelley's office.

"Sure, AP is anatomic pathology and covers things like surgical pathology with all its sub-specialties, then there's autopsy pathology—you know what that is—and cytopathology, which is the study of cells and fluids. CP is clinical pathology, which is most of laboratory medicine. Things like chemistry, hematology, toxicology, micro, or transfusion medicine. Sound familiar?"

"Yes, yes. Thanks for that. I don't know yet. I'm open at this point. What's your case about?" asked Rose.

Kelley told Rose about a 46-year-old man with a history of chronic abdominal pain, vomiting, diarrhea, and ringing in the ears. His symptoms got progressively worse, and he was admitted to the hospital after experiencing convulsions. He was now in a coma and facing renal failure.

"Wow, and you think this could be from something toxic?" asked Rose.

"His tox screen was negative for illicit drugs and the common analgesics; you know, things like cocaine, amphetamines, aspirin, acetaminophen. But there are so many drugs and poisons out there that you need a clue or two to point you in the right direction. Otherwise, it's a bit of a rabbit hunt."

Rose laughed and felt herself enjoying her conversation with Kelley. He was an unexpected find in her search for her mentor and her new career.

"Did you find any clues?" Rose asked, moving a strand of hair from her face to behind her right ear.

"Yes, one or two curious clues," answered Kelley, jumping up to the whiteboard in his office and scribbling pieces of the case with a volatile dry erase marker. Rose could smell it.

"Other than results associated with his kidney failure, most of his chemistries were normal except for one."

He wrote out the electrolytes on the board: sodium, potassium, bicarbonate, and chloride. Then he circled the chloride. "Our patient has a very high chloride concentration. And the other interesting bit of info I was able to find out is that his estranged wife is a hairdresser. This is a case Dr. Robinson would love."

Kelley stopped talking when he heard the buzz coming from his beeper. He looked at the message and turned to Rose to let her know that he had to go.

"Sorry to cut this short, but this is an emergency I need to take care of. Catch you another time."

Rose was disappointed to not only have missed out on a personal tour by the engaging Dr. Kelley but, most importantly, not having some conclusion regarding the case. *What was this patient's problem?* she thought. Given that Rose was only in her first year of medical school, she didn't know very much. She had no idea what the values would be for any of the lab tests and how this would relate to this patient's stomach problems and failing kidneys. As she walked back to the office to collect her pack, she decided to research the clues of the case and reunite with Dr. Kelley later.

*   *   *

The first year of medical school was challenging. Sheer memorization, and long and exhausting hours, left little time for anything else. Medicine has a language of its own: lytes, ROS, PE, CAD, and endless acronyms that still meant nothing in year one, but would mean everything in a new career after year four wound down. Work-life balance was hard to come by. Rose signed up for a student meditation class to help channel the stress and provide comfort for her alone times. Deep breathing helped focus the mind and gave her a way to deal with her childhood trauma. She also found that if she concentrated on her medical studies, she could drive out emotions that made her feel vulnerable. It was difficult to bury the abduction of her sister while in Colombia. And at times, more difficult to understand her own beginnings.

An irresistible urge in Rose propelled her to the small set of drawers in her apartment bedroom. She opened the topmost one, pushed aside her socks and underwear, and found the letter. Adrienne had given it to her the Christmas after Rose's horseback riding accident that left her comatose. The same Christmas that Adrienne had given Rose the gold and diamond ring. Her mother's instructions had been quite clear at the time. The letter should be opened only after Adrienne's death and not before. It had seemed odd to Rose that her mother would choose to give her such a letter at that time in both their lives. She wondered whether Adrienne had been uncertain about her own fate and felt the need to leave something in writing, something of importance, that would impact her heir's future. Rose never asked, and Adrienne never brought up the subject again, knowing that her daughter had a strong mind and honest values.

Rose was no longer a teenager in high school. Now a young woman embarking on a career in medicine, she could better understand her mother's message and consider ways to help her mother face her challenges working on the vineyards in Reims. But what were those challenges? A blush came over Rose as she was about to open the letter. Was it a blush of betrayal, excitement, or guilt? Rose couldn't say, but she felt compelled to read the missive, embrace its contents no matter the consequences, and move forward with her life. She carefully opened the envelope at the seam, removed the letter, and began to read:

> *My dear beautiful daughter Rose,*
> *If you are reading this now, I have passed on from this world. I*
> *ask for your forgiveness for my part in the story I am about to tell,*
> *but always know that I have loved you as my own daughter from*
> *the very first day they brought you back from the jungle.*

Rose stopped reading abruptly, tears flooding her eyes. *My God,* she thought. *This is the story of my origin, my beginnings.* She pushed her anatomy textbook off the deep-cushioned chair, folded her legs beneath her as she wedged into the upholstery, and continued to read.

CHAPTER 18

FRANCE

Winter in Reims will be cold this year. Despite its oceanic climate, or perhaps because of it, the fall already had some nights dipping into the high 30s Fahrenheit. The Moreau estate was drafty, and Adrienne wanted to make sure that both the plants in her garden and her adopted daughter Rose were protected from the harsh elements.

For years Adrienne had debated whether or not to share the story with Rose of how she had come to be at the coffee plantation. Adrienne didn't have all the information, but she did know that a research team that had come from the U.S. to explore the Colombian jungle had vanished. The authorities said so when they stopped by the Compound a few days after Rose's unexpected arrival to see if there had been any sightings of the missing scientists. Adrienne hid the little girl at the time, uncertain of her connection, while her uncle Alberto and all the plantation staff only offered silence when questioned. There had been no further follow-up in the newspapers after the initial report, and the subject was never mentioned again at the Compound.

Unable to share the truth with Rose directly, Adrienne wrote about the incident in a letter which she gave to Rose the winter after she almost lost her. Seeing her daughter lying helpless in a hospital bed and doubtful about their future together impelled Adrienne to provide Rose with some clarity about Colombia, but only after she was gone. Mothers and daughters share a special relationship, one started by an umbilical cord able to nurture the child growing inside them. But, of course, the connection is more than biology—and in Rose and Adrienne's case, a unique and selfless bond of love was formed. Adrienne's tie to her own mother had been profound, and she wished her mother had had the chance to meet both of her granddaughters, Bella and Rose.

After cleaning out much of her mother's belongings, Adrienne made plans to take the gently worn clothes into town and bring them to the church, who, in turn, would give the apparel to the poor. Notre-Dame de Reims or the Reims Cathedral was constructed between the 13th and 15th centuries and remained as an example of Gothic design complete with flying buttresses, stained glass windows, high arches, and spires reaching high into the sky. The predicate church to the cathedral burned in the twelfth century only to be replaced by a more expansive regal structure. Over the centuries, Reims Cathedral, the designated place for the coronation of French kings, had held twenty-five such celebrations for royalty. Overwhelmed by the beauty of the façade, Adrienne stood under the Rose window and counted the Gallery of Kings, fifty-six statues in all. Clovis I prevailed straight and center, commemorating the baptism of the first King of the Franks in the 5th Century. Like Adrienne's ravaged life, the church had weathered fire, revolution, war, liberation, and renovation. They had survived.

Her hesitant footsteps crossed the threshold to behold the North Rose window, its presence a vestige from the 13th century. This circular round window, a hallmark of Gothic architecture, demonstrated a complex design like the multi-petaled rose. Rose. What was Adrienne to do about Rose? Adrienne approached the altar, knelt, and began to pray. Thoughts of her father, her mother, her Bella, now all gone, brought tears to her eyes, and her head dropped between her shoulders. And then there was Rose. For more than twenty years, Adrienne had been a mother to a lost daughter and prayed that she had been worthy—good enough—to raise this child from the jungle. She begged her faith to guide her.

Adrienne stood up, straightened her back, and walked toward the votive candles. Eyeing a wooden matchstick, she picked it up and held the dark edge over a lit candle. A spark erupted at the tip, and she took the flame and lit four candles for prayer intentions. The wick turned black, and then the alabaster wax began to melt. On her exit from the cathedral, an old woman with snow-white hair and blue eyes nestled within gentle crow's feet stopped and engaged Adrienne.

"Oh, *Madame*, we were so sorry to learn of your mother's passing. You had such a wonderful family," she said, pulling her well-worn wool coat around her.

"*Merci*," said Adrienne, reaching out and touching the old woman's forearm, " I miss my mother and have come to pray for her soul."

Thinking that perhaps the woman might know more about her family history, Adrienne then asked, "I wonder, did you know my aunt and uncle who lived at the chateau when my grandparents were alive?"

"Oh, that was so long ago," she answered with a sense of surprise at the question. "Let's see." There was a thoughtful pause while she looked through her memory. "They did live with your parents, and then I believe they moved to Chalandry. *Oui*, Chalandry; they left your vineyards with their little boy. That was before you were born, Adrienne," said the woman, taking a handkerchief from her coat pocket and blowing her nose in the cold air. "*Il fait froid!*" she added, rubbing her bare hands together.

"*Oui, Madame, et merci* for the information. I know Chalandry. And winters do seem to be getting colder. I've donated some of my mother's clothing to the church to be given to those in need; I hope they find a good home," said Adrienne, wishing she had some gloves to give the woman before they parted ways.

The parishioners had been kind to Adrienne since her return to Reims and more so since the death of her mother. She would be sure to tell the priest the next time she saw him.

*   *   *

Adrienne made plans to drive to Chalandry. She knew her uncle and his wife had a son named Jean Paul, and Adrienne was curious if he was still alive.

When she arrived in the small village, the *beffroi de Crécy-sur-Serre* caught her eye. The bell tower shot into the sky, and centered near the top like a cyclops eye, stood a clock. Capping the structure was a dome that housed the bell and sat like a crown on the stone.

In contrast to Reims, Chalandry seemed quaint. There was no iconic cathedral or buzz from the tours of vineyards or wine cellars. Reims, the City of Coronations, boasted Joan of Arc who had walked with kings, had a summer music festival—the *Flâneries Musicales de Reims*—and had an enduring medieval market place. Reims, vibrant and colorful, Chalandry paled by comparison.

Adrienne found her way to the town hall to obtain any records of her aunt and uncle's life in Chalandry. Only scant information could be located—an old address that showed that they had lived on the outskirts of town with their son for many years. Her aunt and uncle had since been buried, and the whereabouts of their son, Adrienne's cousin, was unknown.

"*Oui, Madame.* I am sorry I do not have more information for you," said the clerk. "We have no forwarding address for your cousin."

The air was crisp outside the petite government house. A young mother passed by with two young girls in tow. The woman, her head covered in a brightly colored scarf, had each of her hands entwined with those of her children. Adrienne swallowed hard and grasped for the handkerchief deep within her purse. She had reached a dead end. Needing a refuge from the cold, she stopped at a small café to have a cup of tea. Settled at a corner table, she removed her coat and hat and picked up the menu.

"*Bonjour, Madame.* What can I get for you?" said the older waitress.

"I'll have the chamomile tea and Biscuit rose de Reims, *merci*."

"*Oui, Madame.*"

The Biscuit rose de Reims reminded Adrienne of her mother. Stowed in cupboards out of the reach of children, her mother kept these biscuits for special occasions. Delicious when dipped in tea or even champagne to bring out the flavor, Adrienne recalled sharing the pastry with her parents as a little girl. The rose coloring and vanilla flavoring were what she craved now on this cold, bleak day. Her thoughts wandering, she remembered that she needed to prune her lavender plants when she returned to the estate. Living things required care and love.

Adrienne paid her bill, the chill now chased away by hot tea and warm thoughts of her mother and her daughters, and although disappointed, she entered her car to make the trip back to Reims.

Overwhelmed by all the losses in her life, Adrienne had hoped she could find just one Moreau blood relative to connect with—her father's nephew, Jean Paul Moreau. Slipping onto the A26 from town, she could see the road open before her, and home was only about seventy kilometers away. Brown fields hugged the road on either side, and Adrienne was hypnotized by the sights and the setting sun in her eyes. Her attention wandered as she drove, and the weight of her circumstances clouded her mind and diffused her concentration. The cell phone neatly packed at the top of her pocketbook rang, bringing her back into the present. Reaching her hand inside, she grabbed the phone and peeked at the caller ID. Rose. Adrienne never saw the truck stopped in the road ahead. By the time her foot pressed on the brake pedal, the distance was too short for the car to stop. It slammed into the back end of the formidable vehicle, and Adrienne felt the steering wheel move into her chest, and darkness surround her.

CHAPTER 19

HONG KONG

My flight to Hong Kong was easier than expected. Having landed without any issues at the airport, I'll be heading to the part of the city that is untouched by the protests and free from chaos. Anti-government demonstrators fighting the extradition bill—a bill that would allow criminal suspects to be deported to mainland China if the circumstances were right—continue to clash with police, with the violence only escalating. A few universities are the latest battlegrounds, but I will be away from all of that.

I'm going to connect with John Chi first since his academic appointment is at the same university as that of the bioengineer we saw in Seoul. JP and I have assumed that the two men may have switched places. I'll wait until he can relay more information. Maybe there is some way Dr. Leigh can help me. There he is now. Khaki colored pants with brown shoes peeking beneath, his navy blazer hiding a blue tattersall shirt, and his hair combed neatly to one side of his forehead. Consistent. Leigh's eyes search mine and dig beneath my skin.

"Dr. Robinson, let me help you carry that suitcase," says John Chi, as he shepherds me to his waiting car.

"Good to see you again," I say.

"I didn't expect that you would be back so soon." Leigh waits for me.

I keep my eyes looking at my feet so he can only get a glimpse of my face. Emotion writes with indelible ink.

"Dr. Robinson, should I presume that it did not go as expected in Seoul. How can I help you?"

Here we go. I have to come up with some story again. It's so much easier to tell the truth, but the truth cannot be exposed. Not the whole truth anyway. I don't want to be subpoenaed in front of Congress to explain how I got involved in this mission.

"Dr. Leigh," I answer in a formal tone countering his formal address to me, and then begin my lie, "thank you for helping me. Yes, the conference in Seoul started strong, but I learned that there is a bioengineer in Hong Kong that I need to see. Turns out that this professor has an academic appointment at the same university that you do. I'm hoping you can make some introductions."

"Possibly," he answers. "Who do you want to contact?"

"Oh, I have detailed information in my bag. Let's talk about it later. So, what's happening in the lab? Any new toxins in the pipeline?"

I'm always looking for something exotic.

"Nothing since I worked on the cone snail toxin derivative. Lily, the real reason you need to go to university? Why are you back in Hong Kong?" He questions me with that suspicious tone.

"Okay, okay. I'm looking for a bioengineering professor, as I said. My understanding is that he has created a new detector that can identify extremely low levels of drugs in the air."

Will this lie work? I wonder.

"Bioengineering? That is not exactly in your area of expertise. What kind of device, Lily?"

He's got me squirming now. JP called it. This is difficult. I ignore Leigh's questions. Then, still bluffing, I say, "John Chi, are there any faculty events planned soon?"

"We have a general faculty meeting in two days. Usually, there is an informal meet and greet with some refreshments before the meeting. This is one way for new professors to connect with others. Whether the person you want to meet will be there is unknown."

Of course, John Chi is right. Why would our Dr. Wei Guan go to a faculty meeting unless that is the location for the exchange? No, I don't think so. There's got to be another venue. And I assume that if Markovic and Stone are part of Wei Guan's original plan, then they are likely already here in Hong Kong.

"John Chi, would you please drop me off at my hotel? I need to check in with my fellow and see how our cases are going. I truly appreciate you picking me up at the airport. Are you free for dinner later?"

"Yes, Dr. Robinson. I will see you at dinner tonight. Your hotel is just up ahead; I presume the same hotel you stayed in previously in the Tsim Sha Tsui district."

"Yes, of course."

John Chi is focused dead ahead. I feel a little tingle in my gut. Something is wrong, but what? There's the euphemistic click of his brain cogwheels turning and thinking behind those brown eyes. His face, fixed like that of a wolf stalking his prey, makes me wonder what he knows.

"This is it," I say out loud. "Thank you again. See you later tonight. It's okay; I'll grab my bag out of the back; don't bother getting out."

With that, I exit the car, my cashmere wrap around my shoulders, and set the slim heels of my python-patterned shoes onto the pavement.

* * *

My hotel room is quiet, and I have time to think and make some calls. First, I should check in with my service. I get out my personal cell phone and check emails, noting one from Francis Becker. There have been several more cases of lead poisoning. JP did say they found the source for the lead up at the Hillview Reservoir and are working on a fix. Thank God we made that discovery before more children were harmed. Next, I send Kelley a text. It's late in Boston, but he should still be up. He is. I can call him.

"Hey Kelley, how is the tox service?" I ask. He picked up after only two rings.

"Good, good. No worries. How is your conference going?"

"Great," I reply. There just happens to be an international toxicology conference in Asia, so that's where Kelley thinks I am.

109

"The service has been very busy. We got a lot of fentanyl cocaine cases from patients who thought they were just getting heroin. A few didn't make it. I checked in with the MICU to see about declaring brain death before the transplant team came in to harvest the organs. The MICU's always a challenge for me. I hate the smell. Especially when the bodies begin to deteriorate. Anyway, um, the DA's office called about that possible child homicide case from a few years ago. Remember we thought it could be Munchausen's by proxy, you know, where mom was poisoning the kid just to get attention?"

"Yes, I do remember that case. The sibling got sick after, and that's when child protective services moved in. The mother used rat poison. Yeah, it was brodifacoum; at first, they thought the kids had a bleeding disorder."

"Right. Well, I called the office for you, said you were away, and would get back to the DA when you returned. Which is when? Oh, we also had a med student visiting who wants to shadow you when you get back. Says she's interested in going into pathology. Well, just the usual stuff. And, we did have one cool case I know you would love. A patient with a high chloride and—"

I interrupt Kelley before he finishes. "Kelley, thanks, I haven't got a lot of time. Maybe I can check in with you in a few days. I'm sure you've got everything under control."

"Yeah, sure. Catch up with you soon," he says, and I can hear the disappointment in his voice.

We say our goodbyes; I put that phone down and reach for my secure Agency issue to ring JP.

"Hey, JP. Where are you?"

"*Ma chérie*, I am still in Seoul. But I do have some updates for you. Are you safe?"

"Yes, quite safe. I'm in my hotel room. Dr. Leigh picked me up at the airport. I'll have dinner with him later tonight. Have you found Markovic or Stone?"

"It was Markovic who took Stone from the hospital. We confirmed he had some surgery to alter his face to confound the AI facial recognition programs, but we recognized him by other features. After they left the hospital, they went to Stone's medical office, perhaps for some supplies, and then disappeared. We are trying to get some surveillance footage now to see where they may have gone. Remember, Stone had recently been moved from intensive care to the med-surg floor. He wouldn't have much stamina after your poison cocktail," he says.

"Don't underestimate that man," I say. "He's strong both physically and mentally. You don't advance in martial arts or the military if you are a pussy cat. No, think *wolf*. Besides, you told me he survived some pretty desperate conditions in Afghanistan."

"*Oui, chérie,* you are correct. He and Markovic spent time together there."

"Listen, JP. I'm trying to make sense of all this. Wei Guan's destination was always Hong Kong, not Seoul. Only he wanted all of us to think he was going to Seoul. Hence the decoy. But the exchange is happening here. And I believe Markovic assumed differently, too, and Stone was not part of the original plan. Once they realize what's really happening, then one or both of them will be heading to Hong Kong. Don't you think?"

I can hear JP deliberating over the phone. I'm sure the crow's feet around his eyes and those deep furrows over his brows are pronounced like ripples on the water.

"Lily, I agree with you. Guan is meeting the North Koreans. They are more likely to go with his missile design rather than the Russians'. As you know, the last Russian rocket launch was a debacle. Markovic got wind of this deal and wants to find a buyer for his chemical weapons. And Stone, well, he may be looking to make his own deal. A possibility, *chérie*, a possibility."

"Either way, we must eliminate Wei Guan," I say.

"*Oui.* His technology cannot get into the hands of our enemies."

"So find him, JP. I'll be at my hotel waiting to hear from you."

"I will come to Hong Kong to be with you. I should not have let you go there by yourself anyway, *ma chérie*. I will see you soon. *Et*, you are at your hotel in the Tsim Sha Tsui area, *mai oui?*"

"Yes, yes, of course. Don't forget, I'll be having dinner with Dr. Leigh tonight. There'll be a room key for you at the front desk," I say and hang up the phone.

Not that he needs one.

It's easy when the plan is straight forward, and we all know our roles. But the pieces of this puzzle are moving apart as Pangea did 200 million years ago. Where is this all going?

*   *   *

Here is Leigh, right on time.

"Hello, Lily. How is your hotel?" asks Dr. Leigh.

"Oh, wonderful, as usual," I answer. I'm wearing a silk cranberry-colored blouse over a black wool pencil skirt with a side slit and black suede stilettos.

"I thought maybe we could have dinner near the hotel. This restaurant has Cantonese cuisine with a view of the bay," says Leigh.

"Sounds delightful," I reply.

We enter the restaurant and are greeted by an exquisite hand-carved jade corridor and silkscreens with floral embroidery. The carpet is a creamy beige with brown swatches that reflect in the ceiling above. Very refined and modern. Leigh chose wisely. Hong Kong is sophisticated; it's a cosmopolitan city that blends the cultures of Asia and Great Britain. Most of the Chinese are Cantonese-speaking, and the young people of today's Hong Kong seek a brighter future with more freedom and full democracy.

We settle into the table and order Peking Duck, defined by its exquisite preparation. It will come in two courses: the first, the crispy skin with thin pancakes surrounded by delicate sauces and condiments; next, the duck meat itself minced and served in lettuce leaves. After we order, I see Dr. Leigh fidgeting in his seat. He's agitated.

"Lily, enough with the small talk. I ask you again. Why are you here?" Leigh says.

His eyes stare deep into mine, and I hear the annoyance in his voice. What do I say? How do I deal with this? My mind drifts. What were the details of Kelley's case that were so interesting? The patient with the high chloride. For a moment, I close my eyes, and I'm back in Boston where I should be.

"Lily, did you hear me? Do you want to tell me what is going on?"

"Sorry, John Chi, I was just thinking about a case my fellow called me about earlier."

What the hell. Leigh has been involved in enough of my government's escapades at some level.

"Again, sorry, my friend. I'm here looking for a Chinese scientist. I don't know that he's actually in Hong Kong, but that's the suspicion."

"You know, for an academic, you seem to stray considerably from the mark. However, given my own dubious past, I understand."

"No, you don't, Leigh. It's complicated. There's a scientist who works at your university by the name of Guan. Do you know him?"

"I cannot say," says Leigh.

"Well, I heard about his work while at the conference in Seoul."

"Then why are you in Hong Kong, Lily?"

The lie.

"Because I'm hoping I can find him in his lab. He's a bioengineer."

"Hmm, I am not sure why you would be interested in this scientific area," he says.

"Leigh, bioengineers are making all sorts of tiny detectors for drug identification," I tell him. This is true, although this is not the reason for my search. I make it through the rest of the evening on small talk—strictly science.

*   *   *

I'm looking forward to a quiet sleep so I can get my mind in order. My hotel room has a view looking over the water. Skyscrapers light the distant shore across Victoria Harbour while boats linger at the water's edge. My room

113

is decorated in neutrals, lavish yet soothing, and the bathroom is a beige marble with a fabulous soaking tub. Looks decadent, and I can't wait to dive in. My makeup comes off in one easy swipe as the tub fills with water and the lavender fragrance from the bath bomb fizz rides the steam wildly into my nostrils. It smells good. I dip my toe in to test the temperature. It's the Goldilocks sweet spot. Just right. I sink to the bottom and close my eyes.

Where in Hong Kong is Wei Guan? Is it only our team that has discovered the proxy is in Seoul? Is the man with the same name attending the conference in Seoul even aware of this? Maybe not. And what about Stone and Markovic? Leigh didn't have anything to add, but under the guise of visiting him, I will try and get a look at the bioengineer's lab space. There may be a clue there.

I'm tired and off to bed. A good night's sleep is hard to come by these days. I drift off thinking of how I'll get…

I'm suddenly awakened by the sound of a closing door. Now, it's quiet, perhaps it's nothing. I feel so groggy, I close my eyes once more. What seems like seconds later, the bedcovers part, and I feel a warm body slip beneath the sheets. I know that body; I know that kiss on the back of my neck. How Jean Paul manages to get into my room without a key is always a mystery. Oh wait, I think I left him a room key this time. I turn over to meet him in the darkness. His face is barely visible and just a silhouette. Warm kisses surround my neck and slowly drift over my breasts and toward my soft belly. I rouse from sleep to engage the tiger in the jungle. This man of a certain age whose toned body and clarity of thought makes love under the dark shadows of the night with only a sliver of moon above. I feel him inside me, and once again, we move as one.

Ma chérie are the only words I hear when I dare go back to sleep. I can't turn off my thoughts like a light switch. If only I could. We think we know someone, but the reality is that we never really know someone truly. Everyone has secrets. Everyone. They may be small and inconsequential, or they may be big, very big. It's the people we least expect that give us the most startling surprises. The perfect mother and wife with her hidden affair, the eloquent

114

priest engaged in clandestine sex, a brilliant scientist with a gambling habit, or an academic pathologist who is a vaporous assassin. On the outside, a person may be outgoing, vivacious, and engaging, but on the inside, they may be praying for anonymity. I don't really know JP, do I? This man who works covertly for the government, who I'm sure has killed, and who says he loves me. But what is his life like when he's not with me? Where does he go, where does he live, and who does he spend his days with? Is Jean Paul even his real name? I only know his first name, and it took me forever to find that out. He had always been the dark-haired man with the blue-green eyes. The problem with asking a question is that you may get an answer you don't like. Trust is so hard to come by. Sometimes it's better not to know.

*   *   *

The next morning the breakfast cart rolls in with steaming hot coffee and our continental choices. We had four prototype breakfasts to choose from—American, Continental, Japanese, or Chinese. The Japanese and Chinese breakfasts have more fish and protein, while our breakfast choices consist mainly of fruit, pastries, and some yogurt. The almond croissants are heavenly, and the coffee, just right.

"JP, I made arrangements to go to the university today to check out the bioengineer's office and lab while he's still in Seoul. I assume you will go with me. Yes?"

"*Mais oui, ma chérie.* What do you mean by 'arrangements'? Our daily agenda is not public record."

"No, what I mean is that I have a pass to visit Dr. Leigh on campus. Security has been ramped up with all the protests going on. So, this will let me onto the grounds, that's all. I assume you have other ways of sneaking anywhere you want to go," I say.

My voice indicates the difference in our status—he's the true spy, not me. He laughs, so I know he gets it.

"I will find you there, my Lily. But we will go to the university at night.

115

Darkness makes a good cover. *Eh*, like last night." JP winks, the crease in his cheek intensifies, and his forehead wrinkles.

"Ha, ha, JP. Okay. So bring me up to date on Markovic and Stone. Do you have any information about their whereabouts?" I'm enjoying the crunchy almonds on my croissant.

"No, not yet. We lost track of them once they left Stone's medical office. On this side of the world, it is a little easier to get lost. We have monitored the airports, but there are ways of escaping even our eyes. Let us meet over at the university today. I will find you."

"Got it," I say, and with that, he is out the door.

*   *   *

I've managed to find my way to the university in the dark. With Leigh's pass, I've gotten onto the campus and now have to find the laboratory. Dr. Guan's office and lab are in one of the obscure back buildings on the campus. From what I understand, he works quietly with only one graduate student and an older laboratory assistant that has been with him for a long time. I don't see JP here yet, but maybe he found the lab ahead of me.

This university is impressive. It has a reputation for being world-class in science and technology. With a coastal campus and gleaming white buildings, it keeps its connections with mainland China. It's quite a walk to where my campus map, courtesy of Dr. Leigh, says I need to go.

I can see the complex up ahead. It looks secure, and I'm not sure if I'm able to get into the building, much less the lab. Then, I see JP. My spy who can get into anywhere, or so it seems. We link up.

"Lily, let us go around to the back," JP says.

He looks serious. The corners of his mouth are in a straight line with his lips. I feel a sense of foreboding.

"JP, what's wrong? What have you found?"

116

There's no response from him—flying full speed ahead, expecting that I will follow. The back of the building looks deserted, and the door is partially ajar. I can see that the security cameras look disabled. I hope so. JP cautiously moves down the hall. There are no other people at this time of night. He opens the door to the lab. Just as I expected. Large coils of wires, huge magnets, and the kind of electrical engineering equipment that is not familiar to me. There's a small office in the back. Any files or papers would be kept there. That's my thought anyway. As we open the door, I see the blood.

"My God, JP, what happened here?"

The Chinese man on the floor, I assume, is our Dr. Wei Guan, the man with the novel missile technology. His face has been bludgeoned, perhaps postmortem, since I don't see a huge amount of blood around the head. Once the heart stops beating, less blood is pumped out of the body.

"You tell me, Lily. You are the pathologist," JP answers.

I kneel next to the body, trying not to touch the small blood pool. It looks like there has been an elbow disarticulation where the lower arm has been divided from the upper arm at the elbow joint. No bones have been cut. Both the radius and the ulna have been separated from the humerus.

"JP, this was a surgical procedure. The bones in the lower arm have been detached from the bone in the upper arm, the humerus. Look at this," I say and point to the area where the elbow should be.

This is a beautiful job done by a skilled surgeon.

"See how the biceps and brachialis tendons have been freed from the radius and ulna?"

"Lily, what is the cause of death?" he asks, ignoring my pathology-speak.

We turn the body over and look for any obvious signs of trauma other than on the face. Nothing apparent, but I see an indistinct puncture wound on the side of the neck.

"JP, it's possible that he was injected with something that knocked him down and ultimately killed him. There's blood here around the arm, but not enough blood to make me think this amputation was premortem. I think the arm was removed after he was dead. My guess is respiratory arrest. Look at this pink foam," I say, pointing to the froth coming from the dead man's mouth and nostrils.

"What pink foam, *chérie*? Does it matter?"

"No, not really. I'm just guessing without an autopsy and postmortem toxicology. However, I'm wondering if this could be an opioid death. An opioid, like some other chemical compounds, works on the receptors in your body that target your breathing. Too much opioid, and you stop breathing."

"*Et*, that makes pink foam?" he asks.

"Well, yes. The small capillaries in the lungs begin to bleed, and the bubbly mixture comes out from the mouth and nose as the lungs fill with fluid. I doubt this surgeon would have used an exotic toxin. He just needed something to knock Guan down quickly so he could perform the surgery."

"What you are telling me is that a skilled surgeon injected Guan with something that killed him, and then he removed the arm?" JP asks.

"Yes, that's correct. Apparently, death was not sufficient. Where is the arm, JP, and what did they want with it?"

"Lily, let me not answer that right now. There is something else. The United States has just killed a high ranking general in the Middle East. Tensions are high throughout the world. Also, a Ukrainian plane has been shot down by Iran, and there is a plea for calm. While the U.S. makes it sometimes appear that they have no part in assassinations for political or military gain, we both know better. The U.S. cannot deny the hit on the general. And it has made for messy world politics. No doubt that anything we do will be scrutinized by many countries. And one more thing, Lily. I'm sure this has crossed your mind, but I suspect that what we see here could be the work of your Dr. Stone."

My God! What to say? Sure, it crossed my mind. I explode in fright.

"So, your team still can't locate those two bastards? Where's your surveillance in South Korea?" I ask, with the pitch of my voice rising higher with every word.

"*Et*, remember Lily, that Markovic altered his appearance, and he and Stone may be traveling separately. There are many ways to move in and around this part of the world, and with our resources drawn to the Middle East with the general's assassination and the Iranian ballistic missile attack on the U.S.-Iraqi base, there may have been a drop in focus on Asia."

Jean Paul pauses when he hears me sigh.

"I am not certain, but I think we should consider that this is Stone's doing. What do you say in medicine? You have told me, bring it all down to the common denominator. All the symptoms to go with one disease rather than many. Yes, I believe that it could be the work of those two or at least the one."

And I thought Markovic was the only villain in my life, until Stone. I should have killed him when I had the chance.

CHAPTER 20

RUSSIA

Scottie knew he had crossed the line and may have put the operation in jeopardy. When emotions get in the way, the risks increase. His mission in Russia—find Alexis and use her to track down Markovic. Falling in love with her hadn't been part of the plan. And Jackson Scott felt that Alexis shared those feelings. This created significant complications. After their first intimate engagement, they had spent considerable time together. Scottie found Alexis to be lost, directionless, and even remorseful at times. Although she had not yet revealed his name to Scottie, she believed that Markovic, her leader, and tormentor, was dead.

The Agency reported to Scottie that Markovic had been discovered in Seoul, South Korea, after reuniting with his former associate Dr. Aaron Stone. From the surveillance they obtained, it was clear that he had had some plastic surgery done, a nose job, to alter his facial features dramatically. While this made him less recognizable in general, facial recognition programs used additional parameters to help with identification. Pattern recognition could include gait, gestures, and posture.

From the torn photograph that Scottie had found, the Agency determined that the blonde girl in the picture was Alexis at a younger age. A digitally enhanced image outlined her exquisite bone structure and gray-blue eyes. Scottie had been asked to get additional information regarding her origins, birth, and initial connection with Markovic. Alexis had only revealed to him that she grew up on a coffee plantation in Colombia. But which one? The Agency found many plantations that fit the description.

Not all government agencies shared data freely with one another. Assigned to virtual silos, the wide distribution of information did not occur, and usually remained with the collector. Those working in drug enforcement did not connect with those at the Agency, and why should they? Each had different missions and goals. Over time, uncatalogued information became lost. Corporate memories faded. And although there had been an effort to close down as many drug cartels as possible, not all the illegal operations were discovered.

Adrienne's Uncle Alberto's plantation had escaped detection, as coffee remained its principal product. Meanwhile, cocaine production continued and thrived, making significant profits for her uncle over the years. Later, someone at the Agency learned that there had been an incident near the plantation area, but that person never revealed or shared the details. Manifests of the expedition were incomplete. Researchers from the United States had reportedly been lost in the jungle. They had simply vanished into the rainforest while on a scientific mission to capture and study poison dart frogs. Bodies were never found. Foul play had been suspected, but with no proof, investigations in the Colombian jungle never happened.

Lily Robinson's revelations to her therapist about a bloody camp in the bush where the slaughter took place were never revealed and kept confidential between Lily and her doctor. Her memory had been repressed for years, and only recently, after working with a professional specializing in post-traumatic stress disorder, did she reluctantly reclaim it. At the time of the disappearance, the authorities investigating the incident recalled visiting a coffee plantation and seeing a woman, the niece of the plantation manager, with a little blonde-haired girl in tow.

The current whereabouts of both the mother and the child from that plantation were unknown. Authorities from the U.S. working to unravel the mystery found Alberto, now in failing health, uncooperative, even noncommunicative, citing difficulty with his hearing and vision. However, interviews with some of the plantation workers uncovered a story of another child who lived on the plantation around the same time. As young teens, both girls had simply, and quietly, disappeared.

* * *

Scottie was to spend the weekend with Alexis and hoped to get more of her story. Over the last several weeks, only pieces of her past life had been revealed to him, and he struggled with his sense of duty and his feelings for Alexis. They had driven from Moscow the day before, bound for St. Petersburg, some 634 kilometers north. The first night had been blissful. Their inn sat near the river and the opera house, and their room—with cozy red brocade wallpaper, flowing drapes, and opulent furniture—was a sharp contrast to their small and stark flats in Moscow. Tonight, Alexis and Scottie were planning to go to the Potseleuv Bridge, also known as the St. Petersburg Bridge of Kisses. With its spectacular view of St. Isaac's Cathedral, it stood as the setting for Scottie's declaration. He wanted to tell Alexis that he loved her.

Scottie stared into the mirror, knotting his tie with sweaty palms. He poked a finger between his neck and shirt collar, fighting back the cotton-polyester blend that seemed to choke him. A small drip dotted the silk tie.

"God damn it," he said out loud, "Now I've got to change the tie."

He looked for his suitcase sitting on the bench at the end of the bed and unzipped the outermost compartment. One additional tie nestled between the underwear, body-hugging briefs folded in small squares with bright white T-shirts by their side. The red tie stared up at him. No, it beckoned him. Scottie lifted it from its cozy nest and proceeded to try again while facing the mirror. Satisfied with his creation, he checked his digital watch with the cock of his wrist. Alexis was supposed to be back by now. She had gone out earlier for some shopping, which Scottie had declined. He would give her another thirty minutes, and then would consider whether or not to worry. Her clock-like promptness was something he had learned to expect.

Alexis enjoyed walking the streets of St. Petersburg. Compared to Moscow, this was the true seat of antiquity. Art and culture flourished here, as it had centuries ago, and existed in sharp contrast to her one-dimensional upbringing in the jungles of Colombia, and the harsh edges of Moscow and Markovic. Once the imperial capital of Russia, St. Petersburg operated as a port city on the Baltic Sea and served as home to Peter the Great. Its beauty stunned Alexis. For a moment, she let her protective armor slide from her body. She could see its shiny shadow beneath her feet. Markovic could no longer hurt her, and she had broken away from a faction that had brainwashed and abused her. Almost a decade of frustration in the isolation of the plantation had stifled her. She had always wanted to spread her wings, to fly, to be free to grow as a little girl. Those had been her formative years—years where her mother's caring and loving were present but shared, and homeschooling left too much to the imagination. Life had been limited.

Alexis closed her eyes as her mind rolled back to the days she lived on the coffee plantation. She could see herself as little Bella, not Alexis, corralled within the verdant beauty of the jungle. Alexis had only been born after the kidnapping. At first, Bella had been frightened and struggled to get free. Who was this man who dragged her by the hair and threw her into the backseat of a car after striking her mother down? Another man had been waiting at the wheel and took off the moment Bella and her captor landed on the stiff leather. A scarf had been fastened around Bella's eyes and mouth so she couldn't see or talk. There was a slight opening in the material to let air reach her nostrils, but thoughts of suffocation consumed her. The man next to her struck her face to quiet her sobbing, but Bella had only cried harder.

Ultimately, Bella found herself in a foreign country. Markovic, who confessed to being her captor, told her that she was a useful pawn in his dealings with her uncle. Bella had been forced into an environment where she became Markovic's slave. At first, it was household chores, cooking and cleaning, then business chores, fetching papers, and running errands, but within a year, it became much more. Markovic regularly sexually abused her. Still a child, Bella had been terrified and fought back, but time and Markovic's sheer physical power overwhelmed her. She became Alexis, and her former little girl-self dissolved into ashes.

123

Disassociation became a survival strategy, and then cocaine became her pacifier of choice. The cocaine numbed her spirit—a true anesthetic—and lived up to its potential of constricting her blood vessels, boosting her heart rate, and screaming euphoria into her brain. Markovic found that manipulating Alexis into coercion by withholding food as a punishment or allowing her to train with the best language instructors Russia had to offer as a reward gave him leverage over her. She succumbed to Markovic's abuse.

Alexis became multilingual, a gift recognized in her childhood, and was therefore a strategic asset to Markovic regarding the Colombian coffee/cocaine operation, and became hardened to her situation. Markovic, in turn, had kept the rest of his men out of her way. Any challenge to his property meant certain punishment. Markovic and his men instilled in Alexis a hatred of the United States and all it stood for. She had been a good soldier.

Then there was Rose. Just how Rose came to be at the plantation had always been a mystery. Alexis suspected that Rose had been part of the lost group of researchers from the U.S. Over the years, there had been much chatter on the plantation and much speculation. Others suggested she was Uncle Alberto's secret love child, and when the child's mother died, Alberto arranged to have the little girl move in with Adrienne. Wherever Rose came from was irrelevant.

A feeling of heat crept into Alexis's cheeks. She hadn't thought much about Rose in the last several years. Alexis recalled that as a child, she had been intensely envious of Rose. The dark-haired girl with green eyes had always brought smiles and happy tears to their shared mother that Bella could not. That Adrienne sometimes diverted her eyes from the gray-blue eyes of her blonde daughter filled Alexis with doubt. Her self-esteem suffered, and she wondered if there were secrets that held Adrienne back from true unconditional love for her natural daughter. Yes, Alexis felt sure that Adrienne loved her, but with reservation.

Sadness now oozed from her memories just enough to touch an exposed heart, even for a moment. Alexis never expected to see Rose, or her mother, ever again. And yet, even though his moral compass was broken, Markovic had provided her with a new direction. He was gone, but his damage remained. And cocaine was the only bandage that held the wound together.

From the first date with Sasha, her Scottie, Alexis felt something more between them. She had called it right. Scottie had been her redeemer, and Alexis knew that her feelings for him had grown in these last few months. A sensation of warmth filled her body as she stopped by the store window to peep. The arcade had provided a wealth of luxury boutiques, jewelry shops, and often overlooked clothing stores for her entertainment. Her shoulders dropped, and her blonde hair shone in the light. She felt happy for the first time—in a long time.

Alexis checked her phone. Seeing the time, she turned around to make her way back to the hotel. She zeroed in on the street map on her phone before striking out when a man approached her and asked her for directions. He had an American accent. Alexis was about to answer when she felt someone grab her around the waist and hold something to her face. Dizziness and nausea overwhelmed her. *No, not again; I cannot do this again* was the only thought that entered her mind before there was nothing else.

*   *   *

Scottie had waited long enough. Alexis should have been back by now. Donning his coat, he left the hotel and traveled to where Alexis had sent him her last text. He looked around the arcade but didn't see the striking blonde anywhere. Scottie took a deep breath. As a trained operative, he could think this through and, with the help of the Agency, find her.

The Agency wanted Alexis in their custody. This woman had infiltrated the United States as an inconspicuous event planner. Her masquerade had been remarkable. She had not been on a single watch list and had slipped into New York under deep cover. They hoped she could provide a lead that could get them to one of Markovic's secluded safe houses—or more. Unit

29155, the Russian G.R.U.'s military intelligence organization, was just as eager as the Americans to find Alexis. They, too, discovered her recent trail in Russia.

It was just a matter of who got to her first. The tick of the game timer indicated the next move.

CHAPTER 21

BOSTON

The loud ring woke Rose from a sound sleep. She had drifted off after reading the letter from her mother. Although it wasn't meant to be read until after Adrienne's death, its discovery in a box at the back of her dresser drawer took hold of Rose's curiosity and left her no choice. Adrienne's writings told the story of a little girl who called herself Rose and how she was found alone in the jungle, only to be rescued by her uncle Alberto's men. Adrienne assumed that Rose may have been with the missing American research party but had never been able to confirm this. After the kidnapping of Bella, Uncle Alberto had sent Rose to the United States, and Adrienne went back to France. Rose remembered her separation from her mother at that time and still felt the sting from their parting.

The most painful revelation in her mother's story was that Bella had been a child of rape. Adrienne admitted that the Russian man who had brutally sexually assaulted her was also the man who kidnapped Bella. Adrienne had never divulged this secret to anyone, except her Uncle Alberto. With Bella gone, Adrienne explained that Rose should know the truth. When Rose came to that point in her reading, she fled the comfort of her armchair and ran to her bed, shaking and crying. The trauma of the kidnapping and the revelation of the rape overwhelmed her. Rose started to shut down. Cortisol poured into her bloodstream, and blood rushed to her trembling muscles as guilt consumed her. Her body and mind dissociated, and numbness entered her fingers. She buried her face in the down pillow fixed at the head of the bed and wished she had never read the letter. How could she face her mother knowing she had betrayed her trust?

The phone kept ringing, and Rose reached for this noisemaker that had jolted her back to the present. Crackling on the line made Rose think the call originated from overseas. She guessed it was her mother returning her missed call.

"Hello, yes, this is Rose. Mother, is that you? I'm having difficulty with the connection. Who's calling?"

Her voice more settled now, her breathing slowed, and her self-control returned—the letter still beside her.

The woman's voice on the other end of the line spoke in French and then in English. At first, Rose did not understand what she was saying.

"Yes, this is Rose Moreau. What? What do you mean? My mother's been in a serious accident? Yes, yes, *oui, je comprend.* Let me get a pen and write down where I can reach you—where my mother is. Yes, I will make arrangements to fly as soon as I can. No, no, there is no other family, just me. What is my mother's condition?"

Rose could barely hold the pen steady enough to write down the information. Her fingers did not bend around the barrel the way they were supposed to, and the pen rolled to the floor. Rose could hear the pause on the other end of the phone. It was the absence of sound that penetrated Rose's essence and brought her to the ground. Her self-control lost, she could feel her heart rate increase, and her breathing became shallow. *Oh please, God, do not take her from me,* Rose thought. *Do not abandon me.* Something inside her felt familiar and frightening. Chaos followed by silence. She reached back into her mind, but there was no memory to grab onto, just a feeling—*mommy, mommy.* Then the voice on the other end of the phone began to speak once again. Rose strained to listen to the words, which sounded muffled like there was a box over her head.

"Oh, my God. Please don't let her die. Please don't let her die," she sobbed into the phone and then hung up. *No, not again; I cannot do this again* was the only thought that entered her mind before there was nothing else.

*   *   *

Rose called the medical school to make arrangements with the Dean of Students for a leave of absence.

"Rose, Rose," said the dean. "I can't understand you. What's happened? Why are you crying? Please try and calm down."

"It's my mother," Rose sobbed. "She's dying. I, I have to go. I need a leave of absence. They, they said she has a collapsed lung, cardiac contusions, brain injury. She's on a respirator," Rose said through tears.

"Rose, is there someone there who can sit with you now, help you? Let me send someone over to you," said the dean, recognizing that Rose was in no condition at the moment to do much of anything.

"I, I need to go right away. My mother needs me. I need to go."

"Yes, Rose. I'll have my assistant get the necessary paperwork together. Don't worry; do whatever you need to do. I'm very sorry, Rose. Take care."

The dean knew that Rose was a good student and could most likely make up her studies on her return. If the time away was too great, she could always continue her courses for a few months after the end of the first year.

Rose ended the call with the dean, still crying. Then she heard a gentle knock on her door.

"Rosie, Rose, you okay?" said a soft voice. It was one of her roommates. She pushed the door open. "Rose?"

She could see Rose was sobbing, walked over to the bed, and wrapped her arms around her.

"What's happened, Rosie?" she said.

Rose looked up from the bed. "Oh, Claudia, it's my mother. She's been in a horrible car accident, and they said she will probably die."

"Oh, Rose. I'm so sorry."

"You don't understand. I can't lose my mother. She's the only mother I've ever known. I don't know who my birth parents are or even where they're from, and I lost my sister when I was young. I have no one else," Rose cried.

"Oh, Rosie, that's horrible. What happened to your sister?"

129

"She was kidnapped, and they never found the body."

The words just fell out of Rose's mouth. She had not revealed that to anyone before and now regretted having spoken out of despair. Rose's hands shook, and Claudia was saddened by the wet, twisted face of her friend. Her roommate sensed Rose's struggle and changed the conversation. Claudia told her not to worry about the apartment or the courses at the medical school. She would look after both for Rose.

Rose's heartache lingered in the secure Boston rooms on Commonwealth Avenue long after she left; her two roommates could feel it, and a sense of sadness covered them. Prayer and hope were all that remained at the bottom of their newly-minted leather doctor's bags idle at the side of their beds. These were the only medicines they could offer Rose and her mother.

*　　*　　*

The flight to France was unremarkable. Rose remained silent during the six-plus hour journey. Able to rent a car at the airport, she drove to the outskirts of Reims, where her mother lay in a surgical intensive care bed at the largest hospital in the region. Rose gathered her strength and her thoughts and entered the building, standing tall with her tears held back by a wall of intellect.

"*Bonjour*, hello, *parlez-vous Anglais? Je m'appelle* Rose Moreau," said Rose to the woman dressed in scrubs standing at the central hub for the Surgical Intensive Care Unit.

Computer terminals located on the workstations surrounded the cluster of busy doctors, nurses, and assistants.

"*Un moment*," answered the woman. Rose strained to see the ID strung around her neck by a bright blue lanyard. The bottom of the ID said *Médecin*, and Rose realized that she was speaking with a junior doctor. As the young woman disappeared into another room, Rose reflected on her desire to become a physician. She hoped that once things settled down, she would be back on track in medical school and that her mother, Adrienne, would someday see her daughter's dream come alive.

"Hello, Miss. I am Dr. Pasteur, and I am the one caring for your mother, Adrienne Moreau."

He was a tall man, with a bloom of white hair on his head and a grayish-white goatee. Rose thought he looked kind.

"Oh, thank you. I'm so relieved. You speak English," Rose said, the words accompanied by several deep breaths.

"Yes, I did my medical training both in the United States and in England. Are you coming from the U.S.?"

"I am," Rose added quickly. "I'm a medical student in Boston. I came as soon as I got the call about my mother. How is she?"

"Rose, let us go see your mother now. As a student of medicine, you understand that her injuries are quite severe," he said as they walked down the hall and stopped outside one of the glass-enclosed rooms.

Rose could see her mother hooked up to a respirator, IVs streaming from her arms, and monitors connected to her chest. The bruising on Adrienne's face created a marbling, not unlike the mixture of dark and light rye bread. Rose pushed back the tears, and all but one obeyed. She let out a sniff and entered the room. She took hold of Adrienne's hand. It was limp, almost lifeless, and Rose closed her eyes tight and clenched her teeth until they hurt.

"Dr. Pasteur, what is her prognosis?" Rose asked as she caressed her mother's arm.

"I am sorry, Rose, but at this point, it does not look good. There is still brain activity, but her injuries and blood loss were substantial. We are not certain that she will ever regain consciousness even if she survives her internal injuries. We have done everything we can do at this point. She will remain in intensive care for some time and then, and then, we will see. I'm so sorry."

Dr. Pasteur could see the lids of Rose's eyes and the rolling in of her lips as she tried to absorb his words.

"*Bonjour*, hello," said a voice outside the room.

A short man dressed in black pants and a black shirt with a snip of white at the collar stood with a rosary dangling from his hand.

131

"Oh, Père Berger. Come in, come in," said Dr. Pasteur. "This is Rose Moreau. Adrienne Moreau's daughter."

"*Oui*, yes, yes. I know," said Père Berger.

Rose turned and looked directly into his soft green eyes. She clasped his outreached hand and started to cry. Her tears could no longer be diverted and spilled onto her cheeks, letting gravity have its way.

"Rose, the police found your name as the only contact in your mother's handbag after the accident. We have that purse locked up with security. Perhaps you would like to have it with you. If it comforts you, I have been with your mother since she was brought into the hospital. She is a beloved member of our church."

Père Berger held tightly onto Rose's hand. He understood she could not let go.

"Thank you. Thank you," said Rose.

The priest embraced her, and Rose felt her shoulders sink. Amid smells of disinfectant and sickness, Rose inhaled the scent of vanilla. Père Berger's graying hair smelled like warm vanilla milk, and Rose couldn't let him go, lest she inhale the scent of impending loss. Her amygdala and hippocampus—the seats of her sensory memory, her emotions—evoked a hot summer day, steam rising from the jungle floor filling her nostrils with heavy air, air weighted with the smell of death. Yet, her conscious brain only recognized that the scent of vanilla stayed the anxiety that Rose could not understand, only feel.

"Rose, let us pray together for your mother," said the priest.

He held Rose's hand and spoke a common prayer, "Do not fear nor be dismayed, for the Lord, your God, is with you wherever you go. He will restore you to health and heal your wounds."

Then turning to Rose, he said, "Now, let us leave your mother with Dr. Pasteur for the moment. I will get you her handbag, and you can drive to the estate to spend the night there. Have you ever been to the house in Reims?"

Rose had never given it a thought. No arrangements had been made to accommodate her stay. Not once before had there been an opportunity to spend time in France with her mother, and now that she was here, she felt alone and vulnerable. The priest could see the tears well up in Rose's eyes as she bit her lower lip.

"Père Berger, would you be able to take me to the house? I've never been there. I'm afraid to go alone," said Rose, not sure if fear or comfort drove her need for company.

"*Mais oui*, Rose. First, let me get that handbag for you, and I will meet you at the entrance to the hospital," he said and exited the glass room, distancing himself from the sounds of buzzers and bells.

Dr. Pasteur nodded to Rose and left the room. Rose squeezed her mother's hand as the tears again flowed freely like rain.

"Mother, I'm so sorry. You have suffered so much, lost so much, and have given so much. I wish I could have been more for you. I love you," she said as she gently kissed Adrienne's forehead, bandages and all.

Rose couldn't tell her that she was sorry that she had read the letter. Rose's guilt percolated up into the back of her throat, and she let out a little cough. Maybe now it didn't matter since it was not likely that Adrienne would survive her injuries. Some things were best left unsaid.

*   *   *

Rose followed Père Berger's navy-blue car to the estate. She had no idea of the vast expanse of the property. Stunned by the sprawling vineyards that lined the way to the main house, Rose inhaled deeply and let her shoulders relax as she turned off the engine. Now parked in front of the stone building, the priest exited his vehicle and walked to Rose's car's open window.

"This is it," he said. "It is a beautiful piece of property. You will find the keys to the house in the handbag. Would you like me to come in with you?"

"Oh, please, if you wouldn't mind. I would appreciate that," said Rose, feeling drained.

She stepped out of the car and felt her legs give a little underneath her. Catching herself, she straightened her body and collected her suitcase from the backseat.

"*Magnifique!*" exclaimed the priest as he opened his arms and embraced the estate. "Rose, this house, these vineyards have been here for centuries. What an extraordinary heritage you have."

Rose hesitated and then said, "Father, do you know that I am the adopted daughter of Adrienne? I don't think she ever shared this information with anyone."

"*Eh*, no frankly, I did not know that. Are you certain you are adopted? You have the Moreau coloring—dark hair and light eyes. Adrienne only mentioned she had one daughter living in America."

"Well, actually, she had two daughters." Rose felt that if she could confide in anyone, it would be this priest. "Please, Father, keep my mother's confidences."

"Yes, of course, *mais oui*," he said as Rose found the key and unlocked the front door.

They crossed the threshold together. Tall ceilings and a drafty interior greeted them. Rose let out a sigh, and the priest put a reassuring hand on her shoulder, shepherding her into the large living room. The couch by the window offered comfort, and as she nestled into the soft cushions, Rose told Père Berger everything she knew about her life with Adrienne. From the jungles of Colombia, the kidnapping, the escape to the U.S., and her brush with death in the horseback riding accident. She ended with the story of her inspiration for a career in medicine—her teacher, Lily Robinson. And now, here they were in Reims, in the Moreau house, without Adrienne.

"Oh, Father, I feel terrible. I betrayed my mother's trust by reading a letter she wrote to me that was only to be read after her death. Maybe by reading it before, um, before, you know… have I brought death to her door? I can't stop thinking about this."

"Now, Rose, you must not think so. Sometimes God has his plan. When the police went through your mother's things, they found this slip of paper with an address in Chalandry. From what I could determine from the church records, your mother had a Moreau uncle who lived there with his wife and son. I do not know what happened to them, and I am not sure that your mother found her answer."

By this time, Rose had left the peach-colored velvet couch and was looking at the papers on top of the desk in the corner of the room. The eight-legged desk was veneered in ebony with fine copper marquetry of horses and falconers—an exceptional French Mazarin writing desk from the master Andre-Charles Boulle. Rose had enjoyed reading about art while on the Compound and recognized the piece. But Rose's attention was not captured totally by the desk, but rather what was on the desk. It was a letter—a letter from Colombia informing Adrienne that her uncle, Alberto Rosario, was dead. He had inherited the coffee plantation from his dead wife's father, and now authorities could find no living relative other than Adrienne. Although no legal will was found, the lawyers assumed the plantation would most likely go to Adrienne. Rose sat down hard in the chair at the ornate desk and let out a cry.

"Rose, Rose, what is it? Did you hear what I said about your mother's journey to Chalandry?"

"Father, my mother's uncle on her mother's side, is dead. That's what this letter says."

The priest stood up and joined Rose at the desk.

"What does this mean, Rose?" he asked.

"I'm not sure, but if my mother does not survive, then I may inherit not only this vineyard but also a coffee plantation in Colombia. Having said that, I don't believe I have any formal paperwork saying that I am her heir and her child. You do understand that I don't know where I came from."

"Yes, I gathered that from our earlier conversation. But Rose, most adopted children have uncertain origins. There is no shame in that. So, let us pray that your mother survives. I know that it doesn't seem possible, but you know they always say that God works in mysterious ways."

Rose was not a very religious person. She didn't go to any church or identify with any formal religion, but she believed in the spirit of something beyond the visible.

"Father, you said that you found an address and some information on my mother's uncle on her father's side."

"Why, yes, Rose. In Chalandry."

Rose widened her look at the desk surface and saw a neat pile of black and white photographs. There was one picture of a handsome man and woman holding hands with a small boy. Rose turned the photo over and saw "*avec JP.*"

Rose turned to the priest. "Père Berger, Do you know who JP is?"

"I am sorry, Rose, I do not. Perhaps one of the older parishioners might know. You could bring the photo to Mass on Sunday, and I could introduce you to some of the women who knew Adrienne's mother, your grandmother."

Rose always felt better when she had a goal. Perhaps her mother couldn't figure out the mystery of the family tree, but maybe Rose could. Her mind bounced. There was also the puzzle of the poisoned patient Dr. Kelley had told her about. The one with the high chloride. Rose had given it some thought and had done a little research before she left for France. What if it wasn't chloride at all, but bromide?

CHAPTER 22

HONG KONG

"That was quite the mess to clean up, JP."

"*Oui*, my Lily. You of all people know that death is a messy business," JP responds.

"I find it curious that Wei Guan would use the lab of his namesake as a venue for the information exchange. It seems too obvious. But clearly, that was the case because we found him murdered and missing a forearm. Who do you think did this?"

"It could have been Guan's North Korean contact, but more likely, this is the work of Stone. You said the removal of the arm looked like a surgical procedure. Anyone else would have just hacked off the arm. *Et*, we did not expect to find both Stone and Markovic in Seoul. The information we had put Markovic in Russia and Stone under the radar. Whether they planned to meet or that occurred because of the plastic surgery is unknown. *Mais*, someone knew about Wei Guan and his missile designs and knew he would be here in Hong Kong," says JP.

"JP, why the arm? Why take his forearm?"

"Lily, someone cut it off, thinking it contained something, *eh*, like a microchip concealed under the skin. We do not know if the missile technology plans have already fallen into the hands of the North Koreans."

"So if the plans were on the chip, then why not just cut out the microchip? Why cut off an arm and have to carry that away?"

"You are assuming that the killer knew precisely where the chip was located. Perhaps he did not, so in haste, took the arm. *Et*, of course, he

137

would also have to know which arm to take—right or left," JP answered.

"JP, you know we need a complete forensic autopsy on that body we found in the bioengineering lab. We need to be sure it's really our Wei Guan and whether or not there is a microchip possibly in the remaining arm."

"*Oui*, that is being done as we speak," says JP.

"Should we return to the U.S.?" I ask. "I mean, if I don't have a target, what are we doing here?"

The crinkles around his eyes deepen. He is at a loss, shifts his weight in his seat, and thinks.

* * *

We're back in the hotel room, working to determine our next move. I focus my brainpower, all my thoughts on the facts in front of me. It's both a challenge and a puzzle. JP's phone rings.

"*Oui, oui*, you have the body now? Did they start the autopsy?" he says into the microphone using a soft voice.

I can only hear one side of the conversation, JP's questions. What are they saying to him?

"*Et*, additional DNA testing will be sent back to the U.S., *je comprends*. How long will that take for results? *Oui, oui*. What did you say? You have heard from Jackson Scott? *Et*, yes, I understand."

Then I hear a long pause. I am staring right at JP as if to will him to switch to speakerphone, and then all I hear is, "*Merci*."

"What? What?" I say with growing impatience.

I'm now in JP's face. I keep asking myself, what am I doing here? I can see that crease in his cheek. All of a sudden, JP looks older, and I now feel the acid beginning to swirl in my stomach again.

"Lily, we have the ability to perform rapid DNA testing in the field. You know about this?"

"Of course, JP. There are a few small portable machines like the ANDE, used in forensic, military, and law enforcement circles that use rapid DNA technology. These can turn a result around in two hours."

"*Eh, oui*. We have been using it in the field for some years now and…" JP adds, stopping mid-sentence.

He wants to say something else. The hesitation in his voice is apparent to me, so I continue for him.

"I believe the technology was developed in Boston. This automated process allows for the extraction, amplification, separation, and detection of alleles without the complicated hands-on processes. In the end, you get information on the DNA profile of the individual in question. It has been a game-changer, especially in disasters where identifying the victims quickly is critically important. Is that what you were going to say?"

Now I pause. He is looking at me strangely.

"JP, what is it?"

"*Eh*, no. *Ma chérie*, there is something else. The DNA from the body we discovered is not that of Wei Guan according to the results from the rapid test," JP says.

"What!"

I sit down on the couch and try and remain calm. I'm a pathologist, a toxicologist. I'm a physician; I'm part of a healthcare team. I work in a hospital. What in God's name am I doing in this circus? I should not be here. I take a deep breath and close my eyes.

*   *   *

Back in college, I took a summer off to go on a mountain climbing trip. Hiking up to base camp, a thirty-pound pack on my back, challenged every muscle in my body. Endless switchbacks eventually transitioned from evergreen forests to pure rock-scape—the timberline. And the journey had only just begun. Hours later, tents pitched, freeze-dried dinner shared by the campfire. Then, settling in for the night, the anticipation growing for the final climb the following day, thoughtful calm ensued as we reviewed the route.

Daybreak came, and we checked our gear, ready for the rock climb to the summit. As I followed the lead climber, bound to him through my harness with a red-and-blue kernmantle rope linked between us, I questioned my every anxiety-provoking reach upward. I would ask myself: why am I doing this? Why am I putting myself in danger? I could be relaxing and reading a book several hundred feet below. The leader, seeing my angst, would shout out at me: *Lily, don't look down! There's a small handhold on your left, and get your foot onto that little outcropping of rock on the right. You can do this, Lily!*

Just keep going forward. I heard myself say, *don't look down.* When I reached the top of the peak and stood firmly on my own two feet, I did look down. And I looked outward at the glorious view of the mountain tops that enveloped the entire valley below. Chin tilted to the sky, I inhaled the thin, fresh air and understood why I had chosen to put myself at risk and climb the mountain. For the sheer beauty and accomplishment of it.

I know, you're probably saying right now, too, that I should be back in Boston, teaching the next generation of doctors and caring for patients. Isn't there beauty and accomplishment in that? But here I am. In Hong Kong, with the man I adore, an arsenal of poisons by my side, and the hope that I can do something big to save the world. Crazy, I know. I open my eyes, hearing only my voice telling me *don't look down, just keep moving forward,* while studying those blue-green eyes sitting across from me.

*　　*　　*

"JP, what are you saying? That the DNA from the body in the research lab didn't match that of Wei Guan?"

"*Oui,* that is correct."

"Come on. What the hell? What's going on, JP?"

"I am not certain, Lily. First, we need a positive ID of the body we found in the lab. The question is, did the person, perhaps Stone, who murdered this man believe him to be Wei Guan from mainland China, or is he just playing with us?"

"This is scary, JP. That arm was definitely disarticulated by someone who knew what they were doing."

"*Oui*, Lily, Stone is in this for something. He left behind a lucrative medical practice. And I do not know if he was coerced or went willingly with Markovic after you poisoned him. Not anticipating his or Markovic's presence in our operation reflects badly on the Agency. An intelligence opportunity missed, so we acted, *eh*, spontaneously, to try and slow down Aaron Stone and get him out of your way. But, *ma chérie*, we failed. In retrospect, you should have killed him while you had the chance."

I hear what he says, my thoughts exactly, and then I find myself angry, my heart pumping full-speed.

"JP, I am *not* a murderer. I'm not."

I feel my cheeks getting warm. Yes, I know, I've already been a sometime-assassin for government purposes, a contract killer, but I plan those missions thoroughly. Am I making excuses for my behavior? Guilt consumes me at the frank reality of my situation.

"Let us not discuss this now, Lily."

"And what was that you said of Jackson Scott? What's the story there?"

I change the subject so I can cool off a bit. The topic of what I do for the Agency always sends acid swirling from my stomach to the lower junction of my esophagus.

"The story? *Eh*, the story, *ma chérie*, is that Scottie did make a connection with Alexis, but now she has gone missing." JP says, looking intently at my face.

"Markovic?" I ask.

"The man cannot be everywhere, Lily—Russia, South Korea, Hong Kong. I do not have the details of Scottie's encounter with Alexis or any additional information on her disappearance. However, they did identify one of the two girls in the photograph that Scottie found to be Alexis when she was younger, perhaps twelve or thirteen."

"Did they identify the other girl and the woman with her?" I ask.

"No, not yet. They had photographs of Alexis, and therefore by using AI aging programs, they could determine that the blonde girl in the picture matched Alexis."

"JP, have you seen the photograph?" I ask.

"I have not. Why these questions?"

He closes one eye as if to get a better read on my face.

"Just curious. So, what's our next move? Is there a small handhold on the right, or the left? You are the lead climber, *mais oui*." I say, pushing the words out of my mouth.

"My Lily," he says as he strokes my hair, taking that same errant strand and hooking it behind my ear. "Always a puzzle, talking in a riddle. Let me make some phone calls, and we can then plan for our next move. I believe the next move is on the side of right."

He kisses me for my comfort before I get up from the couch, ready for a change. My hands and arms quaver as a wave of energy ripples downward through my body, shaking loose the doubts.

"Okay, look. I'm going to take a walk, get out of the hotel, and put my brain to work. I may have to rethink some of these toxins I brought with me, JP."

"*Oui, ma chérie*, but with an abundance of caution."

"Got it."

*   *   *

I'm back walking the streets of Hong Kong. I'm surprised I haven't heard from John Chi. I only saw him a few days ago. He knew I was interested in meeting Dr. Guan, or I believed he surmised it when I gave him some specifics of my journey. Where is Wei Guan?

It's times like these, walking alone, that my mind wanders from one subject to another. Was it Stone or possibly even Markovic who killed that man? Who is the dead guy we found in the lab, and where is the target I was originally set out to eliminate?

I think back to the meeting with JP in my cottage. The images of chemical warfare are hard to shake. I wonder if the United States is ready for a full-on terrorist attack with chemical agents that could wipe out our largest cities. There would have to be self-imposed isolation and rationing of food if that were to happen. Food and water could become contaminated and thus scarce, leaving farmers to struggle to earn a living. Only dry goods or canned food would be available. Are the citizens of America capable of self-quarantine for months? I don't think we are prepared for an event like this, and I don't believe the government has even considered a large-scale, countrywide disaster plan.

How do I fit into this world? In my fantasy life, would I have a rational relationship with Jean Paul, the two of us living together on a defined plot of land, enjoying the world around us instead of always having to work to protect it? Sometimes I wonder. How would my life have been different if I hadn't lost my baby in Colombia, if I had lived a less adventurous life? But living a safer existence would mean betraying my true self. I am a risk-taker by nature.

When I say you don't really know someone, you don't. Because all of us project a particular exterior, one that is viewed by the world, and it may be different than what's floating around on the inside. I know that others have remarked on my steely, clinical exterior, and it serves me well. Distancing myself from emotion allows me to function at the most difficult of times. Yet I know that the most self-assured of us, particularly women, can suffer from impostor syndrome. We question our accomplishments and worry that we will be exposed as a fraud. Even though we are competent, smart, and intelligent, we need only to believe in ourselves. Project a confident exterior, yes, but understand that in the quiet of our alone time, that our self-doubts need not negatively drive us or defeat us, but rather propel us forward. Yes, I am a risk-taker, and despite moments of uncertainty, that's why I am here. Now, where can I find a new pair of shoes?

When I arrived earlier in Hong Kong to pick up the toxin, I found the shoe shop in the Tsim Sha Tsui district and planned on getting the rainbow stilettos in the window, but it never happened. This might be a good time to find something else to occupy my mind—those shoes. As I enter the store, there is a dazzling array of new pumps, stilettos, and handbags. White shoes are trending right now, but I still have my eye on those that look like camouflage for the jungle. I turn the pretty ones over, and even though the price is not in U.S. dollars, I can see that most are way above what I can afford. No matter, window shopping is one way to distract me for the time being. Finally, overcome with desire, I talk myself into the rainbow suede heels and wait until the salesperson rings me up. I might just have to mail these back home.

I leave the store and send a text to JP that I will be returning to the hotel soon after I grab a coffee. On my way to the café, a car pulls up to the curb, and a smartly dressed Asian man wearing a surgical mask exits from the rear seat, and is now walking towards me. Surgical masks are not that unusual in Asian countries, but why is he approaching me?

"Doctor," he says in Hong Kong English, "would you come this way?"

He opens up his arm and points to the car. Now, of course, I'm not going to get into that car. Why would I? Just as that thought enters my head, he's on top of me, the sweet smell of anesthetic in my face and his arm around my waist.

*   *   *

JP checked his watch, anticipating Lily's arrival when the phone rang. His posture stiffened, and he left the couch behind.

"*Oui, je comprends.* Yes, yes. I understand."

His voice reflected his anger, and his right hand curled into a fist.

"*Mais,* what I don't understand is how you let this happen. Your strict instructions were to watch her from a distance, yes, but you should have been able to prevent an abduction. Did you get a good look at the car or the man who took her?"

JP paused, garnering every detail. Closing his eyes, he thought, *Why is it when Lily Robinson goes for a walk, something always happens?* He could feel the muscles of his jaw tighten and his teeth clamp down. His cheeks puffed out as he let a big breath escape between his lips.

"*Oui*, I see, you collected the shoebox and the phone she dropped on the pavement. *Eh*, she was out buying shoes."

These last words abandoned him with another long breath, a breath of exasperation.

"Yes, bring them to me, *tout de suite, merci*," said JP as he hung up the phone.

The dark-haired man retreated into the bedroom of the suite and pulled out his briefcase. Opening it, he removed a small device from the back pocket, switched it on, and waited for the pulsating light to give him a signal. He knew Lily had stayed true to her word. When they were together in Paris, years ago, he declared his love for her, and gave her a beautiful platinum bracelet of a fine mesh weave and asked her always to wear it. Lily wore very little jewelry, only her grandmother's gold ring in the shape of a serpent, a ruby at its head, on her right ring finger, and the bracelet. A dazzling diamond on her left hand might be attributed to romantic attachment and would invite risk.

The Agency agreed with JP that Lily Robinson had no personal relationships. No family, no husband, no children, and as far as the world knew, no lover. The bracelet had become the subtle symbol of their bond. An eternal circle of love that kept them together, but it was so much more. Inside the platinum, JP had embedded a small tracking device that would allow Lily's every move to be followed. Months ago, when Markovic's men captured her while she was in front of the Metropolitan Museum in New York and then took her up to the Hillview Reservoir, he knew exactly where to find her. This simple technology became his way to keep her safe and keep her close when they were apart.

Now he could see the blinking dot of Lily on the map of Hong Kong in front of him. He knew where she had been taken, but getting to her would be difficult. The New York reservoir had been relatively isolated, and at the time, JP did not expect that many of Markovic's men would be there. But Hong Kong? Was this Markovic's work, or someone else's doing, someone who had been dogging them since they arrived in Asia?

145

JP got out his phone and made the call. While it rang, a knock on the door to the hotel suite caught his attention. It was strident and persistent. He looked away from his phone and headed toward the door. A loud but muffled sound took him by surprise. The PSS silent pistol fired at subsonic speed. Driving through the door, the bullet splintered the wood as it entered the room. JP fell to the floor, the phone next to his body. It had stopped ringing. A small voice from the speaker called out.

"Hello, hello. JP, are you there?"

Chapter 23

RUSSIA

"Get your hands off me," she said in English rather than Russian. Alexis found herself sitting on a hard metal chair with her hands tied behind her back. The man in front of her worked at loosening the ties to make her more comfortable, but she resisted.

"Who the hell are you, and where am I?" she shouted.

"Let's just say you are safe here with us for the time being," answered the man with a distinctly American accent.

"I asked you, where am I?"

Alexis looked around the modest, sparsely furnished room. A few more of the tan metal chairs clung to one white wall that hadn't seen paint in years. A small table crouched in the corner, holding up a brass lamp with an off-white textured shade. The door had a mirrored window cut into the upper half. Alexis assumed that this was one-way glass, allowing those outside the room to look in.

"Look, we know your name is Alexis Popov, and you work with a man called Grigory Markovic," said her interviewer in a calm monotone voice.

Alexis stiffened at the mere mention of Markovic's name. Her escape as a result of his death had been an unexpected gift. Meeting Scottie turned out to be her ticket back to civilization and hope that she could have a different future than the one she saw for herself more than a year ago.

"Come on, Alexis, we know you and Markovic were behind the ricin poisonings in New York City. Do you know where Markovic is now?"

The agent stepped back from the chair and took a pack of cigarettes out of his shirt pocket. He shook the box until a single cigarette emerged. Carefully placing it between his lips, he set the tip on fire. With a deep breath, he inhaled the smoke and then let the return escape from his mouth.

Alexis wasn't sure how to respond, but she recognized that she was not in a position to bargain. At one time, she thought she might lead Markovic's cause after his death, but she had no status and no power. A spent servant to Markovic, they told her. Released like a bird from a cage, she sought a new existence as she faded into the folds of Mother Russia. Life on her own suddenly tasted sweet without her master's dominance and cruelty. And then there was her relationship with Scottie, introduced to her as Sasha. Convinced that what she felt for him was real and not just her imagination uncorralled, there had been tangible love and trust. Yet her capture now would change the course of her life once again. It seemed like only moments ago while back in the hotel that her dream was coming true. But now Scottie was gone, and soon, she would be gone, too.

"Markovic is dead. I last saw him in New York, months ago," she said defiantly.

"Why do you say Markovic is dead? Who told you that?"

A puff of smoke filled the air and settled near her face. Alexis felt her nose drip, and she wished she had a hit of cocaine. Now that her hands were free, she ran her sleeve across her face and moved her body in the chair as if to settle in. Her body's true desire screamed escape.

"Markovic was killed by the Americans in New York. Now, why do you have me here? Where are we exactly, and who are you?" Alexis said with renewed confidence in her voice.

A knock at the door produced a head turn for all. The man interviewing Alexis got up from his chair and tapped on the glass. He opened the door slightly and spoke with someone on the other side. After he closed the door, the agent walked back toward Alexis with a large manila envelope in his hand. He sat back down in front of her, opened the packet, and removed three eight-by-eleven color photos of a stocky, balding man. Alexis watched the agent closely for any sign of emotion as he scanned through each picture; there was none. He handed the first photograph to Alexis and now waited for her response.

"Do you recognize this man? Is that Markovic?" asked the agent.

She quickly viewed the picture, not interested in helping. Alexis saw a man who looked not exactly like Markovic. His nose appeared different.

"That's not Markovic," she said. "It's someone who looks closely like him, but that's not him."

"Why do you say that?" the American asked.

"Because it's not his face."

But when Alexis looked again at the photograph, instead of her Gestalt impression, she focused on each of the features of the face, forgetting the nose for the moment. There they were. Those telltale steel-gray eyes. Of course, how could she have been so rash as to overlook his most defining feature? She felt a wave of nausea sweep through her body, and her upper torso fell, her head resting on her thighs.

"Hey, are you okay? Do you want a drink of water or something?"

Alexis tasted the bitter fluid climbing up to the back of her throat. She vomited over her shoes as well as those of her captor. Her face was white, yet on fire—burning cheeks and burning throat.

"What the fuck," the man said as he jumped up out of his chair, noticing bits of digested food and froth on his black shoes and socks.

The door to the room opened spontaneously, and a woman dressed in black pants and a white shirt handed the agent a roll of paper towels.

"Here you go," she said.

He carried the roll over to where Alexis sat and handed her some dry paper towels to clean her shoes while he did the same. The woman stood behind him with a wet washcloth and then handed it to Alexis.

"Here, wipe your face with this," she said.

She picked up the glass of water on the table and gave that to Alexis, too.

Alexis swallowed hard. The cool water was refreshing, but she could still taste the bitter vomit in her mouth. She had come so close to her dream, and then just like that, it was gone. The American agent nodded to the woman to leave the room and then turned to Alexis.

"So, you do recognize this man as Markovic? We believe he got a nose job to slow us down, but it takes more than minor plastic surgery to get by us. Why did he go to Korea?"

Her cheeks were still warm to the touch, and now her heart was pounding. Markovic had given her a cyanide pill when they were in New York in the event of her capture. She wished she had it now. Sitting upright, Alexis inhaled one big breath and tried to compose herself. It didn't matter anymore.

"I, I thought he was killed in New York. I didn't know he was still alive. Where is he now?"

"We were hoping that you could tell us. Have you ever heard of a man called Aaron Stone? He's a doctor who lives in Seoul, South Korea."

The American agent went into his pocket for another cigarette. He could see that Alexis's cheeks were flush and that her nose produced a slow but steady drip.

"No, I've never heard of Stone. I don't know who he is. What has he got to do with Markovic?" asked Alexis.

"We believe he is the plastic surgeon that Markovic saw in South Korea," said the agent speaking with the cigarette in his mouth. He could smoke and talk at the same time.

Then he took the butt from his mouth and said, "So how and where did you and Markovic meet?"

Alexis still didn't know who she was talking to, but she had a good idea. American accent, looking for Markovic, aware of the ricin poisonings, he must be with U.S. Intelligence. She couldn't envision a rescue coming her way, but maybe there was an opportunity to trade information for a deal.

"If I tell you what I know about Markovic, can we come to some kind of arrangement?"

Alexis felt exhausted, and her mind ground to a halt. Her concentration wandered, her eyes moving across images around the room left her feeling trapped and anxious. Sweat leaked from under her arms and between her breasts.

"I think we could work something out, but it depends on how useful to us you are."

The agent, already aware that she had made contact with Scottie, was not about to blow his colleague's cover. He knew Jackson Scott had strayed from his mission, and that's why the Agency bypassed him and picked up Alexis directly. When Scottie first reported Alexis missing, they withheld that information from him. Better to let him think someone else picked her up—at least for now. And, as far as Alexis knew, Scottie remained her Sasha from Moscow—his cover secure. Another agent had been sent to see Scottie in St. Petersburg, debrief him, and bring him in.

"I'll ask you again. How and where did you meet Markovic?"

Alexis closed her eyes and took in a big breath. With Scottie, telling her tale had been much easier. He had been someone she had a relationship with, a man who wasn't a government agent, who cared for her as a person, and not as an object or possession. Now she had to tell the story all over again, and to a man she didn't know, couldn't trust, and didn't like.

The creases in the crooks of her elbows felt damp, and her stomach remained queasy. If there were just one chance that she could cut a deal, then she would try. Looking back at her time on the plantation, Alexis saw her mother running after her to rescue her, before Markovic struck Adrienne down. *A courageous woman*, Alexis thought with renewed appreciation. Alexis blinked and started to unravel her tale. She didn't start with the kidnapping; she began with the day that Rose came to the coffee plantation. The day that changed Bella's life forever.

* * *

The smoke from Jackson Scott's cigarette swirled around in space like the feelings in his chest. He had jeopardized the operation. His emotions, rather than his head, had driven the narrative. Now he was about to meet with one

151

of his contacts, someone they had sent from Moscow to St. Petersburg to clean up the mess. Scottie knew he was fucked. He dunked the tip of the cigarette in the water glass and went over to the door to open it only after he peered through the peephole.

"Jackson Scott?" asked the man standing in front of him.

He wore a crisp white shirt under his navy blazer, a blue tie, and khaki trousers.

"Yeah, I'm Scott. Come on in," responded Scottie scanning the hallway to make sure no one had seen his visitor.

He shut the door behind him and showed the man to a seat near the desk. Scottie sat on the bed, back straight up and his feet flat on the floor.

"Look, Jackson," said the man as he settled into the chair.

"It's Scottie. I prefer Scottie."

"Sure, Scottie. I'm Agent Dan Springer, and as you know, the shop sent me down to debrief you."

Dan could see that a woman had been in the hotel room. A sleek black dress hung over the top of the door to the bathroom, and two small suitcases propped on individual luggage racks peeked out from inside the closet.

"We understand you had contact with Alexis Popov. So, what can you tell me?"

Dan took off his glasses and cleaned them with a small, soft cloth he had in his jacket pocket. Scottie could see that the color of his eyes was brown, now that the glasses were off.

"I did make contact with her. I reported in already," he said.

Scottie shifted his weight on the bed. He was sure they knew everything already anyway and that there wasn't any point in pretending otherwise.

"Did you ever ID the picture of the woman and two girls in the photo I sent in?"

Agent Springer eyed his shoes. It appeared he'd missed a spot with the brown polish when he had buffed them earlier that day.

"Look, Scottie, I don't want to get into too many details here. We know you've had contact with Popov, and then you said she went missing."

Agent Springer was a master at keeping all his cards close to his chest.

"Did she say anything about Markovic?" he continued.

"I believe that Alexis thinks he's dead. She told me that when she left the United States, her captor was killed. Her captor, presumably the man who kidnapped her when she was just a teenager, was most likely Markovic. He kept her in the fold and abused her in more ways than one."

"So, Scottie," said Agent Springer as he removed his glasses again and polished the lenses as if the first time had been inadequate. "So," he said, pointing to the luggage and clothing around the room, "is this stuff Popov's?"

Scottie stood up from the bed and walked around the small hotel room. He found his cigarettes again and lit another one. He took a large drag and then blew the smoke out.

"I know, I fucked up. I crossed the line. Yeah, these are her things. I never planned on falling in love."

"No, 'course you didn't. She must be a real piece of ass for a fuckin' Russian spy."

Scottie felt his insides boil, and if Agent Springer had been anyone else, he would have torn him apart. Instead, he just stood there, ignoring the smirk on Springer's face.

"Ok, get your shit together; we're going to take you back to Moscow while we sort out this mess. Your instructions are to assume your regular day job. Do not try and contact Popov. Oh, but then she's missing, isn't she? I'll take the girl's stuff, just in case there's anything we can find in there."

"Springer, do you know if they found her? Ah, where she is? I know that factions of Russian Intelligence have also been looking for her. They'll kill her if they get the chance," Scottie asked, keeping his voice even.

"I haven't a clue, lover boy, but whoever finds her, I'm sure she'll be getting the screwing she deserves."

Red-faced, Scottie took a big deep breath, wound his right arm back, and punched Agent Springer in the face. Springer was hit so hard that he temporarily lost consciousness as he fell to the ground giving Scottie just enough time to grab his car keys, wallet—and run.

CHAPTER 24

HONG KONG

My eyes feel heavy, and my mouth is dry like I'm just coming out of surgery after having been under anesthesia. I feel disoriented, but I quickly realize what has happened. While taking a walk to release some energy (and buying a pair of shoes as a distraction—crazy me), someone grabbed me in front of the store.

The room I'm in looks like it could be in an office building. There's no phone that I can see, and the door is locked, so I can't get out. Looking out the window, the curtain's pushed to one side, I appear to be in a skyscraper, maybe twenty-plus floors up. My purse. Where is my purse? I don't remember dropping that since it was slung over my shoulder, and I see I've lost my phone, too.

I tell myself to focus, like the fine focus of my microscope, and drill down on the problem. What's going on, and who wants me alive? I say 'alive' because they could have already killed me if they wanted to. I'll just wait and see what my abductor's pleasure is.

He must sense that I've come to; I hear someone outside the door, and my heart rate increases. My breathing, too, quickens. I look around the room for something, anything I could use in self-defense, but there's nothing. The door opens.

"It's you, Lily Robinson, isn't it?" says the short man now standing a foot from my face. "I thought that was you when I saw you at the conference in Seoul."

I can see him clearly now. It's Stone. He looks a little beaten down, and he's got a small cast on his left wrist. That break must have happened when he hit the ground during the seizure. What is his game? And why does he want me? Yet, if he is with Markovic, then I guess I already have my answer. I say nothing.

"So, now. Yes, I remember you quite well from our time together. Smart, photographic memory for all kinds of scientific facts. I can't imagine how you are involved with all of this. But, my good buddy Markovic wants a piece of you, too. I told him, only after I got to you first. So, Lily, what have you got to say for yourself?"

"Nice to see you, too, Stone. You're the same piece of shit you were back in the day. Still controlling people's lives, are you? And I might ask you the same question. What have you got to do with Markovic?"

The disgusted look on my face does not escape Stone.

"It's not going to matter anyhow, my precious flower. I thought of you once as my precious flower, my angel. But that was not to be. You were too independent, too free to be mine," says Stone with great sarcasm.

"As I said, you were an abusive control freak," I respond. "All you wanted was for people to admire you, to kowtow to you. You never cared about them. Now, you change people's faces not to help them overcome some horrible disfigurement, but as a way to escape their criminal life—as a means to avoid being captured by the authorities. You're in it up to your eyeballs, and there's no turning back, Stone. You walked out of that hospital and essentially gave up your medical practice. And for what? You're a traitor."

I can't contain myself now. There's no denying the edge in my voice. Sharp enough to create a gaping wound right through his torso. He was always clever but getting into this thing with Markovic, I don't know. I feel my heart pounding in my chest. How do I avoid a lethal blow from a true martial arts master? Stay calm, Lily. You can handle this.

"So, what is your game with Markovic, Stone?"

"Markovic and I go way back. Back to Afghanistan. Yes, he needed a little help with his face, and so he came to me. I didn't want him in my life again, but then, here we are. Up until now, life has been good for me. Markovic

155

fucked that up, but there's always a new start somewhere around the globe. And, leaving the United States was velvet for me. I've made more money in Korea than I ever could have stateside, and there are some women here who like being dominated by men like me. That's my experience."

His lips curl a little. Not a smile, just a smirk. His arrogance is making the vessels in my neck constrict and my blood pressure rise.

"Did you kill that scientist in the Hong Kong lab?" I ask.

"Of course, angel. I'm surprised to hear that you went to that lab. Did you like my work?" he says with a smooth voice.

No wobbles there. He's cool. I'm not sure he knows who he killed.

"Dr. Wei Guan?" I ask.

He takes his right forefinger and taps his temple, then says, "It's all right here, Lily Robinson."

I can feel a shudder go through my body. He's toying with me. It's only a matter of time. How much I have, I don't know.

"What was Markovic doing in Seoul other than getting his nose rearranged by you? Does he have anything to do with selling chemical warheads to the North Koreans?"

I take advantage of my humble position, the non-threatening little lady. Ha! Will he spill it all out to me?

"You seem to know an awful lot for just a pathologist. What's your real role, Lily?"

I truly hate surgeons who minimize the work of pathologists! My fangs come out.

"Stone, I'm a doctor just like you. Only I decided to use my skills for the good of the many, and you chose evil. I think it's pretty simple, isn't it? We just work on different sides of the Pearly Gates."

"You mean you deal with the dead, and I deal with the living," he says.

I laugh in his face.

"No, Stone. You keep company in hell, not me."

He doesn't like it when I challenge him. I can see his teeth clench and his body stiffen.

156

"Yes, Lily. Markovic's got chemical weapons, and Guan's technology is the key to making it all fly. I know the North Koreans, so when I thread the needle, their plan will go forward. I may not have been in on the original deal, but China is making it worth my while. North Korea will get the missile technology they have been looking for, and China will work at brokering some kind of agreement after the U.S. suffers a blow that will knock it down into its place. We are creating a little chaos. Not a bad plan to disrupt the world order. You know me, I'm just a facilitator, angel."

"I don't understand what Russia gets out of all this," I say to him, trying to learn as much as I can.

"Come on, Lily. Russia wants to interfere with anything that has to do with the U.S. Elections, fake news stories, bullshit on social media. They stir up political rallies and make America look worse than it is. As long as they can sow the seeds of doubt, mistrust, derision, and division, they have accomplished their goal. It seems to be working for them. The U.S. is rockier than ever before."

I can see that he has relaxed. Even through his shirt sleeves, his biceps do not appear as contracted as they were moments ago.

"Stone," I say, softening my voice, "where will you go after this?"

"I'm headed to Vietnam. South Korea was a plastic surgeon's dream, but with the money I'll get from this shit diversion, I can set up another practice in Vietnam. My contacts in China and North Korea are on board with me. If Markovic wants to throw in some chemical weapons, he can do it without me."

Stone tells me this, knowing that he's going to kill me, so it doesn't matter to him. I can almost feel his carotid pulse as I watch it blink on his neck. I try and focus. I feel my carotid pulse, too. Keep it together, Lily. It's just one more pitch up the rock slope.

"You said you were going to hand me over to Markovic. Where is he?" I'm thinking it doesn't hurt to keep talking, to keep asking him questions even if he doesn't answer. It's called 'buying time'. I'm scared.

"You are a curious bitch, aren't you, angel. I did tell you I was going to hand you over to Markovic, but I'm not. I don't think he would mind if I had the pleasure of killing you myself. It's been quite some time since I had the satisfaction of taking a life. Not since Afghanistan. But the joy of using my bare hands again, well, that would be something. They say martial arts should be used defensively, but there are exceptions. And like your poisons, Lily, not that messy. It was you, wasn't it, who poisoned me?"

His voice is more intense. He is turning. I see his arms flexing. I've got to slow this down. Softly, Lily, softly.

"Aaron, what happened to you in Afghanistan?"

I ask in a quiet tone using his first name, hoping to de-escalate the exchange.

"Afghanistan? It was shit over there. Heat, desert, drugs, and death. An unbearable hell hole. I stitched men back together only to see them blown up later. One night I went for a walk and was ambushed by some rebels. They hauled my ass back to some fucking cave. Wanted me to stitch up one of their wounded. Added in a little torture to make it worth my while. I have the marks on my back to prove it. Provenance. After I stitched their guy up, under gunpoint, that fucking piece of shit handed me a cup of something to drink. I threw it back in his face, the gun dropped, and I was able to strangle him with my bare hands. It was surprisingly satisfying. I found my way back to my own camp."

He hesitates. Stone stops his story. He's thinking.

"I'm sorry, Aaron. Is Markovic in Seoul or here in Hong Kong?"

My heart is pounding. I should be at the medical school teaching or in the lab. Steady; steady.

"Yes, that idiot Russian is in Seoul. I sent him a gift. After all, he's the one who sucked me into this; the rest, well, it's good to know generals in high places. Tomorrow night I'll have the pleasure of introducing my North Korean contact to Wei Guan at a scientific congress dinner right here in Hong Kong. It's a hell of a deal. Now, if we're finished with the chit-chat, angel."

Stone moves in closer to me. Now or never, I tell myself. Disarm him.

"Um, crap. My foot is killing me," I say just matter-of-factly to produce a puzzled look on his face.

"What?"

With a groan, I bend down and take off one of my stiletto shoes. These are the booties I wore for the Mt. Vernon affair. Do you remember that? That's where I assassinated the diplomat while he was enjoying his salad at dinner. The lever is released, and with all the speed I can muster, I leap up and stab Stone in the neck with the heel of my shoe. The carotid blip, my target. He grabs at his throat as I fall back away from him.

"You bitch!"

Here comes his outstretched leg. It originates from the leap into the air— one leg bent while the other, foot first, lands into the opponent's body for a killing blow. But he drops right there on the floor in front of me. Just drops.

My hands are shaking. I'm not going to check for a pulse just yet, either. I have to give the toxin a chance to work. Yes, toxin. The new derivative I planned on using for Dr. Guan. Nothing like a test run. Stone is looking blue. I killed him. My deep breaths follow. One of those big long breaths fills every alveolar sac in my lungs.

Now, how do I get out of here? The door cannot be budged, but Stone has to have a key on him, or how would he get out? His body is in a heap like a bunch of discarded clothes thrown to the floor. Somewhere in that pile, there must be a key.

I'm on my knees now. As I lean in, I can smell his aftershave, reminding me of a smothered past. I move my hand ever so gently into his pockets. There's nothing there. Then I remember. He always wore a chain around his neck. I unbutton his shirt, and sure enough, around his neck are his dog tags with the key dangling in between the rectangular T304 stainless steel identifiers. My fingers travel to his throat to break the chain, and I can sense the hair on the back of my neck and arms stand on end as I feel his hand move onto my back. *Oh, God*!

The door to the room bursts in. I roll off of Stone pushing his arm down, and spin towards the couch. This is the end.

159

"Robinson, Robinson, where are you?" says a voice in a very distinct French accent.

"I'm here, JP. On the floor by the couch. It's Stone. I thought he was dead, but—"

Before I can finish, JP is over me, extending his hand, while someone else is hunched over Stone. He pulls me up, but I can see him wince. He's been hurt.

"JP, what happened to you? I see you guarding your left side?" I ask with concern.

I have to tone it down since we have another agent in the room. JP laughs.

"*Eh*, Lily Robinson. You ask me what happened, and yet here you are kidnapped by Stone, and somehow, you have managed to take him out. You did not need our rescue, *oui*? What will we do with you?" he says, shaking his head.

"JP," says the other agent. "Stone is dead. I'll get someone over here to take care of the body."

"*Merci*. I will take Robinson back to the hotel and catch up with you later," says JP, then turning to me, "Robinson, *et* get your shoe. I found your pocketbook outside this room. Here you go." He hands me my bag, and I put on my bootie while hopping on one foot.

*   *   *

We're in the car now. I'm still pretty shaken. It's been silence since we left the room where Stone held me. JP is not speaking, so I start.

"JP, how did you know where to find me?"

"*Ma chérie*, ever since that first time in Paris, I have been able to find you," he says and reaches for my arm. He fingers the platinum bracelet that circles my wrist.

My lips fall open, and I look at JP intently.

"Jean Paul, are you telling me this bracelet is some kind of a tracking device? Is that it?"

I can't hide the conflict in my voice. He lets out a sigh and winces again as his chest moves in and out with each breath.

"*Chérie*, what I love about you is that you are a free spirit. You are your own woman. Independent. Competent and capable, but you are also a risk-taker. No one climbs those rocky ledges that overlook the air below unless they are willing to embrace danger to reach their goal. And, Lily, all risk-takers need someone to watch over them."

He takes my hand and squeezes it.

"JP, I don't know if I should be angry or grateful. As you could see, I had the situation under control."

I clear my throat and continue.

"No, I'm grateful," I tell him. "Knowing you can find me anywhere on the planet gives me a sense of calm. Thank you. Now, what happened to your side, or do I have to lift your shirt and see for myself?"

"Just a small wound. A bullet grazed my side. I can tell you more about that later," he says, dodging my question for now.

"Really, JP? A bullet grazed your side. How is that not a major and immediate story?"

"*Ma chérie*, and I would like to know what happened to Stone. One of your poisons, *oui*?"

"Touché," I respond. "JP, I have info for you. Since Stone was going to kill me anyway, he didn't mind sharing a few details. I know where Wei Guan will be. Sort of."

"My Lily," he says, making my name into two long syllables. "I want to hear every word. Let us go to the hotel, have a quick bite, and review what we know."

I can't help but think that when we reach our destination, we will embrace each other like mating swans, share stories like sailors in the night, and plan our next moves with the precision of a heart surgeon.

* * *

161

After leaving Lily back at the hotel room, Jean Paul made his way to a small office park in the opposite direction of the Tsim Sha Tsui district. As he entered the building, he checked that his gun remained snug in its holster. Following the recent attempt on his life, he had become more cautious of his surroundings.

Shallow breaths slowed his walk but reduced the ache he felt with each pull of his rib muscles. One stop before the stairs, and a steady hand to buttress his side, before moving on. Only five flights, his head tilted upward. Deeper breaths meant more pain. JP wanted to avoid the elevator. No space to move if he had to. When he reached the fifth floor, he found the designated room and knocked on the door. Familiar sounding footfalls became louder, and then the door opened. It was Parker.

"Hey, hey, JP," said Agent Parker, "how are you feeling, old man? Last time I saw you, I had to pick you up off the floor of your hotel room and take you in for repairs."

"Good to see you too, *mon ami*," said JP shaking Parker's hand, not wishing to be thought of as old.

"Do we know who fired the shot?"

"Not yet. Working on it. But I do have some news from headquarters. Have a seat," said Parker.

Another sparsely furnished room, just enough for the essentials of conversation.

"First, we located Jackson Scott, or at least we had him initially," said the agent, his trim body filling out the silhouette of his shirt while his wavy brown hair careened over his left eye.

"*Et*, what do you mean, you 'had' him?" asked JP.

"Well, you know that stupid fucker Agent Springer? He got a little out of control with Scottie back in Russia, and Scottie bolted. Yeah, he's on the run, but I think we'll be able to bring him in, no sweat."

"What happened?" JP asked, looking around the room.

It was a small office, most likely rented under an assumed name so that there could be private meetings as needed.

"Turns out ol' Scottie got himself mixed up with Alexis, if you know what I mean. We do have her in custody, and she was shocked as hell to learn that Markovic was still alive."

JP sat quietly and listened. He knew his relationship with Lily Robinson would be more than frowned upon.

"There's more, JP. From what Alexis told us, it looks like Markovic kidnapped her from a coffee, or should I say cocaine, operation when she was a budding teen. Then hauled her off to Russia, where he brainwashed her into his way of thinking. We're trying now to find the exact location of that plantation in Colombia."

"So, there was an initial drug connection between the two. That might help explain the relationship between Stone and Markovic," added JP.

"Right. Stone. We just picked up the body. I see it was our doctor who brought him down. Which poison was it this time?" asked Parker with a little laugh, then added, "Last time I pulled her out of the New York reservoir, she had just jammed a syringe full of, what was it?" Parker hesitated.

"Aconite," JP filled in.

"Was it aconite this time, too?" asked Parker.

"I haven't gotten those details yet," said JP.

"Anyway," Parker continued, "remember the photograph that Scottie found on Alexis?"

"*Oui*, the one with the woman and two girls. We already know the one girl was Alexis. Did we determine who were the other girl and woman?" asked JP, wanting to move the conversation along so they could finalize their plans. His side hurt.

"Alexis said the other girl in the photo just showed up one day on the plantation when some men brought her in from the jungle. She was just maybe three years old at the time."

"Do they know where she came from?" asked JP, his curiosity now building.

"Okay, JP, this is where it gets crazy. Turns out that around that same time, there was a research team from the U.S. that just went missing. They vanished, and the story was buried. Only one known survivor," said Parker, his voice now tense like a rubber band about to snap.

"*Et*, the one survivor was the little girl, *oui*?" said JP, anticipating the climax.

"No, JP. Not the girl, one of the scientists; it was Lily Robinson."

JP let out a gasp. He bent his neck back so his eyes faced the ceiling. Why didn't he know this? Why didn't he see this coming? He felt a red wave of heat rising into his face, the furrows in his cheeks deep with crimson. Finally, he spoke.

"I do not understand, Parker. What are you saying?"

"Well, we have to confirm, but the way it looks is that our Robinson was on a biology mission some twenty years ago where everyone but her disappeared. The assumption now is this little girl survived, too, but we have to figure out who she belonged to."

"Parker, I don't understand how we could not know this," asked JP, the heat dissipating now.

"Because, my friend, we operate in silos in this government. We are not the drug operation guys. One section of the government doesn't know what another section of the government is doing, or maybe doesn't want to, and if you go to the trouble of burying any evidence, who the hell is going to remember twenty-something years ago. I sure as hell won't."

"I cannot believe it," said JP.

"Turns out only one person knew about this connection, and that's how they came to bring Robinson to the Agency's attention," added Parker.

"*Et*, who was that?" asked JP.

"Pixie Dust. Yep, the guys back home who are putting this puzzle together for us figured out that Pixie Dust came across the article and found a way to exploit Robinson. I haven't got all the facts for you yet. Still waiting on some intel to come back."

Parker went over to the sink and filled a glass with water. He could see that JP was thinking and was surprisingly subdued. He took a few sips of water and said, "So, what's your take on this, boss?"

JP hesitated. He debated on how much he should share with Parker now, but he thought it was important that he understand the consequences.

"Parker, you and I both know where this is going to lead, *oui*?"

"I have a pretty good idea, JP. The question is how do we handle it, and what do we tell headquarters?"

Parker had finished his glass of water by now.

"Let me think about this. Do not say a word to Robinson. When the time is right, I will speak with her. She trusts me," said JP.

"I know she does," said Parker with a knowing look.

JP thought his friend might have guessed at his affair with Lily, but nothing was ever said or confirmed.

"What about the woman in the photograph? Did they identify her?" asked JP.

"Um, Alexis said it was her mother whose name is Adrienne. Said she used to talk about how she came over from France to help her uncle, and then he never let her return home. The uncle sounded pretty brutal."

This revelation lit JP's mind on fire as he mentally moved squares of information in his mind like those on a Rubik's Cube. Solid red on one side. When he left France for the United States, he assumed a false identity. At that time, an official, long since deceased, changed JP's last name from Moreau to Marchand to create distance from his remaining family as a means of protection. Looking back, Jean Paul now realized that in a tender moment with Lily, he had revealed his true identity to her while in Boston when she asked him to share some details of his life. He was angry with himself for that momentary weakness. Had she been asleep when he told her who he was? He thought so but couldn't be sure. As it was, Parker knew him only as JP Marchand.

"Parker, do we know the woman Adrienne's last name?" asked JP.

"I think they said it was Monroe or Moreau; something like that," said Parker, distracted from the conversation. He opened some cabinets above the sink to see if there were any snacks in there.

"Don't they keep any food in this place? I'm starving. Want to go out and grab something to eat before you go back to your new hotel room with no bullet holes in the door?"

"*Eh*, no. I had a bite earlier. I should check on our doctor before she stabs someone else with poison," said JP, trying to lighten the conversation.

His mind, now at the bursting point, tried to contain all that Parker had shared with him. JP couldn't yet imagine how he would be able to look Lily in the eye. How would she feel about him and their relationship if she knew the truth about the Agency? At some point, he knew he would have to tell her, but not before they completed their mission. First, they had to find Guan, and Markovic. To stay resolute.

"Parker, *eh*, did Alexis say anything else about her time at the plantation?"

"Well, she told the guys in Moscow that when she lived at the Compound, her name was Bella and not Alexis. It was Markovic who changed it."

"Did she happen to tell them the name of the other girl in the photograph?" asked JP.

"Yeah, I think they said the other girl's name was Rose. Yeah, that was it, Rose. You know, like the flower."

"*Je sais*, Parker. I know." And finally, each side of the Rubik's Cube had only a single color.

CHAPTER 25

FRANCE

Certain people love to solve puzzles. Doctors, in particular, are puzzle-solvers and the supreme art of puzzle-solving falls to the pathologist. These physicians take all the clues before them—those in the blood, the urine, any tissue in the body—and information from the patient's signs, symptoms, and history to make a diagnosis. Armed with this diagnosis, the treating physician then creates a plan and helps the patient on their way to recovery. Rose was such a puzzle-solver and chose this sub-specialty of medicine for that very reason. Solving the mystery to her mother's family tree would provide not only an answer to the past but a distraction from her current state of despair.

After speaking with some of the elder parishioners introduced to her by Père Berger, the village priest, Rose heard how her grandmother, Adrienne's mother, had passed away at home after a long illness. Sorting out the estate details had become her mother's obsession. The large property had presented Adrienne with more than a few challenges, given several outbuildings and a large house with many rooms, closets, and hidden locations. The Moreau family had a remarkable history. Rose pored through piles of paperwork and learned about Adrienne's father's brother and his small family that had moved to Chalandry. Now she understood why her mother had made the trip. Finding a connection to her cousin and his parents, if they were still alive, would help cement Adrienne's family heritage in France.

The internet was a good source of information, and Rose had thought to bring her laptop on her journey abroad. She set up a spot in the living room of the big house as a working office. Her cell phone now served as a wireless hot spot since the house did not have a fast and modern Wi-Fi set up. After hours of searching on the internet trying to track down her adopted family's whereabouts, she decided to return to the hospital, now a part of her daily routine, to check on her mother.

Adrienne's condition had not improved. She remained unconscious, and the ventilator worked steadily to keep her breathing. Rose checked the monitors that displayed the only indication of Adrienne's health status. Her heart, her lungs, all performing, registered with little blips and waves on the screens, yet Adrienne slept in silence, unaware of their presence, or of her daughter's. Rose took the opportunity to sit and read to her mother. She thought it would be the sound of her voice, rather than what she read, that might soothe her mother's pain. Choosing to read some medical literature out loud, one paper, in particular, caught Rose's attention while she had been researching a case online. Now sitting by her mother's side, she could use the time to review her findings, and her voice could drown out the intensive care unit beeps and buzzers while giving Adrienne some comfort. Rose focused on the clinical information found in the article. This led her to solve the puzzle of Dr. Kelley's case. So absorbed in her work, she did not hear the doctor come into the room. Rose was startled.

"I am sorry," said Dr. Pasteur in his elegant English. "I hear you are reading to your mother, *oui*?" he said.

"Oh, no problem," said Rose. "I was working on a case that one of the doctors gave me before I left medical school to come here."

She shifted slightly in her chair so she could remove her right leg from under her.

"I see. Yes, I remember you are a medical student. So, *docteur*, what is your case?" asked Dr. Pasteur, taking his hands out of the pockets of his lab coat.

Rose could see his name tag in sharp blue embroidery on the left chest pocket. She felt bold enough to continue.

"Well, after considerable research, I learned that the instrument that determines the chloride concentration in blood—the blood gas analyzer—

can sometimes mistake bromide for chloride. Both chloride and bromide are halides, that is, they are halide anions or a halogen atom with a negative charge. Fluoride is another example."

"I see. So, what were your patient's symptoms that piqued your interest in this case?" he asked with curiosity.

Rose remembered Kelley circling chloride on the whiteboard from the list of electrolytes when she was in his office.

"Dr. Kelley—um, that's the doctor who told me about the case—Dr. Kelley's patient had a history of chronic abdominal pain, vomiting, diarrhea, and a remarkably high chloride concentration."

"I see where you are going with this. A high chloride concentration, or hyperchloremia, would produce different symptoms such as fatigue, high blood pressure, dry mucous membranes, excessive thirst, and muscle weakness. And that is not what your patient had, *n'est-ce pas?*" he said.

"Right. I learned that within the blood gas instrument, there is a small ion-specific electrode that measures chloride, but a high enough bromide concentration will fool the instrument into thinking that the patient has elevated chloride," said Rose.

She felt good about her explanation and glad that she had a chance to think out loud.

"So, my young puzzle-solver, how did your patient get bromide?"

"Dr. Kelley told me that the estranged wife of the patient was a hairdresser. With a little more sleuthing on the internet and some toxicology books, I learned that sodium bromate was a constituent of hair waving or curling lotions. I guess, somehow the wife found a way to use this compound to poison her husband. Do you think I have this right?" Rose asked.

"Rose, you will make a fine doctor," said Dr. Pasteur as he put his hand on Rose's shoulder.

Rose looked back to her laptop, feeling pleased with her detective work. She would send an email to Dr. Kelley and tell him of her theory. The distraction gave her a boost, but when she looked away from the computer, she could see that Adrienne had not moved. Rose squeezed her hand.

"I am sorry, Rose. There has been no change in your mother's condition. Sometimes it takes a long time for the body to heal. Keep your faith. Your being here will be a comfort to her. I will check back tomorrow."

Dr. Pasteur left the room as quietly as he came in. All Rose could hear were the various tones of the monitors.

"I love you, Mother. You are the only mother I remember, and you will always be my mother," said Rose.

Rose thought she saw a momentary flicker in Adrienne's eyelid and dismissed it as only wishful thinking. With the laptop securely loaded into her backpack, the Moreau estate remained the only destination for Rose's tired mind and body.

*   *   *

Silence accompanied Rose on the drive to her mother's home, and when she entered the big house, she felt the chilly draft, and a strong sense of loneliness overwhelmed her. She longed to be back in Boston with her roommates and studying in the library, not in her mother's hospital room. The mirror at the end of the room over the side table reflected Rose accurately—her dark hair was tousled carelessly, and her clothes displayed wrinkles from top to bottom. The weight of her situation sat squarely on the young woman's shoulders, and Rose began to cry. She saw the tears spilling over her eyeliner and down her blushed cheeks while the mirror captured all her sorrow. Only the ping from her computer broke the spell.

Rose wiped away the tears and went over to the desk. It was an email from one of the registries with information on her mother's relatives. According to the email, both Adrienne's aunt and uncle were deceased, but her cousin had moved to the United States in the vicinity of Washington, D.C. However, once he reached the U.S., no further information or record of Jean Paul Moreau could be found. Rose's disappointment brought more tears. The single clue of immigration to America was probably a dead end. She wondered if Adrienne had uncovered the same facts when she went to Chalandry.

Rose was about to close down her computer when again, she heard the familiar ping again. An email from Dr. Kelley popped up in the inbox. Rose's theory had been correct. Kelley, excited that she was such an astute student, encouraged her to spend more time in the laboratory when she resumed her studies at the medical school. He suggested a few hours a week of learning the backbone of pathology and laboratory medicine. He said he thought that Dr. Robinson would like her, too, as she enjoyed teaching students, but unfortunately traveled all too frequently. Rose felt buoyed again. A smile passed over her face. She had never gotten the opportunity to have a one-on-one with Lily Robinson, but she would change that on her return to Boston. Rose closed the laptop.

Despite the early hour, Rose decided to go to bed. She was physically and emotionally drained. Leaving her phone to charge in the living room on the great desk, she headed up the stairs where the rooms located off the landing felt cavernous and cold. Rose found her way to the bathroom and ran the water until it was hot. She soaked her washcloth with lavender soap and removed any remaining makeup painting her face.

Done with her routine, she pulled on her fleece pajamas, the ones with the pink top and cozy bottoms covered with designs of palm trees and flowers. Rose closed her eyes and imagined herself back at the boarding school, riding her favorite horse around the outdoor course. Her breathing slowed, and she drifted off to sleep.

The ornate desk in the downstairs great room started buzzing. The cell phone slid across the surface, muted in its attempt to notify the young medical student. Dr. Pasteur hung up the phone, unable to reach Rose, and debated whether to drive out to the estate. He decided to wait until morning. Some things are better left said in daylight, and in person.

CHAPTER 26

HONG KONG

I've been waiting for JP to come back from his meeting. He's been wounded, and he's running around the city like it doesn't matter. I'm not happy about that, and I'll let him know how I feel when he gets back. Meanwhile, I've had the chance to answer a few text messages from Kelley whose been holding down the toxicology consult service in my absence. He's working on a case of a young patient who presented with symptoms consistent with a stimulant and now having hallucinations. The standard tox screens have been negative, so I tell him to look for cathinones that come from the khat plant. This African species, *Catha edulis*... ah, finally, I hear a knock at the door between our two rooms.

"My God, Jean Paul. What's going on? Let me take a look at that wound again and see if it's bleeding through the bandage. You shouldn't be out there; you should be resting," I tell him.

I can see from the scowl on his face that he doesn't like me telling him what he can and cannot do.

"*Ma chérie*, thank you for thinking of me, but I am all right. Let us talk some more about what Stone told you, and then we need to make plans."

He looks tired. The furrows in his face reflect trouble.

"Jean Paul, what is it? I sense some distance in you. Are you sure you're okay?"

He doesn't answer. There's something hidden, but what? Is he not telling me all there is to know about the attempt on his life or the extent of his injury? I wait.

172

"Lily, the information you got from Stone was correct. We know where to find our Dr. Wei Guan, *oui*, our elusive Dr. Guan. He will be attending a gala dinner for a technology symposium in Hong Kong. Stone planned to meet him there with his North Korean contact. *Et*, we do not believe Guan, or the North Koreans, know Stone is dead. We've obtained tickets for this event. Can you find something suitable to wear for tomorrow?"

This is unexpected. I know JP can see my nose scrunch up on my face, and my lips press into one another. I'll need my very best swimsuit as we are about to dive into the deep end of the pool that has no bottom.

"Lily, we will be going as scientific colleagues. Here," he says.

He hands me some business cards. One says Dr. David Lavigne, Senior Research Scientist from Global Tech, France, and the second card reads Dr. Eve Laurent, Senior Research Scientist from Global Tech, France.

"I see; we are both senior research scientists. What do we research?" I ask him, leaving my wardrobe issue aside.

"*Et* Lily, this brochure explains our company's mission and products."

It looks professional enough and has a few pages with photos and information on technology. JP continues.

"Years ago, we purchased some offices in France to serve as a front for the company *du jour*. *Eh*, you see, we can create a brochure depending on our business needs. I think you will find all you need to know here," he says, tapping the pamphlet.

"JP, I have collected a few business cards from my travels. I will also be using one of those."

"How so, Lily?" he asks.

"I'll tell you later, JP. It's better that you don't know upfront. It reduces the anxiety," I tell him as if I have none of my own. He can see the closed smile on my face indicating a wink.

"JP, one more thing. Will we be wearing a disguise? Some basics like hair and glasses?"

"*Mais oui*. I know you love wearing all those wigs you have been carrying around. Will you be blonde or brunette, curly or straight?"

173

He lets out a little laugh, and the corners of his eyes crinkle. I ignore his banter and ask him about his attire. He's easy, but I need more information.

"Will I need a formal dress? What kind of dinner is this?"

"*Oui*, something *tres jolie*, to match your sparkling eyes," he says and pulls me in close.

I feel him. He's breathing deeply, and so am I. I gently touch his side, and he flinches.

"Let us go, Lily, *tout de suite*," he says.

God knows I've been dragging my luggage and toxins all over Asia.

* * *

This is it. JP and I are going in. A toe in the water before we stand on the edge of the springboard, ten digits dangling on their own, hands straight up in the air, and with a full twist, enter the proverbial deep end.

The great room is already packed, and I can see company executives and scientists filling the space in non-business attire. The room is octagonally shaped with a matching ceiling that looks like a spider's web spun in glass. In the center is a five-pointed star penetrating slightly from the overhead glass panes. My eye catches the beautiful panels in the walls that contain photographic land- and seascapes. I wonder if the photos change like those in the digital frames you keep on your living room end table. The fifty large round tables almost seem engulfed by the vast space. Each, holding up to ten guests, is surrounded by bland gray straight-backed chairs while the centerpiece, a floral arrangement in the shape of a Christmas tree, floats above red circular doilies. There are many technology giants here from several countries, and JP and I fit right in. I'm nervous, but I'm prepared.

I'm wearing a simple but elegant ensemble. The high neckline of this ankle-length stretchy column dress has a keyhole opening in the back and a thigh-high slit on the left. A satin ribbon defines the waist of this whipped apricot-colored classic, and I've paired the dress with open-toed satin stilettos wrapped with a crystal vine around the ankle. My wig of blonde hair rises in a twisted up-do that I've secured with a sparkly hair clip, and my beaded clutch is slung neatly across my body. I'm dressed to kill.

"Robinson, you are ready, *oui*?" JP asks me under his breath while smiling.

Jean Paul is wearing a handsome tuxedo and has added extra gray to his dark hair. I just smile back at him. He is mic'd up, so addresses me by my last name. JP has assured me that the man standing over near the seascape is Dr. Guan. Yes, Dr. Wei Guan. Finally. Confirmed by facial recognition and whatever else my spy is using. JP is wearing dark horn-rimmed glasses that contain a small camera device feeding into a monitored computer sitting with our guys observing the feed. Don't ask me how that all works. That's not my area of expertise.

I'm the poison lady, some even say, the queen of all poisons. My job is to make this look like absolutely nothing unusual occurred to cause Guan's unfortunate death. And if I can get to him before he sits down at the table, even better. The local police, or whoever, on review of the surveillance cameras, will not see how it was done.

Our target is speaking with a Korean man, and I have no idea who he is. Could he be the North Korean waiting for the intel transfer? I hope we are not too late.

"JP, you don't think that's the North Korean who is supposed to meet with Guan, do you?" I ask, now feeling acid creep into my mouth.

"Robinson, we expect that Guan is waiting for the introduction via Stone. *Mais*, let me see if I can get a read on him," answers JP as he turns his head so that he is looking directly at the man.

He goes silent, and then says, "*Et*, we are good."

The Korean is distracted by another guest, and we move in on Guan. The room is crowded. Everyone is greeting each other with bows and business cards. We have sufficient cover.

"Good evening," says JP in the thickest French accent he can muster.

He speaks to him in English, expecting this is the universal language of science.

"I am Dr. Lavigne," JP says.

Since we are in Asia, JP bows before Dr. Guan instead of extending his hand and reaches into his jacket pocket to retrieve his business card case. He presents a card to Guan with two hands as a sign of respect, and in turn, Guan returns the gesture. Each man studies the card intently since it is an extension of the bearer.

"Dr. Lavigne," says Dr. Guan, having difficulty pronouncing the name. He smiles brightly. "Hallo," he adds, then graciously bows again.

"Dr. Guan, I would like to introduce you to my colleague, Dr. Laurent," JP says slowly while looking at me. "As you can see, we both work at Global Tech."

Dr. Guan nods his head in agreement. We know he understands some English, but he may be slow on the uptake on the finer points, as English is such a challenge to learn.

With that cue, I open my clutch and hand Guan my business card, also using two hands. He customarily accepts the card and brings it closer to his face.

"Doctor," he says, having difficulty with my name as well, "You are not Dr. Hyeon, Materials Diagnostics?" he says questioningly.

The card is written in Chinese.

"Oh, *pardonne-moi*," I answer in as thick a French accent as I can muster, "That must be a card given to me from one of the other guests. My apologies."

I extend my hand toward him. He gives me back my card, and I retrieve another card from my purse. We once again go through the presentation ritual.

"Thank you," he says, resuming his scanning.

We can see that this conversation will go nowhere, given that communication is so difficult. I look down at his card. A fake since we both know he is not from Hong Kong and does not work on nanomaterials. I give a smile, and JP and I back away politely. Dr. Guan moves off in another direction, seemingly looking for his contact.

"Robinson, you are okay with your poison?" JP asks.

"Yes. But I would like to get back to our hotel as soon as possible. And before they start serving dinner."

"*Oui*, we can exit over here," he says, gently steering me toward one of the large openings.

I look behind us. Guan is still standing, but not for long.

"JP, what's to stop someone from digging into his arm after Guan's dead, or at least rifling through his clothes for that precious chip?"

"Robinson, we do not believe anyone knows the location of the chip. Except maybe Stone, and he is dead. *Et*, for additional insurance, I have this."

He reaches into his pocket and pulls out something that looks like a key fob to me.

"This will erase all information on any chip he is carrying. *Et*, if the chip is still under the skin, I am told it will work to erase it there, too."

So that's what JP was fumbling with when I handed Dr. Guan my business card.

"And if the chip is in a locker somewhere?" I ask nervously.

"If that is the case, well, then we will see. As a woman of medicine, you should know that once a chip is in the tissue, the body surrounds it and makes it very hard to extract physically unless it is placed very superficially. How Guan was going to do the transfer, I am not entirely sure, *et* I am hoping there is not a copy somewhere."

JP and I smile at each other. We leave understanding there are many cameras throughout this area, and our images have certainly been captured. The exit brings fresh air and reduced anxiety. I need to get back to the hotel, now.

*   *   *

I am physically and emotionally drained. There's a trembling going on inside of me. My heart is running the bases within my chest, and I just want it to reach home plate and stop. Home. I want to go home. Mysteriously my hands appear before my eyes with dusty pink polish adorning manicured nails. Hands can caress a face, lovingly hold onto a child, strangle another human, or deliver poison. Where I put them, what I brush, matters.

Finally, we are back within the security of our hotel, and hope fills me, knowing we might soon leave Asia and fly back to Boston.

First things first, I go to the sink in the bathroom, and donning latex gloves, open my purse to retrieve Dr. Hyeon's business card, and place it inside a plastic bag. I look up and am startled. Who is that staring back at me in the mirror? No, not the professor, not the healer, not even the still despondent mother, but the assassin. Oh, Lily, you've done it again. There was no personal anger toward Guan and no self-defense argument as in the battle with Stone. I need a moment to reflect.

It's times like these that my analytical mind must repress my feeling so I can keep it all together. My heart rate has returned to baseline, but my stomach still feels queasy. Unsettled. The battle of good versus evil. My thoughts—fighting each other—knowing what I sacrifice. I was a healer before I became an assassin. The world is now my patient. The good of the many outweighs the good of the one.

From the mirror to my hands. The business card is no longer necessary, and I will dispose of it later. Block emotion and carry on. After removing my gloves and carefully dumping them, I wash my hands with acetone, followed by lots of warm soapy water. My knees buckle uncontrollably, and I land on the toilet lid. JP is calling out to me from the other room.

"Just a minute," I shout back, "you know I can't hear you with the water running."

I turn off the faucet, dry my hands, and return to the outer room.

"Lily, I just got word from our asset in Hong Kong. Wei Guan is dead. He had just sat down at the dinner table when he collapsed. A commotion followed, and then the dinner resumed. The word is that it appears to be a heart attack. Well done. Since Stone never arrived, it is unlikely that Guan connected with the North Koreans. His work will likely die with him since we know he did not keep detailed records of his design. Unfortunate. Those plans could have helped our side. We will meet tomorrow with the team and go over the details. One more loose end, my Lily—Markovic. Lily, are you listening to me? You look flushed. Are you okay, *ma chérie?*"

"JP, do you think they'll do an autopsy?"

"I do not know. That could be problematic, Lily, and not because of your poison either. You have assured me it is not detectable, *oui?*"

"Yes, of course," I tell him.

No one knows this poison exists.

"JP, you read the name on the business card he handed us. The card wasn't his. The authorities will have to do some searching to find his true identity."

"*C'est vrai.* Tomorrow, the safe house across town for the debriefing. Let us go now to bed, *ma chérie.*"

And just like that, he takes me in his arms and kisses me like it's our last kiss on earth. No time to feel sorry for myself.

*   *   *

"Dr. Robinson, nice to see you again," says Agent Parker, looking fresh and fit, a cup of coffee in his hand.

Our safe house in Hong Kong is dismal. Sparsely furnished with little color.

"Yes, good to see you too, Parker," I answer.

"Say Doc, you're knocking it out of the park; two down, one to go. Don't know if ol' JP here can keep up with you," he says, laughing, putting his arm around Jean Paul.

"Parker, enough with the old man talk. You are only jealous of my mature looks and years of wisdom," says JP, sounding slightly annoyed.

Do I detect a bromance, or is this just banter to ease our tension? I'll keep quiet until they play themselves out.

"JP, we have one of our assets from Asia here with us, you know, Sam. You saw him last night at the dinner," says Parker, pointing to the younger man in the room with us.

"Thank you, Parker. Hello again JP and Dr. Robinson," says Sam, turning toward us.

I do remember seeing Sam at the dinner but only briefly. A handsome Korean man with a pleasing face, broad smile, and deep-set brown eyes.

"After you introduced yourselves to Dr. Guan, he was seen talking to several other guests. We observed him exchange business cards with at least two Koreans, and several Middle Easterners. JP, you and Dr. Robinson were in the minority as Westerners. You two had already gone when the signal sounded announcing for everyone to take their place at dinner. As Wei Guan approached the table, he grabbed his chest and collapsed. Someone started CPR, but as you all know, resuscitation attempts failed. So, Dr. Robinson, how did you get the poison to him?" finishes Sam.

"Thanks, Sam. Gentlemen, I brought several toxins with me to Asia, there's nothing like options, but the one I used last night worked as expected. It's a potent derivative of a Geographic Cone Snail toxin or conotoxin and acts by blocking the heart."

"What the hell is a cone snail, Robinson? Are these the ones that crawl around your garden, and you can trap in a beer can?" asks Parker.

He looks at the other men and hopes that they, too, will find him funny. I ignore him and press on.

"Parker, the cone snails are predatory mollusks. The most toxic of the *Conus* species are the piscivores, or for you, I should say they feed on fish."

Parker makes a face, but he is listening now.

"They hunt prey in the water using a harpoon, or modified radula tooth, that shoots out from the snail once it locates its prey. It's through this proboscis that the snail snares its target and then injects the venom. The Geographic Cone is the most venomous of all the cone snails and hails from the Indo-Pacific. Its shell is also renowned for its beauty—with a brown and white peg tooth pattern in a delicate and intricate design."

"Robinson, that is fascinating, but how did you get this, this conotoxin into Guan's body?" asks Parker.

"I'll explain in a minute, Parker. My chemist friend and I were able to isolate one of the conotoxin peptides and one that specifically works on blocking calcium channels. We just tweaked a little molecule here and there to make it more potent—and undiscoverable," I tell them.

"But Guan," says Sam, "I watched you. I didn't see you do anything different than the other guests. You kept your distance from him."

"I did, Sam, but like everyone else in the room, we engaged in the ritual of exchanging business cards. The business card I handed him was saturated in the novel conotoxin."

"Wait, wouldn't that mean that if authorities sift through the business cards he collected that night that they could also become exposed and tip our hand?" Parker asks.

"No, not at all. You see, the toxin was embedded in the first card I handed Guan. After scrutinizing it carefully and for at least twenty seconds, he recognized it as not representing me. I apologized for my ineptness, he handed me back the card, and then I proceeded to hand him the correct card with my cover name. That would be the card he would have on his person at his death," I explain.

"*Et*, Robinson, how is it that you did not become exposed to this toxin? I saw you handle the card with your bare hands," says JP.

"Surgical glue," I say matter-of-factly.

I can see a look of surprise on all their faces.

"I dipped my fingers in tissue adhesive or surgical glue. You may know of it as liquid stitches. Instead of staples, surgeons use the glue to close wounds. It forms a waterproof covering of the incision and reduces the chance of infection. In this case, it created a clear barrier between my skin and the toxin."

Looking into their faces, I see the parting of their lips, their O-shaped mouths, but no words are coming forth.

"I see," says Parker. "Guan handled the card and absorbed the toxin through his fingertips. No residual toxin. I guess you built in enough of a delay to give him some time to move around the room before the toxin kicked in and killed him. And you, Doc, were untouched because you were sort of wearing invisible surgical gloves."

"Precisely," I respond with a smile, letting them know I appreciate their listening to the science lesson.

Then I add, "Do we know where they brought the body?"

"Doctor, they brought him to the mortuary for review by the Coroner. I think it's best if I stop there. Let the specialists take it to where they will," says Sam.

"Yes, of course. But won't they realize he's not who he claimed to be?" I ask.

"Not necessarily, but it won't matter. The authorities will see this as a tech dinner with a casualty. When they try to contact next of kin, we will intervene. Sam, you're on that, right?" says Parker.

"Yes, sir. We will intercept the call," says Sam.

"I just received an interesting message," JP adds after checking his phone. He is now speaking to all of us.

"Our people combed through the Hong Kong bioengineering lab after we discovered the body with the missing arm. We did not find any plans or blueprints for missile designs. We did, however, find out who Stone murdered."

All at once, Parker, Sam, and I say, "Who was it?"

"*Et*, the man Stone killed worked as a research associate for years in that laboratory," says JP. "He was around the same age as the professor who ran the lab."

"How are you going to explain that to the professor when he comes back to Hong Kong?" says Parker, reminding us that we did leave another man with the name Wei Guan in Seoul attending a conference.

"JP, my head is spinning. I hope we got the right Wei Guan after all this," I add.

"*Oui*, Dr. Robinson, it is most confusing. *Eh*, let it go. With this part of the mission secure, it is time to reset the scene."

"What do you mean?" I ask.

"Now we must find the chemical warfare agents and finish off Markovic," says JP.

JP pauses, and I jump in to fill the space. I raise my hand.

"Guys, can I go home now? I have a lecture coming up, and I need to prepare," I say with sarcasm.

They know this is a ploy. Do I work at a flat rate or fee for service? I press my case.

"You recall my role was to assassinate Guan. I did that *and* murdered Stone, too; that was not part of the playbook."

They all look at me like I'm crazy. And well, maybe I am just a little.

"No, seriously," I say, "do you still need me? I did my part."

"Dr. Robinson, you're the one who knows the most about the chemical agents," says Parker.

"True, but I don't know a thing about bombs or missiles. I think I should go back to Boston. I'm needed there."

I can see JP giving me that look. An eyebrow moves up, colliding into his furrowed brow. "No, really," I say.

For me, it's about recovery time. These missions always feel so surreal. I'm just playing a part, and my real life is back in Boston. Or is it the other way around?

"*Eh*, Robinson, we did discuss this back in your home state if you remember. Stay sequestered for the time being. Perhaps meet with your staff via the internet until we have more information. Remember, Markovic is looking for you, just as we are looking for him," says JP.

That's a thought.

"Okay. Deal. I'll stay quiet until you come and get me. Any chance you can find a secure laptop so I can connect back to Beantown with more than a phone?" I ask.

"Bean what?" asks Sam.

"Sorry, Sam. Just a nickname for Boston. Haven't you heard of Boston baked beans?"

I let him know about the beans.

"Um, Dr. Robinson, I'm more of a kimchi guy," Sam says with a smile.

CHAPTER 27

RUSSIA

Alexis felt she had made the best deal she could. Information regarding a Markovic safe house and operations in Russia were exchanged for her getting a new identity. She would plead "brainwashing," and the government would create another life for her in the United States with a new name and fresh start. Though seemingly the perfect solution, Alexis would likely never see her Scottie again. She would have to leave Russia—and Scottie—behind.

The Agency learned that Markovic had a central operation on the outskirts of Moscow, the sole purpose of which was the coordination of illegal and catastrophic actions—namely, to disrupt and destroy life in America and other nations. Here they utilized the internet as a terrorist weapon by planting fake news stories, data, and misinformation so the American public would receive a continuous feed of contrary, confusing and derisive messages. And synchronization of the distribution of illicit drugs and chemical weapons around the world for both monetary and political gain became a primary objective. Grigory Markovic had been in the business since his days in the opium fields of Afghanistan and the cocaine jungles of Colombia. But it was Colombia that provided him with his most talented asset, his 'daughter' Alexis.

Russian leaders would tout the three essential elements of the party line regarding espionage: deny, deny, deny. The operation outside of Moscow would be expected to have significant security despite its façade. Only someone familiar with the layout could help the Agency gain entry—Alexis. But would she be able to return to her base and get them the information they needed to find the chemical weapons? They could try. Alexis couldn't be trusted, so they needed an insurance policy. Someone from the Agency would have to work with her and keep the mission on track. An asset they knew who could speak the language and improvise on the fly. A plan to locate Markovic's chemical warheads in South Korea before they could be incorporated into North Korean missiles emerged.

*　　*　　*

Jackson Scott had been on the run for several days. And for what? Yes, he knew he loved Alexis, and he also knew he loved his job—no, his country, even more. He decided to go back to Moscow, to his flat, and turn himself in. When he arrived in the city, he drove around his neighborhood's streets to determine if he could spot any unusual activity. He had swapped out his car a few days back to evade detection by his colleagues. Now it seemed irrelevant since he planned to come in, out of the cold.

He parked the car on a narrow side street, made his way to his building and into the elevator without being followed. When he reached his flat, the door seemed intact, and his key found its way without compromise. Pushing the door in ahead of him, Scottie flipped on a light switch and surveyed the room. A big sigh escaped his mouth, acknowledging a successful transition. With no one in view, he turned to shut the door when an arm thrust into the flat, pushed Scottie away, and blocked the exit. Scottie fell backward as his feet failed to follow his torso in the same direction.

"Get up," the man said to him in English. "Get up."

The muscle-bound man offered an outstretched hand. Jackson Scott accepted the help and got back on his feet.

"Who the hell are you?" he asked, rubbing his left hip that had been the landing spot for his fall.

"Hey, look, I'm just the messenger. Here to pick you up and bring you in. They want to talk with you. No funny business. I'm in no mood. You got it, cowboy?" said the agent.

Scottie agreed to the terms, and the two left the flat and drove to an Agency safe house off the city streets of Moscow.

* * *

"Scottie, so nice of you to join us," said the man now standing from out behind the desk, his voice sounding sardonic.

Scottie remained silent.

"You want a cigarette?" he offered.

Scottie nodded. The agent lit his own cigarette, then lit another with the tip of his and gave it to Scottie.

"So, look, Scottie. I know Springer is a ball buster and not a diplomat. You broke some of the rules, and sometimes, yes, sometimes, the 'fuck it' happens. You know what I mean?"

He blew the smoke into the air as if he were blowing out imaginary candles around the room. Scottie listened intently.

"We got your girl here, Alexis. Now she doesn't know about you, so we've got to think this through," the agent said, and took another puff.

Jackson Scott could feel the red entering his cheeks and the sweat under his arms. He took a long drag on his cigarette.

"Alexis knows where Markovic hides when he's in Russia. But at the moment, he's somewhere in South Korea. Turns out, he hooked up with his old buddy Aaron Stone. He asked Stone for a meet-n-greet with the North Koreans so he could unload his payload of chemical warheads," said the agent. "Hey, are you following me?" he added.

Scottie looked at the agent in front of him. He looked like all the others, brown hair, brown eyes, brown clothes.

"Yes, I'm following you. Aren't you going to arrest me for something? Treason, desertion, *fucking up*?" asked Scottie.

"Not at the moment, Scottie, because I think we have a way that we can rectify this mess. You need to go with Alexis to Markovic's hiding place and find out anything you can on their operation."

"How can I do that? She knows me as, as, a boyfriend. She has no idea I'm an undercover agent," said Scottie.

"Exactly, and we'd like to keep it that way. We will tell her we picked up her boyfriend and interrogated him. She will be obliged to take you with her to the Russian's little shop of horrors, as collateral. I don't think she would like to see you get hurt, now would she?"

Scottie thought about it. He had nothing to lose.

"And what happens after?" asked Scottie.

"Alexis was promised a new identity and a new life somewhere in the United States. As for you—"

"As for me," Scottie interrupted, "how about I get a new life in good ol' America, too. I've been living too long in Russia. I need a change."

"We'll have to see. That's not my call," he replied. "So, are we done here? I'll have the boys fill you in on the details. We'll give you some reunion time with Popov; you feign shock, whatever, she knows it's your life on the line if she fucks up, and we go from there. Got it?"

"Got it," said Scottie, crushing his cigarette into the ashtray until it splintered into bits and pieces.

* * *

"Ms. Popov," said the agent. "We picked up one of your comrades; you want to tell us about him?" he added, handing her a photograph of Scottie in an interrogation room.

Alexis closed her eyes. *So, they got Scottie, too.*

"He's not part of any of this," she said.

"Are you sure?" said the agent.

"*Da, Da*, yes, I'm sure," Alexis said.

Her right hand was squeezing her left hand so hard that her fingernails left marks on her skin.

"Well, we want you to take him with you to Markovic's place as a little insurance policy," said the agent. "You behave and keep him safe, or both of

187

you will end up dead. Understand?"

Alexis had tried to leave this life behind, and the thought of going back to where Markovic had used her—had *abused* her—made her sick. She could feel the vomit creeping up. She gagged, and the agent quickly moved away, not wanting another mess. It was only a little spittle, and Alexis wiped her mouth with the end of her sleeve.

Scottie, too, felt sick watching this unfold through the one-way glass. If only he had stuck to the plan and not deviated from the course. He let his emotions run the play. Jackson Scott felt like a failure, but he would do whatever he could to regain the trust of his colleagues and save Alexis. The curtain rose, and he entered the stage. Act 2 Scene 1.

"My God," he said in Russian when they opened the door and let him in the room with Alexis. He went to her like a bee to a flower and hugged her tight in his arms. The agent stood right behind him.

"Alexis, what is going on? Why are we here?" Scottie said to her in English. "Are you all right?"

Alexis started to cry. She, too, felt the heat within her creep. Shame and deception. Scottie didn't deserve any of this.

"I'm sorry," said Alexis, "You once asked me about the man who kidnapped me, who raped me, who twisted me. I thought he was dead, but he's not. The people here want me to go back to his base of operation and find out any information I can about his plans. I, I didn't want to drag you into this, but I have no choice."

Scottie squeezed her hand and swallowed hard, pushing down the guilt from the deceit.

"I'll help you, but after, after... what will happen to us?" asked Scottie, feigning ignorance.

He eyed the agent overseeing this reunion and detected the look of disgust on his face. Scottie ignored him and caressed Alexis's hand in his, his focus back on her.

"I don't know," Alexis said, looking at the agent, too. "It's up to them."

Scottie's heart pumped wildly, and his mind raced as he carried out his part in the Agency's play. There were no cue cards to give him his lines. They were improvised. The moment felt like the rush of cocaine that Alexis had shared with him, except that they were not sharing a bed; they were sharing a nightmare. Scottie had to make this right.

CHAPTER 28

SOUTH KOREA

Markovic unwrapped the package. Inside the box was a plastic bag surrounded by large sheets of bubble wrap. The odor permeated the room as soon as he opened the container, and Markovic ran his sleeve up under his nose to catch the mucus and block the smell. He stopped. Rummaging around the room, he found some matches and lit several at once, finally lighting some paper in a trash bin to keep the smoke alive. He could still taste the stench on his tongue and imagined a decayed animal roasting over an open fire pit.

Stone had come through. The disarticulated arm appeared intact. There were no visible signs on the exterior skin surface to indicate that anything unusual had been planted underneath. Markovic placed the limb on the counter in the kitchenette, took out a knife, and cut into the underside of the forearm in parallel slices. Using his bare hands, he moved pieces of tendon and muscle to one side then the other, poking his fingers in the slits and fishing for the chip. Nothing. He flipped the arm over and started hacking into the other side. The cuts became longer and deeper as Markovic felt his anger grow.

Information that an aeronautic engineer would be carrying a small chip with novel missile design plans had come from a reliable source. Stone had told Markovic that the North Koreans not only planned a deal with the Russian but with a Chinese scientist as well. Russia had chemical weapons for sale, the Chinese had superior missile technology, and the North Koreans wanted both. The surgeon agreed to help secure the information chip so that Markovic would hold all the cards.

The Russian learned from Stone that the data would be embedded beneath the surface of the skin on the left forearm. But it wasn't there. Markovic threw the knife across the room, and its tip stuck firmly in the closet door. A shudder could be heard throughout the space as the blade reverberated. Craving nicotine, the Russian dug into his shirt pocket and pulled out his cigarettes. Using the remaining embers in the waste bin, he lit his cigarette and sat on the hard kitchen chair. Markovic looked around his meager room, one that Stone said would be cheap and out of the way, and pinched his lower lip between his thumb and forefinger.

Where is Stone? he thought. There hadn't been any contact since they parted ways several days after leaving the hospital and agreeing to the arrangement. Markovic decided to push forward with his original plan with the North Koreans. They had only been given a sample, but the results had been spectacular. Though the missile had flown off course and hit the outskirts of Alaska, alerting the Americans, there had been no retaliation. Markovic sent assurances to his contacts that he had more and better poisons to offer—a niche that begged to be filled.

Grigory Markovic was not a man to be double-crossed. He stood up and crushed the remaining life from the cigarette onto the kitchen counter. A black crescent marked the spot. Seeing the mutilated arm, he picked it up off the now-wet red surface, placed it back into the plastic bag, and surrounded it once again in bubble wrap. He needed to dump it somewhere. It couldn't stay in the flat.

This was all Lily Robinson's fault, crossed Markovic's mind. Somehow, she had gotten in the way, again. Stone had said he knew her, too, from years ago, a deadly flower not to be reckoned with, but that he wanted to "have a go" at her. *Silly American expression.* Markovic laughed at the thought. She was a mere nuisance and would not interfere with his latest plans. Yet, if Aaron Stone said that he saw her at the conference, she might still be in Seoul. But how to find her? He dismissed the thought. Why bother? She could easily be defeated if he wanted it to happen. There were more important things to take care of now.

191

Markovic made a call before leaving the flat. He needed to get to Gunsan soon. An associate planned to meet him there, a comrade who oversaw operations at another base located in Songtan close to North Korea. With or without Stone, Markovic would make the deal. The hallway looked empty when Markovic finally emerged. He carried the box under his arm, hoping that he had sufficiently secured the wrapping. Yet the putrescent odor oozed from the container. It was a foul-smelling breakdown product he was familiar with from his days in Afghanistan.

The walk to Namdaemun Market allowed Markovic to stretch his legs and rethink his plan. The streets were bustling, teeming with people, food, and merchandise all displayed in the open. Shirts were stacked on tables next to piles of bananas displayed on an adjacent corner. Trays of colorful cooked food lingered in stainless steel pans, waiting for the next hungry customer, while the smells of sizzled skewers of roasted meat wafted across the street— an endless parade of humanity and all their needs.

Leaving the more commercial area, he turned down the back of a narrow alley where several food vendors were preparing their meals. In essence, he walked behind the scenes that faced the public. He could see butchered pig legs, chickens, and other animals that had encountered the meat cleaver. Markovic relished this view and imagined the disarticulated arm among them. When he reached the end of the alley, the street opened up and was busy again. Women passed him with food trays balanced on their heads. He was sure that they were looking at him. He stood out in the crowd as a non-Asian, with storm cloud–colored eyes and telltale residual bruising around his nose. Markovic wasn't familiar with the market but continued to search for just the right venue. He passed the fresh kimchi, more green produce, and unfamiliar roots until he arrived at the Hairtail Fish Alley. This was the spot. When he reached a large trash bin near a particularly pungent fish vendor, he dumped the box.

Retracing his steps proved harder than he imagined. Without Stone as a guide, it was easy to get turned around on the busy passageways through Namdaemun Market. Its origins were in the 15th century during the years of the Joseon Dynasty. Stone had told him that it had been burned to the ground during the Korean War, but now, fully reconstructed, it existed as the place to come to get almost anything a consumer could want. With more than 10,000 shops, crowds of people worked to navigate the same maze as Markovic.

Seeing a vendor with piles of blackened meat on a stick sitting on metal trays, he walked by slowly, looked around, and with sleight of the left hand, grabbed two, neatly balanced on the top of the pile. When he brought the barbecued pork to his mouth, he could smell the residual bits of tissue and blood that had stuck to his hand from the severed arm. Markovic spit out the first chunk of meat, wanting to just coat his tongue with its smell, and then packed the rest of the skewer in his mouth using his teeth to pull off the remaining pieces. It provided a distraction while he found his way. Eventually, he reached an alley he remembered following to the market and proceeded to work his way back to his furnished flat.

In preparation for the trip to the south, the Russian reviewed the instructions he had received earlier and stuffed them in his jacket pocket along with the keys. These provided crucial information on the location of the warheads. However, what he needed now were directions for getting out of Seoul and for the drive to the shipyard in Gunsan. Namdaemun Market had been a challenge to navigate, but Markovic anticipated this trip would present an even bigger challenge. No longer a job for two, the Russian would have to go it alone. Stone never arrived at flat 224 as planned.

Markovic checked his watch and then his phone. Pulling up a map app, he punched in the address of where he needed to go. Road signs would be mostly in Korean, making it problematic to follow the directions; Markovic could not read Korean. Not being able to rely on recognizable street names meant that the only helpful information he could obtain from his GPS was to follow the arrow marker of his car on the map and the information indicating where he needed to turn. He studied the route on his phone to get a gist of the journey. Pulling out another cigarette from his pocket, he cursed Stone for his desertion. *Fucking bastard, I should have killed him when I had the chance*, he thought.

Markovic closed the car door, oriented himself to the interior cabin dials, and proceeded to head south. Neon signs shouted their messages in the night air as he drove through narrow streets. The markets were still open, and pedestrians straddled the sidewalks and pathways. Confusion entered his brain as he tried to navigate. There were too many people and bright lights, and while the GPS was working, he found it difficult to follow and keep his eyes on the road.

One little street looked to escape the masses, so Markovic made a hard left, hitting the curb. Students out for a night stroll reeled back onto the sidewalk as the car shot around the corner. They avoided a collision, but just barely. A large, bony dog was not so lucky. She had darted into the road ahead of the students after following them for some time. The front bumper struck her full-on, tossing her body into the air. She landed down the sidewalk several yards ahead. Some students, cell phones filming the incident, waved and shouted at Markovic to stop, while others ran to attend to the dog's motionless body. Markovic hit the gas pedal and pushed the car faster down the street. The dog was the least of his problems.

Mindlessly, he drove, watching the compass on the rear-view mirror indicating south until he reached the Dongho Bridge. Crossing the Han River would take only minutes, and Markovic could see a train crossing in parallel in the center of the structure and then finally passing him as he steered over the crossing. When he reached the other riverbank, Markovic looked for any prominent roadway that would continue to take him south. He headed for Seongnam and assumed he could keep going until Daejeon when he would need to go west to Gunsan.

Uncertain of the exact time he would meet up with his contact, Markovic expected to send a text when he got close to the destination. As the car picked up speed on the highway, he could hear a rattle but chose to ignore it. By the time he reached Daejeon, the rattle had turned into a shimmy, and he had to pull the car over to the side of the road. The encounter with the dog and the curb back on the streets of Seoul did more damage than he thought. Not only was the bumper dented, but to Markovic, it appeared as if the front axle had considerable damage. He had managed to get this far but now would need to find other transportation. He checked his watch. It was getting late, and he needed to come up with an alternate plan.

CHAPTER 29

FRANCE

Rose woke up refreshed and went downstairs to make a cup of coffee. The aroma filled the kitchen as the coffee dripped noisily into the mug while Rose wandered into the main living room. The sun shone brightly, making filigree patterns on the desk after being filtered by the lace curtains. Rose could see flowers and leaves outlined in shadows on the wooden top. *Oh, there's my phone*, she thought. She picked it up and immediately noticed a missed call. It had come in sometime last night after Rose had retired to bed, and she recognized the hospital's phone exchange. A sense of dread overcame her, and she debated if she should call first or just drive over directly. Rose chose the latter. Whatever the news, she didn't want to hear it while alone in the house.

Rose drank her coffee in one gulp, ran back up the stairs, and decided that there was no time for a shower. Hopping on one foot to get into a black pair of pants, she saw herself in the mirror. Her hair was tousled, and despite the efforts of a ready and willing comb, her hair would not obey. Buttoning her pink blouse, she sprinted back down the stairs and out to her car, carrying her large bag with her.

Rose took several deep breaths as she entered the car and sat for a moment before turning on the engine. *I need to drive slowly, and under control*, she thought. *I don't want to risk an accident.*

*　　*　　*

She arrived at the hospital in due time and collected her thoughts once again before she went in. At the nurses' station, she inquired after Dr. Pasteur.

"*Bonjour*, Rose. The nurses alerted me that you were here," said Dr. Pasteur. "I tried to reach you last night."

"I know, I know. I'm so sorry I missed the call. Mother is... Is Mother...?" asked Rose, having difficultly finishing her sentence.

Dr. Pasteur could see her pale face and the sadness in her eyes.

"Rose, that is why I called you last night. Your mother has been extubated. She's breathing on her own," said Dr. Pasteur. "Truly miraculous."

He saw the blush come back in Rose's cheeks, and a big breath escape her chest. Uninhibited, Rose threw her arms around the white-haired doctor and hugged him.

"Now Rose, there is one thing. Your mother has not regained consciousness; that may take some more time. I suggest we move her to a step-down unit and care for her there. Would you like to see her now?" he said.

"Of course," said Rose.

They headed off to the hospital room. Everything appeared the same as when Rose left the night before, except that now she could see Adrienne's face clearly. The bruises were still there, but her lips were dry and exposed, and only oxygen prongs entered her nose. The breathing tube was out. Rose pulled up the chair by the bedside, took Adrienne's hand in her own, and put her head down on the bed, resting it on their intertwined union. After a moment, she picked her head up and turned to Dr. Pasteur.

"Thank you," she said. "How long do you think it will take before she wakes up?"

"Ah, Rose. Sometimes the best medicine is the tincture of time. As I said, we were all shocked by her spontaneous breathing so soon after the accident. Perhaps you could think about making plans to return to Boston while we care for your mother. When she has regained her consciousness, she will still need rehabilitation. Why don't you resume your medical studies?" said Dr. Pasteur stroking his goatee.

"I'm not sure I can leave her," said Rose. "And I wasn't able to locate any next of kin. Her uncles on both sides are deceased, and well, she had one cousin who went to the U.S. and just disappeared. Dead end."

"Rose, I will have the case manager work out the details here. Go back to Boston. Become the physician that both you and your mother dreamed of," said the doctor putting one hand on Rose's shoulder.

Dr. Pasteur stood up straight, nodded his head, ran his fingers through his hair, and left the room.

Rose sat quietly. So many thoughts flooded her mind. She prayed that her mother would wake up so they could discuss the contents of the letter. Guilt still consumed her, along with fears of loneliness and abandonment. The familiar tingle fanned across her tummy, its appearance heralding fear— feelings from a time Rose couldn't quite remember. But that uneasiness was deep inside her. Rose just couldn't explain it.

Having her mind engaged in her clinical work helped bury uncomfortable emotions. Collecting her composure, Rose proceeded to read to Adrienne from one of her medical textbooks while occasionally glancing at her mother, looking for any signs of consciousness. There would be time before she would leave France and return to Boston. Here she could hold her mother's hand and will the love from her body into the almost lifeless body that lay before her.

CHAPTER 30

RUSSIA

"This is it," said Alexis.

Scottie stopped the car two doors down from a bleak beige building in the vicinity of Novye Cheryomushki, "New Cherry Town." The late afternoon carried billowy dark clouds hinting of rain.

"How are you going to handle this?" asked Scottie, having to feign ignorance of intelligence operations to protect his cover.

"Follow my lead," said Alexis, not sure that her arrival after a long absence would be met with anything but suspicion.

Alexis reached for the car door handle, and Scottie grabbed her hand before she could push the door open.

"Wait a minute, wait a minute," said Scottie. "I don't know what will happen, but I can tell you this. The night you went missing, the night we were supposed to meet on the bridge, I wanted to tell you that I loved you," Scottie said softly, now holding Alexis's hand in his. He waited patiently for her to respond.

"My Sasha," Alexis said, "I feel the same way. It's not been easy for me. I felt so broken, but you changed that. You gave me hope that I could trust again. I don't know what will happen either, but if we get through this, maybe we can find a path forward," she said, and leaned toward him just enough so her lips could meet his.

Jackson Scott's eyes were closed when Alexis' lips brushed his, and he hoped that the underlying deception that ran through his mind would not escape out his mouth.

"Okay, let's go," he said, and pushed open the door and got out, leaving his jacket behind.

Scottie followed Alexis up the street to the dwelling. He knew the team would have activated a tracking device to identify their location, but they had agreed not to interfere unless needed. Any intelligence that could be obtained from this meeting might prove critical in blocking Markovic's game with North Korea. Time didn't choose sides.

Alexis turned to Scottie, indicating her readiness. They both could see typical surveillance cameras surrounding the building, and a camera at the door. The exterior looked ordinary enough, only a sign fixed to the stone façade noting 'The Research Institute of Novye Cheryomushki'. Alexis rang the bell, knowing full well that those inside already knew they were on the front steps.

"Hello," said Alexis, "I am Alexis Popov," she said in Russian, looking directly into the door camera.

Turning to Scottie, she stepped back and waited for the response. Scottie checked his watch. Five minutes passed before anything happened. Then the door opened, and a woman with long dark hair and bold red lipstick slightly smeared below her lower lip stood in front of them. She spoke in Russian.

"Well, Alexis. It is true. You did not die with Maxim," the woman said.

Then looking at Scottie, she added, "And who the hell is this?"

"A friend," said Alexis.

She heard the tremble in her voice and wondered if anyone else did. Alexis soothed herself as only a survivor could. She would manage this.

"Come in," said the woman as she quickly closed the door behind Alexis and Scottie.

The entryway appeared as nondescript as the building. Bland. The woman led them into a waiting area, almost like a parlor, with a few wooden chairs and a well-worn couch. She signaled Alexis and Scottie to take a seat and then disappeared into another room.

Scottie and Alexis dared not speak a word while they waited. A short time later, a man with a black beard and black-framed glasses entered the room.

"Popov," said the man with the glasses. "Where have you been?" he asked, glancing at Scottie and evaluating him from a distance. "I understand that you returned with the others, but then disappeared."

Alexis tried to get a read on his face. Scorn, disdain, contempt? Her pulse quickened while she formulated her answer.

"I thought Maxim and Markovic were both killed in New York, so I came to Russia and have been hiding out. This is my friend Sasha. We are together," said Alexis in a soft tone.

The Russian man sitting opposite them raised a single thick dark brow and squinted an eye but chose not to speak, forcing Alexis to fill the silence.

"So, is Markovic here? Can I speak with him?" she asked.

The man with the beard let out a laugh as if to mock her, then said, "Really? If Markovic were here, do you think we would let you near him, and with a stranger at your side? No, Popov, Markovic has moved on to bigger things, and he no longer plays with us. So, if you have nothing else to tell us, perhaps you and your friend should go."

Alexis felt the sting, but then she didn't know the bearded man or the woman with dark hair and bright red lipstick. Yes, she had spent time in this house with Markovic and Maxim, planning certain aspects of their trip to the United States. She looked around the room again, this time scrutinizing every corner and every surface.

"Would you mind if I used the bathroom before we go? It is a long drive back for us," said Alexis.

The bearded man opened his arm as if to show her a direction when Alexis said, "I know the way; it's down the hall and off to the right."

The Russian chose to wait with Scottie while Alexis got up and walked away from the room.

"Make it fast," he said as she moved down the corridor.

Alexis remembered that a desk with a telephone sat outside a small kitchen area near the downstairs bathroom. If she could only have a few minutes to view the contents on that desk, she might learn something. As she approached the bathroom, she could see the break area with the sink in the next room—just like she remembered it.

Alexis heard Scottie speaking with the man in Russian as if to distract him, while the woman with the dark hair had seemingly disappeared. Only the desk stood in front of her, and looking around once more, Alexis saw she was alone. Papers piled high on one corner, and a writing pad on the other side of the desk drew her attention. The disarray of bills and notes prompted her to sort through the pile quickly. Unsure of what she was looking for, any clue would be helpful. And then, there it was—a short, handwritten note. A record of a phone call from Markovic dated only a few days ago. Alexis read through the message and quickly memorized it. Her phone wasn't available as they had been asked to leave them in a basket at the door when they entered the building. Alexis looked up and headed for the nearby bathroom just as the woman with the dark hair moved toward her. Alexis quickly closed the door and flushed the toilet. Then she ran the water for a minute, dried her hands, and came out of the lavatory finding the woman standing right in front of her.

"Everything all right?" she asked Alexis.

"*Da, Da.* It's my critical days. Sorry," Alexis said, referring to her period.

With that, she and Scottie were escorted to the door. They hurried to the car without saying a word.

"Did you find anything?" Scottie asked, glancing at the rearview mirror and then pulling out into the street.

"I think so. We can discuss it when we get back to, to where? Where are you going, Scottie?" Alexis asked when the car took a sharp turn to the right.

"Alexis, I think there is someone following us."

Scottie looked into the rearview mirror again and could see the shadowing car's headlights glued to his rear bumper. He pressed his foot to the gas.

"Hold on," he said to Alexis.

The car darted around and through a maze of streets until both Scottie and Alexis were dizzy. Alexis found herself sliding from one side of the vehicle to the other as Scottie navigated in and around other autos and obstacles. He turned down a narrow one-way street, hoping this final push would shake those tailing them. Then he saw headlights coming directly toward him. Classic.

"Watch out!" screamed Alexis.

Scottie hit the brakes hard, forcing Alexis to crack her knees on the dash. He thrust the car into reverse and drove the gas pedal to the floor. The car whirred backward down the alley while the sounds of gunfire could be heard in the night. Sprinkles of rain splashed the windshield, and Alexis and Scottie instinctively lowered their heads, dodging broken glass and hot lead. Their car swerved from side to side to avoid the line of fire, still pushing ever faster as the headlights kept coming.

"Take the wheel, take the wheel!" yelled Scottie.

Alexis grabbed the wheel while Scottie kept his foot directly on the gas; he reached for his jacket and pulled out a gun. Opening the driver's side window, he leaned out and aimed at the approaching car.

"Where the hell did you get that?" shouted Alexis, trying her best to navigate the road as she drove backwards from the passenger seat.

A single shot fired from the gun and drove through the windshield of the oncoming car, which veered abruptly onto the sidewalk, hit one of the bollards and flipped over, bursting into flames. Now at the end of the street, Scottie grabbed the steering wheel and turned the car in a sharp one-eighty degree turn, and sped off.

After what seemed like a reasonable length of time, Scottie let his foot off the pedal, watching the numbers on the speedometer slowly drop. The car slid silently into a car park, lights and engine off, signifying an end to the chase. Neither of them said a word. Then Scottie took a single labored breath.

"Are you all right, Alexis?" he said, running his hands over her knees.

"*Da, Da*, I am, but Scottie, you have blood coming from your side," said Alexis.

Her voice registered alarm, and her heart pounded when she saw red oozing from beneath Scottie's shirt. The stain got larger by the second, and she frantically scanned the car for something to stem the bleeding. Alexis squirmed in her seat from side to side, searching like a shark hunting for prey.

Scottie looked at his shirt, and his left hand cupped his side while his right hand flipped on a hidden microphone set by the Agency in the car before he left the safe house with Alexis. Anything he or Alexis would say from now on would be captured and sent back to his superiors. He turned toward Alexis, still feeling a sense of guilt over his deception. Alexis saw the sadness in his eyes.

"Scottie, take this and press it against the wound, hurry; we need to get help," said Alexis handing him the sweater she had in the back of the car.

Then picking up her phone, she began to make a call.

"No, wait," said Scottie. "Do you have the number of the agents that picked you up earlier? Call them, hurry."

Scottie already knew they would be listening, and with his tracking device turned on, they shouldn't have any difficulties finding them. He began to feel light-headed and nauseous. Seeing Scottie's color turning pale, Alexis felt a sense of dread.

"Scottie, Scottie! Stay with me. Do you hear me? Listen to me," she shouted. She tried to distract him. "I may have found something the Americans can use," said Alexis as she moved closer to him to keep him warm.

His body was quivering.

"Alexis, what's going on?" Scottie asked, his mind now confused about what had happened. The bloodstain was expanding, soaking his shirt.

He wasn't sure if he heard sirens in the background or just noise in his clouded brain. Alexis felt the need to keep up pretenses even though she, too, was experiencing queasiness and could feel herself starting to gag on the creeping vomit. The thought of losing her Scottie after everything she had been through was too much to bear, so she continued to talk to him, making sure her sweater pushed deep into the wound and that her body was as close as possible to his. Heat moved out from her and into him.

"Scottie," she said, speaking to him in a voice as if they were sharing a pew at church. "There was a note written down on a pad by the phone. It contained some numbers and a location," said Alexis.

"Well, what did it say?" said Scottie, trying to focus, his voice also soft, matching hers.

"There's a locker at a shipyard in South Korea near the military base in Gunsan. The locker number is A-234. I think that's where Markovic will be going. Scottie, Scottie did you hear me?" asked Alexis.

Scottie forced his eyes open. The car door broke away in a blur, and he felt a cool breeze float in. Within minutes, their car was surrounded, and a man grabbed Alexis, covering her mouth before she could call out. Once again, she found herself overpowered and pushed into the backseat of a waiting vehicle. The door slammed, nipping her toe in the process while adding to the pain in her knees. And then, without care or notice, the car jetted into the night.

Scottie, now slumped over in the front seat, called out to Alexis.

"Are they here?"

He closed his eyes. *Yes, those are sirens*, he thought.

Scottie's body was taken into the ambulance. Two of the agents remained with the car to examine the contents, the bullet holes, the blood spatter, and anything else left behind. Uncertainty loomed over Alexis' absence. She was nowhere in sight.

*   *   *

The black sedan sped from the city and out to the countryside. Alexis remained frozen in her seat, imaginary Velcro keeping her secured to the leather. Too petrified to move and too petrified to speak. Yet, her two bruised knees felt differently and moved in and out like a bellows.

"Ah, nice to see you again, Alexis," said the man sitting opposite her.

At that moment, Alexis let the entire contents of her stomach explode out of her mouth.

205

CHAPTER 31

SOUTH KOREA

"Robinson, open up the door."

I know that voice. It's Parker. Why the fuss when I only asked for a secure computer. I look through the peephole. It's Parker, all right. But no boss. JP would be the one normally to come by. I open the door.

"Parker, what's going on?" I ask.

"JP sent me over to get you. We got a bead on Markovic. Are you up for this?"

"What the hell is that supposed to mean?" I say.

"I mean, we can always use guns and knives, but we like your poisons, Doc. And I suppose we might need you if we have questions about chemical weapons. Come on, Robinson, this could be our chance to get the bastard that sent us his poison perfume cards. It's sexy," says Parker.

"What's sexy?" I ask.

"The power of poison. You know that, Doc. Come on. Get your bag of goodies, your whatever shoes, and let's go. JP is waiting."

Parker can be persuasive, especially when he's on a mission for Jean Paul. Ha. I leave my room, not so sure I want to, but making certain I have enough of... of whatever I will need.

"Parker, exactly where are we going?" I ask him as we get into the car.

"We're going to a shipyard near the military base to the south. We got some intel from our contacts in Russia that Markovic may have chemical weapons stored there. We also know the adjacent military base has an old missiles stash. Two plus two, Robinson," says Parker.

Our first stop is to pick up JP across the city as he had to make some arrangements before we go to the base. Parker says that we are heading toward the Yellow Sea. Reaching like an outstretched hand, the Shandong province of China invades the Yellow Sea as it tries to touch the dividing line between North and South Korea. The opposite coast of the Korean Peninsula yields the Sea of Japan. Parker stops the car.

"What are we doing?" I ask.

"We're going to switch cars, Robinson. Over there, see," he says, pointing to a large black van. "That's our ride."

I get out of the car, and JP is standing at the ready to greet me. I see those tired eyes. He's conflicted.

"Robinson, sorry, but we are going to need you and any knowledge you have of chemical warfare agents," he says.

"Did your guys figure out what chemical weapons they're going to use? There's not just one kind, you know. And, I hate to ask, but do we even know where Markovic is?"

"The answer to both questions is not exactly. We believe he is in South Korea and possibly heading to the same destination that we are. But we do not know his timeline. Let us hope we get to the warheads first," says JP.

There is a pause, then he says, "Everyone, get into the van, *tout de suite*."

I climb back to a seat in the third row. I'm scared. Small bumps show up on my arms, heralding my terror. As always, my stomach is churning, and my heart is bouncing around my chest. *What am I* doing *here*? Standard self-interrogation.

Parker gets in the front seat next to Sam, who is driving. Jean Paul occupies the middle row. Behind me is just what I would call 'gear'. I don't know what it is, and I don't want to know.

"Sam, where are we going?" I ask.

"Hi, Doc. We're going about 240 km south of Seoul; that's about 150 miles for you. We're headed to Gunsan, near the coast," says Sam.

Sam starts in about the American military bases in South Korea. He said there are about fifteen or so bases in the region, varying in size and importance. Different branches of the military are in charge of separate stations. We're headed to one that falls under the command of the United States Air Force. This airbase existed prior to World War II when it was established by the Japanese in 1938. When they withdrew from the peninsula, the U.S. took over the base, only to vacate it by 1949. Later, it was commandeered by the North Koreans during the start of the Korean War. They recognized its strategic importance. A big wake-up call for the United States, who ultimately recaptured the base with their hard-fighting troops. At that time, it became a major player in the Korean War, and a network of bases seeded South Korea.

Sam, I learn, knows Tae kwon do, and tackles the roads like a master of martial arts; he knows how to kick on the high roads or duck on the low roads, depending on our needs for coverage. I don't know him well like I know Parker or, of course, JP, but he seems dedicated to our cause. Funny, he also has those khaki pants and button-down shirts all the agents seem to wear. Except for Jean Paul. He makes his own fashion statement.

Crossing the Han River at dusk is beautiful. We needed to pick JP up near the university—who knows why—and now we're headed over the Yanghwa Bridge. If I look back to the north, I can see Bukhansan National Park in the background, with its mountains looming in the distance. Sam says that it's the only national park in metropolitan Seoul, and it's also known as Samgaksan or Triangle Mountain. There are the three granite peaks that shoot to the sky—Baegunbong the largest at 836.5 meters, not even 3000 feet, followed by the smaller Insubong and Mangyeongbong. Not quite the mountains I climbed back in the day, but still ruggedly enticing. The river looks quiet from my perspective as we cross the bridge. Once we reach the other side, we head south to Gunsan.

The men aren't particularly talkative, and JP is spending a lot of time on his phone, texting with someone who has information he needs, or perhaps he's the one sending information.

"Hey," I say to wake them all up from introspection, "did you ever get more information on Wei Guan? Do you know if he had an autopsy?"

"*Eh*, Dr. Robinson, they did not conduct an autopsy because when they obtained the medical records for this patient, they noted he had a heart ailment, and his symptoms surrounding his death fit his medical condition," says JP.

"I don't understand. He did not attend the dinner under his real name. So how did they get the medical records?" I ask.

I can hear Parker giggle.

"Robinson, we have our ways of making things happen when we need to. Change a few things here and there, and *poof*, you have the documents when and where you need them. Right, guys?" he says, talking to Sam and JP.

I see them both nod their heads. Nothing comes out of their mouths. That's all I'm going to get.

The drive is long. Maybe we've only gone 100 miles so far, but Sam says we are going into Daejeon so we can get a little lost in a metropolitan city, and by that, he means just get off the main roads for a while and switch to another car. That's probably what JP was setting up while we were on the drive down. As we pull into the city, Sam heads towards a military area.

Daejeon serves as a transportation hub for central South Korea, and there are some government complexes located in the area. It's also known as Asia's Silicon Valley and as a very high-tech city. I'm sure we're going to get a new van with more gear in the back. Ironically, it's the lady assassin who travels the lightest. Everything I need can be carried in my handbag.

As we drive to our newest destination, I can see a car that has broken down on the side of the road. The anterior bumper looks dented, and there's a man bent under the front end looking at the damage close up. I don't envy him.

We get to the next spot and sit a while until we get the all-clear signal and then get out of the van. Another vehicle is parked around the corner and waiting for us. Parker takes all the gear and sticks it into the trunk of the new ride. Not sure what we will need; all I hope is that we get to the weapons before Markovic. Where he is, no one can say. He could already be in Gunsan, and JP is waiting for confirmation. The Agency always has gaps in its information, something I've observed for quite some time. And too, we all understand that my killing of Stone may have changed Markovic's plans, and he, like us, may be improvising.

"Robinson, let's go," says Parker.

I take my third-row seat, and we're off again. After a while, I instigate a conversation where there is none.

"Sam, how much farther until we get to the airbase or the marina or wherever?" I ask.

"Hey, Dr. Robinson, you sound like a kid. Are we there yet?" he says with a laugh. Then adds, "Not too much longer. Maybe around another 115 kilometers or so. A little more than an hour."

The quiet ride resumes as the men continue their hush. They are focused, introspective, or just avoiding what we might face. My mind drifts. I try to work my fine focus like on my microscope, reviewing possible chemical weapon threats. After seeing the pictures from Alaska, I'm fairly certain I know what we're up against. Nevertheless, I run down the list while the silence consumes me. Then I disrupt the calm with a loud question.

"JP, I asked this before, but have the boys, I mean the lab, made a final ID on the chemical agent we could encounter? I mean, is there any intelligence to point us in one direction or another?" I ask, trying to initiate a conversation.

"*Eh*, Robinson. I believe it is as we discussed before. Perhaps you can review it for 'the boys,' as you say, sitting with us in the car."

Point well taken.

He wants one of my lectures to fill the time, or maybe he's looking for more clues. A section of the puzzle that only he's working on so only he will recognize the missing piece.

"Well, the Russians have already manipulated one of the toxalbumins—ricin. This worked well since they successfully used microencapsulation technology for the toxin and incorporated it into such innocuous, everyday items like the perfume cards and glue for the football game programs. And it allowed for easy distribution along the Northeast Corridor."

"Have you ever used ricin, Doc?" Parker asks.

Now I've got them talking.

"No, but I used a related compound called abrin in one of my assassinations. You know those special shoes I have with the hidden injection device that I can trigger to release poison?" I say.

"You mean the ones you were wearing when you killed Aaron Stone?" asks Parker.

"Yes, those shoes. That aside, Parker, I don't think ricin or abrin is the direction they'll go if missiles will be used for dispersal. Then there's cyanide. That wouldn't be a good choice either as this is a better agent in a close kill situation such as homicide, suicide, or assassination and is not effective as an 'outdoor' weapon. It was used, of course, in enclosed gas chambers during World War ll," I tell them.

"Robinson, we already know you have used cyanide, *oui*?" says JP, now looking up from his phone.

This is his way of showing me he is listening. It always feels odd to me when he and I have to speak business-talk instead of our usual lover-talk.

"Of course. Good on short notice, reliable and fast. But there are other historic poisons to worry about. We have phosgene, a chlorine gas, or vesicants like the mustard gases that were used during World War I. Sulfur mustard or bis-(2-chloroethyl) sulfide alkylates cellular DNA immediately and—"

"Whoa, whoa, whoa, Doc. I always have to remind you that we are not the scientists in the group. So, what does that mean exactly?" says Parker.

He's right. I eternally seem to have this flag thrown on the playing field between those in science and those in hardcore espionage.

"Parker, when I say that the mustard gas alkylates the cellular DNA, I mean that the protein bonds within the body's cells are disrupted, resulting in cellular death. These chemical compounds are oily liquids that, when dispersed into the air, come into contact with the skin, the eyes, and the respiratory system. And there is a dose-dependent inflammation."

"Meaning the more exposure you get, the more cells die," says Parker.

"Yes, and the cellular necrosis, or cell death, can obstruct the airways. Think chemical burns of your respiratory tract all the way down from the trachea to those little tiny airways that move oxygen from your lungs to your bloodstream," I say.

"There's a whole lot of choking going on," says Parker.

I give him a look that lets him know he's not that funny.

"And the chlorine gases are not much better," I add. "Did you know that after studying the prevailing wind patterns in Ypres, Belgium, in 1915, the Germans released more than 150 tons of chlorine gas against the French? The French didn't see it coming, and toxic fumes wafted toward the trenches. The French soldiers, and perhaps even some of the Germans, were surprised by the effect."

"But I thought we couldn't use those weapons anymore," says Sam, who up until this time, has been paying attention to the road.

"I'll get there, Sam. Not ones to be left behind, the British developed their own chemical weapons, and then, so did the United States. It was a messy business, and it wasn't until 1925 that the Geneva Protocol banned chemical warfare. But we all know that what exists on paper and what exists in the real world are entirely two different things. More than anyone, those of us in this car know the truth," I say.

It gets quiet again, and then Jean Paul speaks up.

"Your best guess, Dr. Robinson?" he says as a question.

"Jean Paul, I told you this before. I'm more worried about the nerve agents, chemicals with an organophosphate base, than anything else. I saw the pictures from Syria and Alaska. You said this was most likely sarin. These agents are potent acetylcholinesterase inhibitors, and there is some recent history of their use."

"Now, don't start using all those big words with us again, Doc," says Parker.

"All I'm saying, Parker, is that weapons that interfere with an enzyme that plays a huge role in the body's chemistry are deadly. This is how our nervous system works. You need to transmit messages from one part of your body to another part. Those messages, or neurotransmitters, are just chemicals. We have our central nervous system—that's the brain, Parker—and we have a peripheral nervous system, the one operating outside the brain."

"I've heard of that," says Parker. "The sympathetic nervous system is responsible for 'fight or flight.' The scared-shitless response. Right?"

"Impressive Parker. You've been holding out on me. Yes, in contrast to the sympathetic nervous system, the parasympathetic nervous system produces the neurotransmitter responsible for activities of rest or feeding rather than fight or flight, such as those experienced after a meal, slowing your heart rate, or even of sexual arousal."

"We're listening, Doc," says Parker.

"Nerve agents that block a major enzyme produce a toxidrome sometimes referred to as DUMBBELS," I say just as Parker interrupts.

"A toxidrome?"

"Yes, signs and symptoms that point to a particular poison. So, getting back to what I was saying, the mnemonic DUMBBELS is used by toxicologists to help identify the signs and symptoms in a patient exposed to these organophosphate compounds: **D**iarrhea, **U**rination, **M**iosis, **B**ronchorrhea, **B**ronchospasms, **E**mesis, **L**acrimation, and **S**weating."

"What are you saying, Doc? In English," says Parker.

His head is turned toward the back seat, and I can see him rolling his eyes.

"Essentially a hot, wet mess of poop, pee, drooling, coughing, vomit, tearing eyes, and pinpoint pupils. Got it?" I answer. "It's a horrible way to die."

"That's disgusting shit, Doc," says Parker.

"Yes. There's more to it, but I think I'll skip the rest for now."

"Good timing, Dr. Robinson, and oh, thanks for the lecture, but we arriving in Gunsan near the port and the yard," says Sam.

There's a vast space in the darkness just ahead. An open void and water beyond. I can smell the sea air. As Sam slows down and points, I see that it's not a boatyard at all; it's a shipyard and a large port of entry. The port's location makes it ideal for trade with China. Sam says that this facility can handle fifty-thousand-ton vessels and has the capability for warehousing and processing cargo. So how are we going to find the proverbial needle in the haystack?

JP has his hand in his hair while he is talking on his cell, Sam's staring at his phone, and Parker is looking after the equipment. Then JP informs us that this shipyard is also Markovic's destination, and he could already be here. We might keep the van at the entry point in case we're the first to arrive. We all know that having Markovic lead us to the chemical weapons would make our job much easier.

"Oh, no," says Sam, a bit of alarm in his voice.

"What is it?" I ask, worried another challenge could loom before us.

"Oh, sorry. I thought I would just check my social media account while we're sitting here," says Sam. "Look. Someone posted a video of a car that killed a dog back near Seoul. Poor thing. Looks like that pup went flying through the air."

"Geez, I hope they get that bastard," says Parker, still fidgeting with our gear. "I hate any hit-and-run, but a dog? Bastard."

"Let me see your phone," I say, taking Sam's phone to scrutinize the video. "Sam, that's the same car we passed back in Daejeon. I saw it by the side of the road. Can you tell if it's a rental?"

I'm not sure why I'm excited about this. Isn't facing Markovic and chemical weapons enough?

"Here, let me have the phone back. Why is that important?" Sam says, looking at the feed.

Now both Parker and JP are listening attentively.

"I guess I want to know if it's a rental. The driver doesn't look Korean to me. I can't see him clearly. But he's familiar in some way."

"I think you're right. Now that I look at the video more closely, I can see a bar code sticker in the window, meaning that it is a rental. Wow, Dr. Robinson, you are very observant. And I agree with you, the driver does not look Korean," says Sam.

"Let me see that," says Parker, almost grabbing the phone from Sam.

Then he shows it to JP. "What do you think, boss?"

Jean Paul looks at the video and turns to look at me. He knows I have this intuition thing. Markovic, of course, is always on my mind. Is he coming to Gunsan by land or by sea? We had a plan in Massachusetts back during the Revolutionary War when Robert John Newman and Captain John Pulling carried two lanterns to the steeple of the Old North Church. Henry Wadsworth Longfellow made it famous in his poem, *Paul Revere's Ride*, "One if by land, and two if by sea."

Markovic scares me. He's coming by land, and he's not far behind. So we wait—Sam, Parker, JP, and me.

CHAPTER 32

SOUTH KOREA

Unable to fix the front wheel axle of his rental car, Markovic needed to find another way to get to Gunsan. He wiped his hands on his trousers, leaving a grease stain on the thigh, and looked up and down the road. Cars buzzed by, and Markovic felt the creep of his looming deadline. With no response to his phone call, he decided to walk into town when a car pulled up next to him. The driver rolled down the window and spoke.

"I see your car has broken down," said the Asian man behind the wheel of a gray sports utility vehicle. "Can I give you a lift somewhere?"

Markovic, surprised at this encounter, but not feeling threatened, thought that, if nothing else, he could kill the driver and steal his car. Then again, he thought, maybe he would wait until he reached the shipyard, since it would be much simpler with someone from the region navigating the roads.

"You speak English." said Markovic trying his best to suppress his Russian accent. "I have to report to my cargo ship in the port at Gunsan. Can you get me close to there?"

The Asian man nodded, and Markovic got into the seat beside him.

"I will take you to Gunsan. It is maybe an hour or so from here. I am on my way to Gochang to visit family. My nephew works at the Gochang Dolmen Museum. This museum has the remains from the Megalithic cultures. Have you been there?" asked the driver.

Markovic could not believe his good luck. A free ride directly to Gunsan.

"Thank you," said Markovic.

He pocketed his dirty hands after wiping the sweat from his brow. Not moved to make any conversation, Markovic remained silent—less chance for unwanted revelations. The driver appreciated the awkward feeling of being with a stranger, so he continued with his description of the museum.

"There are many prehistoric cemeteries around the area that contain dolmens or tombs from the 1st millennium BC made of large stone slabs. They date from the Neolithic and Bronze Age cultures and were simple burial chambers."

Markovic tuned out the man's dialogue, so it became a one-way lecture from driver to passenger. He looked at his watch, hoping he had enough time to meet his contact. The Russian shifted in his seat, his pulse quickening, as the long drive continued. Still no text from his associate.

As they neared the shipyard, Markovic debated again whether to murder his driver or just let him go. If he murdered him, Markovic would have his car, and a body to dispose of. However, by letting him continue on to his family in Gochang, the need to conceal a corpse would not be his problem. Markovic considered the second option preferable as his focus was getting to the locker and to the binary compounds. An exit strategy after they collected the chemicals would have to come later.

"I can drop you off here near the ferry terminal," said the driver, not quite sure where Markovic needed to be.

He had said something about boarding a cargo ship, but which one? Opening the car door, Markovic slipped out and mumbled a thank you. He looked around and didn't see many people or cars. He checked his watch and then checked his phone—still, no text message appeared from his contact from Songtan, north of Seoul. Markovic considered that perhaps he had beaten him to the spot after all.

The Asian man who had given a ride to Markovic drove from the ferry terminal onto an auxiliary road leading from the port harbor, but still within the shipyard. Confident he could no longer see Markovic in his rear-view mirror, he pulled the car in behind one of the large buildings off the road and shut the engine down. It was quiet, and he closed his eyes and collected his thoughts. When the man felt that the timing was right, he exited through

217

the driver's side door, closed it without a sound, and opened the car's rear door.

Sitting across the back seat's full length was a narrow wooden box with intricate carvings on the surface. The driver opened the box and removed a long straight stick. The original seams where the two halves of the cane had been glued back together were apparent. Each half's center had been chiseled, creating a channel so that a borehole ran the entire length of the chamber when they were reunited. An admirer of those cultures that used natural toxins to hunt their prey, he had studied and practiced their techniques until he became proficient in the art. The blowgun had been a gift from a friend, and he thought he might try it out on this occasion. It would be silent and the toxin deadly.

*   *   *

The Asian man knew that the Russians, the French, and the Americans were at this shipyard for one purpose—to collect the binary weapons that would be used in rocketry to shower the United States and unleash mass destruction. Those parties were unaware of his involvement, and he felt confident that his mission would be accomplished. Already, the one Russian near the Songtan base up north would not be keeping his appointment with his comrade here in the south at Gunsan. The Asian man had taken care of that earlier, following this trail for weeks now.

Hong Kong had always been the prearranged designated venue for the meeting between the North Koreans and mainland China's Dr. Wei Guan—not Seoul, South Korea. Aware that other foreign governments could have obtained knowledge of this planned exchange, the Chinese scientist had arranged for a Hong Kong university professor of engineering, with his same name, to attend a conference in Seoul, hoping that this decoy would mislead any outside intelligence organizations. This had created diversion and confusion. In parallel, Dr. Guan had gone to Hong Kong under an assumed name to prepare for his espionage encounter and later attend the symposium dinner where the exchange was to take place. However, the North Koreans never met with Wei Guan in Hong Kong. Someone else got to him first.

The Asian man who was now present at the shipyard knew the real identity of the guest who died at the symposium dinner in Hong Kong—Dr. Wei Guan. After the scientist's demise, it was concluded that the cause of death was myocardial infarction—a heart attack. Falsified medical records supported the deceased's false identity, but DNA does not lie. The Asian man had also seen the surveillance video obtained from the event, and he had focused on two guests, in particular, posing as French doctors to gain entry—Dr. Lavigne, a tall, distinguished man with dark hair graying at the edges, and Dr. Laurent, a blonde-haired woman who appeared fashionably dressed and wearing a platinum weave bracelet and a gold serpent ring. After mingling with several other guests, the two "French doctors" could be seen talking with Wei Guan. After the interchange, the couple left the room while Dr. Guan spoke with a few more guests before assuming his seat at the table.

When the missile scientist clutched his chest as death struck, it was assumed that Guan's groundbreaking technology died with him. That would be what the Americans would believe. The French, too. Yet, the Asian man knew differently. Posing as the contact for the North Koreans, he had met with Wei Guan just before the scientist entered the dinner event and had secured the technology. It would remain safe within his operation, thus blocking hawkish countries from having an advantage. The Asian man would help keep world peace.

Even without the new technology, conventional ICBMs, rockets now filling the silos of North Korea, could be launched and hit the United States. It had already been done, if only inadvertently. But the payload would make the difference. Not all countries had ICBMs with nuclear warhead capabilities. And even for those that did, chemical agents of mass destruction could just as easily kill millions of people. This was the final play on the chessboard. Where were the binary compounds hidden, and who would get to them first?

The Asian man closed the car door of his gray vehicle without a sound.

With the support of his walking stick, he headed toward the building that contained the lockers. Only the sound of the Geumgang River, "a river as beautiful as silk," filled his ears as it rolled into the West Sea. Time too, moves like a river—ever-flowing, never stopping.

CHAPTER 33

SOUTH KOREA

"You don't think that's Markovic in that car, do you? I mean, I know I'm paranoid, but maybe he's stuck in Daejeon and can't get here," I tell them.

No one wants to tackle that question.

"Sam, you come with me, and Parker, stay here with Dr. Robinson. Sam and I will check out the main facility housing the lockers. Blocks of lockers may be designated with both a letter and a number like A-1, B-1, and so on. We need to look in the A-block," says JP.

"Why is that?" I ask. "Do you know the compounds are in the A-block?"

"We just received some information that the material could be in locker 234 in the A-block. This is a huge facility, but it's a start," says Parker.

"Wait a minute, just wait a minute. Where did that information come from?" I ask.

"One of our assets in Russia picked up some intel from a presumed phone call with Markovic pointing to the port in Gunsan, the lockers, and the designation A-234," says Parker.

"*Eh*, Robinson, I can see your mind working. How can it be that your skull is so transparent?" says JP.

"No, no. Listen to me," I say, "I don't think that's a locker number. I think that is the designation of the chemical weapon that Markovic plans to use."

"What do you mean?" says Parker.

"Look, all along, we thought they were going to use nerve gas compounds. Don't you see it? They *are* going to employ Novichok agents. These are binary chemical weapons that were developed in the Soviet Union as far back as the early 1970s. Novichok-5 was known as A-232. A-234 is at least five to eight times more potent than the original VX agents."

I can feel my heart pounding now, remembering the photos taken in Alaska that JP showed me. The destruction from A-234 would be far, far worse.

"So, we have good news and bad news. We know what they're going to use, but we just don't know where to find it," says Parker. "Is that right, Robinson?"

"Well, when you put it that way," I say. "If we can find Markovic, let him lead us to the storage facility. These compounds are not going to be stored in lockers; they're too big, so they would have to be stored in a warehouse or even in a ship's hold, and kept separate from one another. You can't let the binary weapons near each other until you're ready to load them in the munitions. And maybe, there is some additional information in the locker that Markovic needs in order to get into the warehouse or cargo ship."

When I stop talking, I see the three men just looking at me with their mouths in the shape of an "O."

"What, what?" I say the edges of my mouth, not quite making a smile.

"*Et*, Robinson, thank you for that," says JP.

Parker just lets out a "holy shit."

"He must be meeting an accomplice here. There would have to be a plan to drive the compounds north," says Parker.

"Or ship them north," I say.

At this point, our mission is to find Markovic, assuming he is here, and to get the information contained in the locker.

* * *

Emerging from the car, we all head to the building where the lockers are. JP wants me to stay in the vehicle, but I insist on coming along. Yes, I'm committed now because I do want to help save the world. Isn't that what my life has been about? I have my gun with me in my pocketbook; I don't care anymore about using a stealthy poison; I just want to get in and get out. Practicing on the firing range every week while I'm back in Boston has been a challenge, but the groupings on the body target show that I can still handle a good kill. I am, after all, an assassin.

JP is indicating that my presence in the locker facility, this intersection of good and evil, is not necessary. Stand down, he says, because if they run into Markovic, it could get messy. He can't fuss too much with the other men present, but I hear what he is saying. Just a little.

They go on to the primary storage locker area, and I decide to go near the ferry terminal. I'm careful; situational awareness has been ingrained in me. There's no one here. The door to the restroom is unlocked, so I decide to go inside for just a moment.

When I come out, I can see that there is a small set of lockers outside of the ferry terminal. Perhaps a place to store one's things before getting on the boat, assuming one comes back this way. I have no idea. In the distance, I see a man walking toward me. My antennae spring into action because I have a way of memorizing a person's form or shape. It's Markovic, I'm sure.

I step back, out of sight, but I'm certain that he has already seen me. Whether or not he knows it's me, I don't know. I back off behind a group of barrels and listen. I hear footfalls, and now I can see him standing by a locker. *It is Markovic,* and as I think that, his head turns, and he stares directly at me. He knows.

"Dr. Robinson. I assumed my colleague Dr. Stone took care of you while in Hong Kong. Yet, here you are," he says coldly.

He appears unshaken—business as usual. God, that man makes my skin crawl. Those eyes.

I can see the gun come out from under his jacket. Yes, I have my gun with me, but I'm not about to have a draw like it's the Wild West. That's a losing battle under the current circumstances. Welded onto the spot, my eyes search for JP or Parker or even Sam. They're nowhere in sight. And here I am, facing almost certain death unless they emerge from the building

223

across the way like the cavalry. Nothing I have with me can fix this. Plan B is to talk. Heart rate and rhythm, fast and irregular; I'm scared.

"Markovic, what a surprise," I say, holding my cool even though my heartbeats seem loud enough for the whole world to hear.

I decide to let it all go.

"So, are you here to pick up the A-234? That is what you are going to sell to the North Koreans, isn't it?"

"Dr. Robinson, you do impress me. Yes, Novichok agents are ideal for this. You of all people can appreciate the complexities of chemical warfare," he says.

"I can, Markovic. This is a big shipyard. You must have found the perfect place to store the binary compounds," I say, trying to buy time.

JP, where are you? Please come out now, wherever you are, I think, while Markovic continues.

"Yes, we have nice a Russian ship docked here, ready to transfer cargo to another vessel from South Korea that will sail the merchandise north. The ship will, unfortunately, get lost in North Korean waters and have to be confiscated. Your friend Stone did not hold up his end of the bargain, so I had to make other plans. Now, if we have finished talking, Dr. Robinson."

I can see his hand raise the gun. My face is frozen. A man is coming in from behind Markovic, but at a distance. I know that form, too. My eyes widen now; I try and distract Markovic.

"Wait, before you shoot. What if I could share with you a novel poison? A first on the world stage. Wouldn't that be worth an exchange for my life?"

These are meaningless words coming out of my mouth, but I can see Markovic lower the gun for a split second.

The man nearing Markovic from behind raises a long stick and puts it to his mouth. I can hear a puff, and I know Markovic can hear it, too. The hand not holding the gun reaches up to his neck, and he falls to the ground. I dare not move. The Asian man puts down the blowgun and approaches me. I stand my ground.

"John Chi Leigh," I say, shaking, "What you are doing here? Are you about to kill me, too?"

I watch him bend down and collect the keys out of Markovic's hand. He kicks his gun to one side. Dr. Leigh is wearing latex gloves and now picks the dart out of Markovic's neck.

"Kill you, Lily Robinson? Why would I kill you?" he says calmly.

He holds the wooden stick in front of me and says, "Do you recognize this blowgun? It was one of your many gifts. I have been practicing. I believe that our innovative snail toxin has performed beautifully. Stone, Dr. Guan, and now Markovic. Are you pleased?"

I have not moved from my spot. I don't know if I should be thankful, happy, or terrified. I really do need to get back to Boston.

"John Chi, what is going on here?" I ask. I'm trying to keep it all under control.

"Lily Robinson, you are not the only academic who leads a double life. I know you were led to believe that I was a gambler and a chemist for hire, but that makes for a good cover story. Don't you agree?"

"You're not who I think you are?" I ask.

There is a breath inside my chest that is pushing to get out. Reality is fleeting.

"Well, yes and no. I am quite a good chemist, and I do like to bet on the racehorses now and then—after all, I test their urine for drugs for a living—but like you, I work for an organization that would like to maintain world order. I took care of Markovic's comrade in Songtan, and then I drove here to Gunsan. I knew you would be here. My job was to make sure you and your associates were successful. It was sheer luck that I found Markovic with his disabled car," says Leigh, "and I am amused that Caucasians think all Asian people look alike."

"So, it *was* him; it was Markovic I saw by the road," I say with strong conviction. "And seeing that video confirmed my intuition even more so."

"What video?" asks John Chi.

"Oh, there's a video posted on social media of him hitting a dog with his car while he was still in Seoul."

I stop for a minute and then wonder out loud.

"John Chi, am I to assume that you knew the reason that I came over to Asia right from our first meeting in Hong Kong a few weeks ago? You have been shadowing me this entire time, haven't you?"

"You are on my side of the planet, after all," he says.

Now I start looking back to New York and wondering about last winter.

"John, did you have anything to do with the ricin?" I ask, knowing that he saved us in the end, but now feeling confused and having all kinds of doubts.

"True, the ricin was made in my lab, but not by me, Lily Robinson. I took care of the chemist who betrayed me. In fact, I used your tea, your 'queen of all poisons'," he says.

I believe him.

"And there is one more thing," he adds.

I'm not sure what he is going to say next. Silence surrounds us, and I wait for Dr. Leigh to fill the void.

"The snake curls in an unbroken circle. It symbolizes eternity and passionate love," says John Chi as he takes my hand in his and touches my ring. "These rings were popular in the Victorian Era. Do you know where you got this ring, Lily Robinson?"

"My mother gave it to me. She said it was my grandmother's. I never met her, of course, and as it is, my mother also died when I was just a girl," I say. "What's this about, John Chi?"

"You recall that my father was British and married a Chinese woman from Hong Kong."

"Yes, of course," I say.

My eyes widen, and I lean in to listen to him. I'm curious more than I'm scared. My heart rate is slowing down.

"Have you ever wondered why I didn't kill you in our first encounter in California?" he asks. Then adds, "You were on a Hollywood set waiting for a producer."

"Well, I thought perhaps you had a change of heart and wanted to work on the side of good," I tell him. My eyes roll a little, signaling the "where are we going with this" look. I'm not sure I can take any more revelations

226

as the night gets darker. As usual, Leigh remains calm.

"True, but there is more to the story, as one says, Lily Robinson. Yes, I was asked to murder you by the subordinates of the so-called diabetic philanthropist who we both knew to be a drug and slave trafficker. Your death would have been retribution for his death. Remember, too, that I was the chemist who analyzed his blood and discovered that you had substituted the toxin from *Chironex fleckeri*, the box jellyfish, for his insulin. Well done, I might add."

John Chi stops for a moment. I can see his dark eyes through the glasses that frame his face. It's a gentle face. There is no meanness hidden that I can detect. Then he starts again.

"Lily Robinson, my organization knew of your government's plan to assassinate the trafficker. There is a consortium from governments around the world that work together on these sorts of things. I am not sure how much you know. After you carried out that assassination in Hong Kong, we uncovered the revenge plot to kill you. At that time, I learned who you were, and I went to Hollywood to save you."

"I still don't understand. You came to the United States from Hong Kong to save me all those years ago? Why? How?"

"I followed the man in the sharkskin-colored suit; he always had a toothpick between his teeth; he led me right to you."

"I still don't understand. What changed your mind?" I ask again, and Dr. Leigh continues.

"No. You misunderstand. Those who hired me to kill you were led to believe that I went to the United States for that purpose. But that was never my intention. Yes, my organization could have alerted your government to intervene, but I wanted the job. Do you also remember that I killed him with the venom from the Chinese Moccasin snake, the hundred-pace viper? I thought perhaps it was a fitting tribute."

"Yes, John Chi, I've heard of that viper but a fitting tribute to what? It's believed that after the victims are bitten, they will only be able to walk a hundred paces or so before they drop to their death," I say, and then he picks up my hand.

"This ring on your finger," he says, touching the ruby head of the snake. "After my father passed away, I went to his house and found boxes of letters my grandfather had written to an American woman with whom he had had an affair while she was in Hong Kong. This woman, although the love of his life, returned to America, and later, he married my grandmother. Your grandmother married someone else as well. I am certain that he loved my grandmother when they wed, but sometimes Lily Robinson, there is one indelible love of your life. For my ancestor, it was the woman he gifted with this gold serpent ring with a ruby head. From the letters that they exchanged—and I took the time to read them all—I believe they were ill-fated soul mates, a love only destined to live in memories. What was your grandmother's name, Lily?"

I hesitate before I answer. Could this be true?

"Her name was Alice," I answer, now feeling shaky.

There's a small twitch under my lower right eyelid that disturbs me.

"If you take off the ring, you will find an inscription inside that reads: to AW from JL."

The ring resists coming off my finger. A good tug, and it's free. It's very hard to make out anything inside the band and even more so in the dark. I open my bag. There's my gun, and my phone. Neither of which I used when I needed to. Now that I have the phone, I turn on the flashlight feature. There inside the gold band, I see something. Dr. Leigh is right. A faint inscription is etched, and I never really noticed it before. As someone who prides herself on detail, this is one I missed. What to say? So again, I say nothing. Leigh's kept this from me for a long time. I wonder what else there is to know about this mysterious man. Are any of us who we say we are?

"The photograph in your office of the couple. Were they not your grandparents?" I ask.

"You noticed. No, it is a picture of my grandfather with your grandmother. She is wearing the ring in the photo, but it is difficult to see."

I'm stunned. Life is so full of twists and turns I feel as if I'm in a Dickens novel.

"John, why, of all photographs, would you have that in your office? I have been to your lab before and never noticed it. There is almost nothing personal in your office."

"True. To amuse myself, and test you, Lily Robinson. You are the pathologist with the keen powers of observation. And, well, after all these years, I thought we might share a common bond knowing that our grandparents were friends."

Finally, I find my true voice. "John Chi, where do we go from here?" I ask.

"I will fade into the background. You call your team, have them dispose of Markovic. Here are the keys to the locker with all the information you should need to find and secure the binary compounds," he says.

"What about you? What do I tell them?" I ask.

"I am going back to Hong Kong and back to the lab. You will do the right thing, Lily Robinson. You always do."

And just like that, as if he were on a hike, he picks up his walking stick and leaves. It takes me a moment to gather my thoughts. It's what I've said before—how well do we really know someone? I never seem to know.

Now I remember to use my phone, and I get JP on speed dial. I tell him to get over here by the ferry terminal. Markovic is dead. I can hear his fear over the phone as his voice asks if I'm all right. I'm not sure what to tell him. Maybe the details will come out later.

"Robinson, are you okay?" JP says as he, Parker, and Sam break into a little run when they see me standing next to a dead body. He looks terrified—his mouth open, his eyes wide.

"Yes, of course." Then, as if cool as can be, I say, "These are the keys to the locker that contains the information on the Russian ship that's holding the binary compounds. Oh, and this dead person is Markovic."

I wait for their response.

"Dr. Robinson," says Sam. "How did you do this?"

"I didn't do anything, Sam; it was poison that killed the beast." I modified that line from the movie about King Kong, or was it in tribute to someone from Hong Kong…?

*　　*　　*

JP is immediately on his phone, making all kinds of calls. Sam and Parker carry Markovic back to the van. I'm sure the port will be flooded with all sorts of agents soon. We wait quietly together until some backup comes. With help from the South Korean government, JP and I have a new car ready to take us back to Seoul. My body is filled with adrenaline, but the post-excitement exhaustion is crashing in. We get into the car, and Jean Paul starts the verbal journey. We have miles to go.

"*Ma chérie*, now that we are alone, what happened out there? Every time I think to rescue you, you seem to have control of the situation at hand. You either are much more gifted at this line of work than I give you credit for, or you are incredibly lucky."

"Actually, Jean Paul, I *am* incredibly lucky. I have more than one guardian angel in my life."

As I look over at him, I can see the furrows in his face deepen.

"Is that all you are going to tell me?" he asks.

"JP, as you already know, there are operatives from governments all around this planet trying to keep peace and save the world," I say, looking over at his face to see if I can detect a response.

The corner of his eye squints as he concentrates on the road ahead, and he says, "*Ma chérie*." And then he stops, so I continue.

"I guess you and I are just one part of that. I've always said that the good of the many outweighs the good of the one. Now, can you share with me the details of this global consortium that works together to rid this earth of those who provide threats to all nations?"

"My Lily," he says, smoothly dragging out the syllables of my name, "I have told you before that we have tried to keep certain information from you for your protection. These last months between New York and Asia, you have done more than we should have asked."

"JP, how can you say that? I am in this so deep and have been for years. I don't understand why you don't see this. I've jeopardized my job, my life, any chance for a real relationship, and for what?"

He feels the sting in my voice. He shoots a glance sideways at me, sadness in his eyes, and grabs my hand.

"There is a consortium, as you say, that operate together. We work across country boundaries because, as you know, this is one planet, Lily. What happens in Africa, the Middle East, or Asia affects the entire world. Living in silos, isolation policies, and ignoring threats like chemical and nuclear warfare endanger all the peoples of Earth. Softer targets are things like climate change. If you cut down all the trees in the Amazon Rainforest, that has a global effect. It is up to us to shape world order."

Jean Paul pauses for a moment, and I think. The United States should shine as a partner for world order and global responsibility. I hope that's the direction my country is taking.

"My Lily, although there is the desire to have, *eh*, a perfect world, it is near impossible. The expression 'perfect is the enemy of good,' often attributed to the philosopher Voltaire, implies that absolute perfection is likely impossible to attain. We know there are inherently bad people among us, and they cannot be changed. There are dictators, traffickers, traitors, murderers, and worse that surround us. We cannot control everyone or everything."

I know JP is right. As much as we strive for altruism, there is the chemistry that inhabits the bodies of those whose desires do not mirror ours. The Pareto Principle, or the 80-20 rule, tells us that while it takes 20% of the time to complete 80% of the mission, it would take 80% of the time to complete the last 20%. Not worth the effort? I don't know. How long has JP known about John Chi?

"JP, did you know about Dr. Leigh's involvement in tracking the actions of both Markovic and Dr. Guan?" I ask, deciding to tell him what happened back at the shipyard.

"*Et oui.* Only recently, I learned that Leigh operates out of Hong Kong," he answers.

"Why didn't you tell me?"

My voice increases an octave, and JP can tell that I'm agitated. I turn my body to face him, although he is still looking forward as he drives.

"Like all things, my Lily, sometimes it is safer that you do not know the details," he says. "As much as we try to deny it, knowing the truth about someone changes how you interact with them. It is human nature, *oui?*"

"JP, Dr. Leigh killed Markovic using the poison that he and I developed. The same one that I used to kill Wei Guan. Leigh told me that his government was very much interested in what the mainland had to offer. We both know that there is considerable tension between Hong Kong and China."

"*Merci*, Lily. There is still much to sort out. As I said, I am only newly aware of Dr. Leigh's role in this affair, *mais*, it makes sense given that Hong Kong and Korea were the stages for this theater."

I pause again, thinking back to all the unsolved pieces of the puzzle. So I ask, "Whatever happened to Alexis?"

"Alexis Popov is a complicated story. She was picked up by our agents, and in exchange for her cooperation, we would give her a new identity and a new country," he says.

I can see him thinking. He pauses.

"So? Then, what?" I ask, prodding him to tell me more.

"Popov did provide us with some useful information, but in the course of that operation, we believe she was picked up by the G.R.U., you remember, the Russian military intelligence agency. It has been a push-pull with opposing factions. The Agency also thinks that it was someone from the G.R.U. who shot me to derail our mission. They were certainly aware of Markovic's plan. Whether it was sanctioned or not, that I do not know. And concerning Alexis Popov, I do not know if we will get her back. I am sorry, Lily, I cannot tell you any more."

"As you say, there are so many loose ends to tie. Promise me this, JP. That there will no longer be secrets between us. What I mean is, secrets that would affect me or our relationship. I understand that for the purposes of the work you do that you will not—*cannot*—share everything, but please, if it involves me, I need to know."

I'm quiet now, and so is he. He doesn't make me any promises, and well, maybe he can't. That's just who he is.

I could not help but think again of how my life would have been different if I had not gone to Colombia all those years ago. Had I stayed in my academic world, I would have raised a daughter, focused on my science, and had a relationship with a man that was not ephemeral and cloaked in danger. I don't want to think about this anymore.

"My Lily, you do know that I love you," he says, squeezing my hand again. "This is not the life you dreamed of, *chérie*. I cannot be with you at all times, but you are always with me. *Oui, oui*, a cliché, but then again, that is a French word, and as a man, I do not know how better to phrase it."

He stops there and turns to look at me. I can see a smile on his face, and even in the darkness, those blue-green eyes give a sparkle. His eyes turn back to the road.

"I have been thinking, Lily. After we go to Seoul for all the debriefing, would you consider delaying your return to Boston, *eh*, just for a few days?" he asks.

If he could see my face, he would see a look of surprise.

"Why? What did you have in mind?" I say.

"I thought maybe we could go to the Champagne region of France. Consider it a short holiday of sorts. You have been through so much, *ma chérie*. Is this something you would like to do?"

I cannot believe my ears. Is this man that I love and adore asking me to do something ordinary instead of extraordinary? Apparently. I feel my heart running around the bases again. The thought of taking a holiday together, and not going on a mission together, would be a first. How will he explain this? We never meet socially; it's always just about business.

"JP, I don't know what to say. How would we do this? I mean, we've never done this."

233

"I have not heard you say, *oui*," he says.

"*Oui*," I say as fast as I can get the word out of my mouth.

This may be the only time in my life that I will spend with my lover with no other objective than to share each other's company and our bond of love.

Then I ask him, "What do you have in mind for our tryst?" now delighting in the idea of having him all to myself. No Parker, no Sam, no Chad. No, no one from the Agency.

"I have a special place in mind to take you. Let that be a surprise for now. You will need to call your hospital and tell them there have been issues with plane connections, or some kind of delay. You have lied to them all these years, does one more make a *différence*?" he asks, interspacing his French into his English.

Now, why does he have to go and spoil this moment? I hate the lies.

"JP, how long do you think we need to spend in Seoul wrapping things up?"

"I should say a day or two. Much will be dissected after the fact when I leave Asia and get back to headquarters. There will be time later."

*   *   *

As we drive back to Seoul, I consider that maybe I should share more of my life, my past, with Jean Paul. Not that I was aware of what happened to me all those years ago in Colombia. Those are recently recovered memories. I'm still dealing with the fallout. Overwhelming guilt.

No, I will remain silent for now. I have too much to digest with tonight's revelations from John Chi to want to share any more of my history.

My emotions have been trying to regrow roots after all these years. I keep cutting them down, so they can't hurt me. Jean Paul's role has been to fertilize and water my thoughts, and I do see progress during times of self-reflection. There will be opportunities to exchange confidences. Yet, I can't help but think, what else is there to know? I feel wrung out.

I wonder what happened with the case Kelley started telling me about when I had him on the phone in Hong Kong. We never finished the conversation. All I can remember is that he said the patient had a high chloride concentration. I wonder if he checked for bromide poisoning. I'll have to remember to ask him.

As I look over at JP, I can see he's also lost in thought. Sometimes the silence is good. We all need time to hear what's in our own heads before we share it with another. What will the Agency have in store for me for the future? I wonder. Over time, the balance between my academic job and this job has shifted. Will they find my knowledge of poisons and toxins valuable as the world changes? There are new threats every day. I always tell my students that most of the death will come by drugs or bugs. If the illicit drugs that are pushed don't get you, then the bugs will. It is the viruses and bacteria that dominate this world, not us. We just have to learn how to coexist.

JP has the radio on now. Soft music; I don't know what it is. Lovely voices singing. I can see the lights of the city. Beautiful. Neon lights abound, their electrical charge penetrating our car and giving us much needed energy. We are exhausted, mentally and physically. But the bright lights I see in the city and the thought of escaping this reality even for a day or more gives me hope. The U.S. Embassy will soon be in view. I take JP's hand in mine and break the silence.

"JP, are we there yet?" I ask him ever so quietly.

He turns his head, a broad smile on his face, his teeth exposed, and laughs. The laugh I adore.

"My Lily, it depends on what you mean. *Oui*, we are close to the embassy now, but with respect to the rest of our lives, I cannot say. I am not certain that was your question, but you have been quiet for so long, I thought perhaps there was more to it," he says.

I let out a little *ha, ha* out loud, and I can see his smile persisting. So perceptive, this man. I guess it is a bigger question, and I have thought it before. How do you know if you're there, if you have reached your destination, if you don't even know where you are going?

BJ Magnani

Are we at the edge of the universe, or just at its beginning?

CHAPTER 34

FRANCE

"*Ma chérie*, I told you I would take you one day to my childhood place. The beautiful vineyards of Reims," says JP while his foot presses hard on the gas pedal of his small French car.

We speed through the countryside with our windows wide open as the wind wrangles my scarf like an experienced rancher. I can see he enjoys being home, in his country. It is beautiful here. He's right. I ask him to stop so I can take in the sights with my two feet on the ground, but JP is impatient to get to our destination.

As the car rounds the turn, a magnificent chateau looms from the flats capturing my interest and imagination. Its gray Mansard roof, punctured by ornate dormer windows, caps the cream-colored "U" shaped façade below. We inch closer down the driveway seeing cold-hardy flowers of yellow, purple, and pink hugging the edges on either side of the road. The small circular balcony crowning four columns that sequester the front entrance now stands before us. Valets pour out of the building as soon as our car engine quiets down. I can't take my eyes off the majesty. This mythical property created in the early 1900s and once owned by a prominent French family, is surrounded by lush gardens and appointed in French classicism.

"Jean Paul," I say, "this is exquisite."

The chateau is nestled on rolling lawns, edged by trees on the periphery. JP tells me that the head chef here is renowned, a MOF—a Meilleur Ouvrier de France—one of the Best Craftsman in France. It is a prestigious award, and the champagne is without exception. We are, after all, in Champagne country.

My door opens, and a handsome young man asks if he can take my bags. Who am I to say no?

"*Mais oui, merci,*" I reply, and all our luggage is taken into the hotel lobby with JP and me lagging a short distance behind.

Elegant dark wood tones and a grand staircase greet us while twenty-foot tall ceilings tower overhead yielding intricate crystal chandeliers.

"JP, how did you find such a treasure?" I ask.

"*Eh,* Lily, I left Reims as a young boy, but I remember my father driving the countryside many times on a Sunday, and even after we moved, he would occasionally drive back here. *Oui,* the beauty is hard to forget."

* * *

The bags have already been taken to our room. Yes, this time, we have one room, not two rooms with an adjoining door. We are here not as operatives or assets of the government but as two people secured with a pledge of love.

We enter the suite, and I'm immediately taken with the timeless vision of the walls, the pillows, and the bedspread covered in *Toile de Jouy.* Silver fruits and bird patterns on a creamy background encircle the room. The bathroom is also to my liking, the tub large enough for two to soak.

* * *

We enjoy our day sitting in the sun, our view overlooking the Parc, and interacting like any other couple. And yet I know this fantasy can't last for long. I will go back to Boston, and Jean Paul—Jean Paul will go wherever Jean Paul goes until the next time. I find the pain of separation difficult but will try not to let it steal from the moment. The problem is when the moment ceases, it's damn hard to go back to your other life.

We all accommodate and adjust to what life throws at us, and I did just that after my child died. These twists in life mold us into the people we are. I kept that secret deep inside me, buried it, and built a barricade that no one could scale. Except that JP breached the wall and got inside my head and heart. I try and imagine life once again without seeing him daily as I have done these last few weeks. Maybe that's why the fantasy works. Seeing each other every day would be routine, whereas now we intermittently experience danger, intrigue, and love. The light has faded as I sit in deep introspection. I wonder if my dark-haired man with the blue-green eyes would do things differently if he had the chance.

"My Lily, you have been so deep in thought, I did not want to disturb you. But before it gets too late, we should have dinner. The menu looks *magnifique*. Are you hungry?" JP asks.

"Not too hungry at the moment. Would you mind if we dine in our room?" I respond. "I'm enjoying sitting by the fireplace."

"*Oui*, shall I order for both of us?" he says.

So accommodating.

* * *

Dinner is served with candles, roses, and fine silver, and we dine on lobster with caviar, potatoes and watercress, and creamy organic cauliflowers smoked with vine shoots. JP pours the champagne into our glasses filled with raspberries, and we toast to love and peace. Dessert is naturally a chocolate mousse, so delicate that it could float in the air like a cloud. He knows I have a weakness for chocolate, and him.

With dinner over, JP asks if I would like to soak in the tub. I tell him yes, and he retreats to the bathroom to prepare. I can hear the water falling from the Roman faucet, and in my mind, I see the water rising to the edge. Will he surprise me with bubbles or fragrant bath salts? In due time, I pry the door open and peek inside while French music fills the room.

Candles light the window above the bathtub and surround the marble rim. Blueberry vanilla bouquet fills the air, and the subdued light flickers on the tiles like images from a rotating glass disk projector. Ceramic starfish pool at the tub's edge, their center a volcanic core holding a votive candle deep within. Tiny holes trickle down the starfish arms, letting beads of light shine through the dark.

JP takes my hand, and we step into the pristine tub facing each other. We sink into the steamy mist. His head rests at one end, my head at the other, my feet resting on his chest. Large hands clasp my foot in a delicate embrace. Blue-green eyes stare at me from across the bubbly sea, and the tips of my nipples breach the foam. It's a love ballad that fills the air, the French singer's soft voice, that reminds me of how I felt the first time Jean Paul and I made love.

His callused fingers rub the ball of my foot, his thumb episodically pressing back to my heel. In turn, each toe is gently pulled from its root and makes its way to his mouth. I feel his tongue and lips welcome my tired feet, and then suddenly, both his hands pull me toward him. They slide down the inside of my thighs, and I feel his fingers between my legs. My head falls back against the bath pillow, and I know he is watching me even though my eyes are closed. We now each have one leg laying on top of the other's body, forming an X. Soon, I am on top of him gazing into a blue-green ocean, our eyes meeting somewhere in the middle, and we kiss—this wet embrace signaling the start of good things to come. Later, I lay in his arms, spooning in the warmth, watching the candles flicker, while the music fades with the reality that soon we must leave our primordial sea.

* * *

The next morning JP and I make our way to the dining room for breakfast.

"JP, I read that the pastries here are legendary."

His head nods in quiet agreement.

Soon our table has warm croissants, marmalades and jams, chocolate, and French dark roast. JP takes his coffee black, while I make mine light with cream to subdue the dark side. A splash of fresh-squeezed orange juice and a bowl of just-picked berries with fresh whipped cream, *crème fraiche*, complete the experience.

We finish our meal, and JP asks if I would like to take a drive around Reims. Yesterday we drove from Paris to Reims after an uneventful flight from Seoul. This unplanned stop is his gift to me after such a difficult and protracted stay in Asia.

"Jean Paul, where are we going today? It's just so pretty here," I say.

"My Lily, I told you, it is a surprise," says JP.

* * *

Jean Paul Moreau—aka Marchand—considered himself a serious man. He had dedicated his life to his work and both his countries, the United States and France. Their shores, linked together since the beaches of Normandy, blended the sands of world order, each grain a soul for hope. Now, JP wondered if he was at the crossroad that inevitably visits all men. Parker had referred to him several times as 'ol' man' and even though he knew he wasn't old, he wasn't young anymore either. He loved his business and was good at it but questioned if his time chasing evil around the globe would soon be overtaken by more time behind the desk. And then there remained the ever-present dilemma of Lily Robinson. Although she was his soul mate, given his circumstances, JP could never fully, or freely, share himself with her. Today, however, would be a start. He would drive to his boyhood home and, without revealing more than he already had, give her a glimpse of his roots—his beginnings as a young man.

JP had never found the right time to tell Lily about the little girl that was found in the jungle. After he and Parker talked, headquarters had determined that Rose was indeed Lily Robinson's daughter. In an ironic twist that he could still not fully accept, he discovered that his cousin Adrienne Moreau raised Rose as her own after their chance encounter in Colombia. But Parker and headquarters had both missed the vital connection that linked him to Adrienne—at least for now. The team back home was in the process of locating Rose Moreau's whereabouts after leaving the Colombian plantation. It was only a matter of time before this final piece of the puzzle would be exposed. After a short drive, he reached the outstretches of vines that lined the land and defined his origins.

* * *

"JP, what is this place? It's gorgeous," I tell him as we approach an old gothic-looking main building with several smaller outer buildings.

He's been quiet on the drive up, thinking deep thoughts, I'm sure.

"JP, this is a stunning vineyard," I say as he turns off the engine. It's cold outside, and I can just detect the scent of chilled wine in the air.

Neither of us moves from our seats. I don't see any cars here. The place looks deserted.

"Lily, let us walk around the grounds," he says as he opens the car door. "This is the house I lived in with my parents and my aunt and uncle. My grandparents owned the estate. Do you remember when I told you about Reims, Lily?" he asks.

I think for a minute but can't quite remember. There is sadness in his eyes and yet a sense of appreciation. I can feel it.

"I'm not sure, JP. That time when we were back in Boston, I only can remember you telling me your name was Jean Paul. I'm sorry."

He takes my arm and loops it through his as we round the grounds. Not a soul in sight, but someone must be looking after the grapes.

When we get back to the driveway after touring the property, we see that there is a navy-colored car parked next to our rental. JP looks concerned. I observe a man with gray hair, his head popped up just slightly above the steering wheel and sitting in the driver's seat. He is getting out. By the way he is dressed, I'm guessing he's a priest. Before I can say a word, JP squeezes my hand, a signal to let him handle this.

"*Bonjour*," says the man.

Now that he has emerged from the car, I can see that he is dressed in clerical black with a white collar marking his faith.

"*Parlez-vous anglais?*" asks the man before us.

JP fires back in rapid French, and they both agree that we will all speak English.

"I am Père Berger," he says and looks to us for our names.

Before I can say a word, JP uses the same aliases we have been using at the chateau and during our mission in Hong Kong.

"Very nice, doctors. Are you friends of the family?" he asks.

"*Eh*, no. We had some wine from the estate and thought we would find the vineyard on our drive," answers JP.

I have hardly said a word beyond hello. I understand JP doesn't want to give us away.

"Hmm," says Père Berger, "I thought you might be related."

He turns directly to me.

"You look just like the young lady who has come from America to take care of her mother. *Oui*," he muses, "poor soul was in a terrible car accident. We did not know if she would survive."

"Do you mean the mother or the daughter?" I ask, finally adding something.

"*Pardonnez-moi*, I did not make myself clear," he says with embarrassed laughter. "The mother. Her daughter is studying to be a doctor, and from what Dr. Pasteur tells me, she will make a fine one, too," he says.

"Who is Dr. Pasteur?" I ask.

"The doctor who is taking care of Adrienne Moreau," answers Père Berger.

JP is shifting his weight back and forth and is finding this conversation uncomfortable. I don't understand why. Yes, he is a chatty priest, but just being friendly. Then he turns to JP and says, "*Monsieur, le docteur*, you resemble the mistress of the house. She, too, has your dark hair and blue-green eyes. You could be brother and sister."

He lets out a gentle laugh, delighted in his revelations.

"Where is the family now?" I ask.

"*Mon Dieu*, I probably said too much. In the countryside, we all know one another, so I tend to babble. Poor Adrienne is still in hospital in Reims. She will have a long recovery. And Rose, sweet Rose, has returned to Boston to resume her medical studies. You know, Dr. Laurent, you do look just like her. It is the dark hair and jewel-green eyes. *Eh*, green eyes are the rarest eye color in the world, you know. As a priest, I tend to pay attention to eyes, the window to the soul, and your eyes are striking. *Oui*, it is Rose's face I see in your *visage. Pardonnez-moi.* I am sorry you missed her. She just left this morning."

I don't know what to say, but I feel my body shudder when someone utters the name Rose. It's jarring to me. Is it because I can relate to the heartbreak of separation between a mother and daughter? I'm taking this too personally. And yes, only two percent of the world has green eyes. Rare indeed. A coincidence? If this Rose is studying medicine in Boston, should I offer to...? Oh no, JP and I are not who we appear to be. Yet, so tempting. I say it again, a woman named Rose is in medical school and in Boston. I dare not ask any more questions.

I can see JP frozen in place as if his shoes are cemented to the ground. He appears more upset than I am. There's that crinkled brow, the slight flush in the creases of his cheeks; he must be afraid I will spill that I also work in Boston, and in medicine. I get it, JP, I get it. We cannot jeopardize our cover, and this side-trip, as it is, has been a stretch. Yet, I can't help think if only the young woman in Père Berger's story was *my* Rose. But that dream ended long ago. Another fantasy, like my ordinary life with JP, illusion, sequestered in my hidden jewelry box full of wishes. So, I shake Père Berger's hand and say *merci.* He says the same.

We watch the navy car spin out of sight and get back into ours. JP is subdued. He squeezes my hand, leans over, and kisses me. Then strokes my hair. Was it something the gray-haired priest said that got him thinking about his own family? Let me take the first step.

"JP, what was that all about?" I say, my voice sounding a little rattled.

I've never shared with him the story of Rose or her death because the memories had been suppressed for years. All I could ever remember was that she died on my trip to Colombia. I'm a little shaken now. I'll wait for his cue. There's silence. None is forthcoming.

*   *   *

The drive back to the chateau is peaceful. Still feeling sad and unsettled, I now think I need to return to Boston. The fantasy must end.

*   *   *

I pick up the conversation again as we sit for a moment in our suite.

"JP, I need to get back home. I don't know how I can explain such a long absence from the hospital and university. And, well, you know, whenever I do this, this work, I always ask myself why."

"*Je sais, ma chérie,*" is all he says.

He wraps me in his arms and kisses my forehead. I know I am strong and self-determined, but I still like the comfort of his arms around me. I hear and feel his heart beating in my ear, nestled against his chest.

"*Eh, ma chérie,*" he says, moving that stubborn strand of hair away from my eye; it always seems to lose its way from the dark center.

"We need to talk," he continues.

Okay, he is scaring me here. It's his tone. Something is bothering him, something that he is finding difficult to share with me. He seems so serious. Maybe this is where he lets me know the Agency no longer needs my services. I wouldn't be surprised. I have practically been begging for that to happen for the past few years. But then, after my regrets, I'm always drawn back in.

"JP, I can tell something is wrong. I thought as much after you returned from the meeting with Parker in Hong Kong. What is it you have to say? Is the Agency reconsidering its relationship with me? I still believe that I'm a valuable asset to the team."

We are both sitting on the edge of the bed now, and he has his arm around me still. This is the pose someone takes when they want to give you bad news. There's that acid creeping up the back of my throat again. I can taste it now. I turn to look him straight in the eyes. Those blue-green eyes that sparkle with his smile, those eyes that I adore.

245

"Come on, JP, what is it? Has this something to do with our mission? I, I thought in the end, it went well. I have to admit, though, I was truly stunned to learn of Dr. Leigh's involvement. Like you said to me when we were driving back to Seoul, knowing who or what someone really is will change how you feel about them. So, what is it, JP?"

My voice is louder, and the pitch more intense.

"My Lily, it is not about our struggles in Hong Kong and South Korea," he says quietly, "it is something else, something I just learned, but we must discuss."

He pulls me in closer, now both arms surround my body, and I hear and feel my own heart thumping in my chest.

I push away and ask, "JP, what? What?"

"*Eh*, Lily, we need to talk about your time in Colombia, *et*, when you were on that scientific exploration."

Panic fills me. My fingers go numb, and my head is spinning; objects in the room become a blur. Those are recently recovered memories I shared only with my therapist. Memories that were blocked, painful memories of death and abandonment. Memories I tried for years to suppress and feelings I never wanted to face. My child died there. I'm responsible for her death, and I've spent the rest of my life since trying to make up for that. I've not shared this with JP, so how does he know, and why is he bringing this up?

"JP, how do you know about this? We've never talked about it. What's happened?"

I know he can feel me trembling. I look down at my hands, and they are red—the blood of my graduate student, Stuart, and of Maggie, dear Maggie, who looked after my baby—stained them forever.

"Lily," he says, making the two syllables as long as possible, "I believe there was a child recovered from that expedition. She was living on a coffee plantation."

He pauses.

I'm reeling now. What does he mean that a child was recovered from the expedition?

"What child?" I ask, my body going limp.

"*Ma chérie*, that child we believe is alive."

Tears obscure my vision and my mind. I can't comprehend what he is telling me. He strokes my hair as he pulls me into him. I feel his chin resting on my head. Why do men feel better when they don't have to look you in the eye when they share feelings or difficult information?

"Lily, the child's name was Rose," he continues, "she was taken in and raised by the niece of a coffee plantation owner. Lily," he says in almost a whisper, "we have been looking for that child for a while now, and today I think we have found her."

Tears are streaming down my face soaking my blouse; the deluge is so vast. I cannot speak.

"My Lily, I believe the Rose in Père Berger's story is your daughter. *Et*, in the most unbelievable twist of fate, I also believe that she was raised by my cousin, Adrienne Moreau."

The wail that escapes my mouth is so loud and so pitiful that it skims like a rock along the water, making ever-larger ripples as it nears the center. Every mother in the world has lifted her head in sympathetic unity, shaken by my cry. I drift off into the blackness, my eyes close. Another blow to my heart, just between beats.

CHAPTER 35

BOSTON

I feel dead inside now. How do I move forward knowing that for all these years, my daughter was alive? Is it worse knowing that I believed she died, or that I abandoned her in the jungle? And what of Rose? Was there a desire to know who her parents were and speculate why they never came to find her? I'm expecting Jean Paul any minute, and I'm not sure what he will say or, for that matter, what I will say.

Life can bring love and joy, but loneliness creeps in between the seams when relationships are not woven tight. At this point in my life, having Rose with me would be a blessing, but I'm not so sure anymore. She sees Adrienne as her mother, and Adrienne, too, has suffered many blows over the years, from what I understand. Perhaps the best possible course is to let the lie continue. And yet, there is such a strong part of me that wants to connect, no, *needs* to connect, at all costs, with my flesh and blood. I hear a knock at my door. It must be JP. I pull myself together.

"Hey, JP," I say, forcing my arms around him and kissing him on the lips, "come in and sit. Can I get you anything?"

Conflicted feelings cloud my brain.

"*Ma chérie,*" he says, hugging me in one of those bear hugs because he knows I need the security of his body engulfing mine.

We sit on the couch together. The Boston apartment is muted in grays and crimson, and the chenille sofa feels soft as I swing my feet under me.

"Lily, I know this has been difficult for you. But we need to agree on some details. I have some information for you," he says, moving his body to face me.

His eyes look sad. Those dark shadows are circling under his lower eyelids.

"Go ahead, JP. What is it?" I respond. My breathing is shallow.

"It is about Rose. We have located her," he says.

Now I've perked up. There's that thumping in my chest again. I'm sitting straighter, my shoulders are back, my eyes wide open, and I wait.

"Yes, JP, where is she?" I ask, now breathless.

"*Eh*, Lily, as you know, she is living in Boston. She is going to medical school at one of the universities right here in the city," JP says, trying to drag this out.

"Yes, JP, we know this. Where is she enrolled?" I ask, swinging my leg out from under me and tapping my foot on the rug.

"Rose is attending, *eh*, attending *your* medical school, Lily," he says, almost in a whisper brushing my hair away from my eyes.

For a few seconds, the world doesn't move. How long have I been this close and never made the connection? And why? Because I was too busy, too wrapped up in the government's work. I feel my heart pounding and spring off the couch.

"JP, what is her address in Boston? I need to find a way to meet with her, to explain everything. This is just wrong. It's all so wrong."

JP gets up from the couch, too. He grabs my wrists to pull me in. There is no smile on his face, and I feel his heavy breath.

"Lily, *écoute*. Please listen to me. This will be the hardest thing you have ever done in your life. For Rose's safety, you have to let her go," he says.

I can't believe what I'm hearing. No, no, this will not happen.

"No, JP. I lost her years ago, and now that I found her, I need to reach out and hold her, tell her everything that has been trapped inside my mind and heart for more than twenty years. How can you possibly think I will just let her go? I don't want to lose her all over again."

Tears are blocking my vision. The room looks blurry. I pull out of his embrace, the register of my voice rising, and walk across the room to escape this confrontation.

"I know you are upset, but you will put Rose in danger if it is revealed

249

that you are her biological mother. You know this, Lily. You know what I am saying to you is true. *C'est vrai?*" he says, and I feel the strain in his voice as he tries to reach me.

I'm back on the couch now. Full circle around the room, spinning on my toes, shoes off. I see them nestled in the corner begging for occupation, but I ignore their plea.

"You're right, JP. And I hate you for being right," I bark back as I wipe away the tears slowly flowing drop by drop down my cheeks. "I know."

"Could you not mentor her, befriend her, and let that be enough?" he asks. His head is bowed in dismay.

"Enough? How do you make up for all the years that I wasn't there to hold her in my arms, to dry her tears when she was frightened, to walk her to school on her first day, to mark her growth on the door frame with a pencil, to…"

"Stop, Lily. *Assez*. Even in your absence, Rose has thrived. Just look at where she is today. This young woman, despite all odds, is now in medical school, and from what Père Berger told us, will become a fine doctor. Perhaps the best doctor, under your watchful eye," says JP.

I see a tear or two in his eyes. He's not a man without feeling, but like me, needs to blunt emotion to get through life.

"Rose has your strength, your mind, your inquisitiveness, and under the loving hand of my cousin, has blossomed," he says, taking a big sniff to clear away the congestion, and then adds, "When do you go back to teach at the medical school?"

"I have a lecture next week, and I have some cases to review with Kelley. Why?" I ask.

"My Lily, you need to be prepared for the inevitable meeting that will occur. Resiliency is part of your make-up, too. Never have I met such a woman with your courage," JP says, taking me in his arms once again.

Yes, tomorrow is another day, and there is no present like the time.

*　*　*

"You're back!" exclaims Lisa. "I didn't know you were coming in today," she says, popping up from her desk like a just-released spring. "Here, let me get the door for you; oh, and I stacked the mail on your desk," she says while she unlocks my office.

"Boy, Dr. Kelley is sure going to be glad to see you. He's been so busy with cases and students, and—"

"Sorry to interrupt, Lisa," I say, tamping down the enthusiasm. "Would you mind? I need a little time to review my mail and gather my thoughts after the conference. And I'm a little jet-lagged, too."

"Of course, Dr. Lily. Let me know when you want me to go over your schedule. I had to rearrange several meetings since you didn't get back when we planned. How awful that you had such difficulty making your connections. Travel can be so unpredictable, and to think you had all these delays after your conference. I—"

"Lisa," I interrupt once again, "Thank you, but can we catch up a little later, please?"

"Sorry. I'm just so excited to see you. Okay, I'll pull the door shut on my way out," says Lisa as she walks out of my office.

She really is a gem; I just need some time to readjust. When you get back on dry land after being at sea for a while, you sometimes feel as if the boat is still rocking. I feel the waves under my feet now and need to sit down so I don't fall over. Being out at sea separates you from your solid surroundings. The farther you move away from the shore, the harder it is to have a sense of wellbeing. There have been times that I have been gone when coming back wasn't so hard. But this time, this time it's different. This time, Rose is also on my mind. A knock at my door. Again, dear Lisa? We really can catch up later.

"Come in," I say.

The door opens an inch or two, and Kelley manages to stick a nose through. "Hey, so glad you are back. We weren't expecting you for another day or so, so this is a surprise. Lisa said not to disturb you, sorry, but it's just so good to have you back."

"Oh, Kelley," I say, actually surprised it's not Lisa, "I'm just exhausted, that's all, and I need to get through all the snail mail and email, you know," I respond.

"I know, I know. Okay, but we've had some incredible cases, and there's a new medical student who's interested in pathology and lab medicine, and you know, that's a rare find. I'm dying for you to meet her," says Kelley, the enthusiasm in his voice is almost overwhelming.

I close my eyes, blocking the sound and light like I'm nursing a hangover. But it's just the emotion.

"Thanks. But not now, Kelley. Maybe a little later in the week. I'm just so behind."

Kelley sees my face and knows me well enough that he needs to back away. So, he does.

"See you later, Doc," he says as he pulls the door shut, and with that, I am in silence once again.

*   *   *

My lecture is prepared, and I'm ready for the medical students. It's been a week since I've been back and it stills feels strange. I'm a different person now. Not the same Dr. Lily Robinson I was just a few months ago. There's a knock at the office door. Kelley and I have some cases to review.

"Hey, Doc. You ready for a couple of cases?" he asks.

"Sure, Kelley. What have you got?" I ask.

"First, we have a seventy-six-year-old man who was admitted to the medicine service, confused, dehydrated, and in metabolic acidosis. They ruled out sepsis, pneumonia, and any GI illness. When I spoke with the attending, I suggested a serum tox screen and guess what popped up?" asks Kelley.

"Salicylates?" I answer.

"Damn, you went right for it!" he exclaims. "But here's the odd part. There is no known source for the aspirin ingestion. He doesn't use any, and his daughter confirms that there is no aspirin in the house. So, what do you think?"

"Let's go see him, Kelley." And we leave the confines of my office to travel to the realm of the inpatients.

As we wait for the elevator, Kelley starts another conversation.

"I don't think I've seen those shoes before," he says, eyeing my rainbow heels.

"Oh, I picked these up during my recent travels. Like camouflage for the jungle."

"So, Dr. Robinson, you haven't talked much about the conference. Was it a bust or what?"

It's the lying that I hate.

"No, Kelley, it was fine. Not as big a turnout as I expected. Some interesting new marine toxins, but that's about it."

Does he wonder about my subdued attitude? Residual dew from the sticky sadness that inhabits my mind.

"Here we are, room 152," I say to Kelley as I pump the hand sanitizer and then make an introduction.

"Hello, Mr. Chen. I'm Dr. Robinson, and this is my colleague Dr. Kelley. How are you feeling today?" I ask.

I've already reviewed his chart in the electronic medical record, and I know he's been getting an IV with sodium bicarbonate and dextrose. By now, we have the translator in our room who is helping us with communication. She lets me know that Mr. Chen says he is doing well.

"Can you please ask Mr. Chen what ointments or lotions he's been using?" I ask the translator.

"Doc, I met with the team earlier, and he wasn't taking any over-the-counter medications," Kelley says.

I nod my head toward Kelley then turn to the interpreter, who is having a conversation with Mr. Chen. I can see him talking to her while he is rubbing each arm up and down with his hands as if he is describing massaging body lotion onto his limbs. I wait patiently for the interpreter to let me know what he is saying.

"Doctor, Mr. Chen says he uses an oil to rub onto his achy joints. He says it helps his arthritis," she tells me.

I make a request that when she sees his daughter, to ask her to bring in the bottle, and let us know when it's here.

"Thank you for your help," I say, and we pump our way out of the room.

"What are you thinking?" Kelley asks me as we head back down to the lab.

"I think he has been using oil of wintergreen for his joint pain. It's used as an analgesic. I know that they sell it in a shop down in Chinatown."

"Oil of wintergreen?" questions Kelley.

"Yes, just one teaspoon of concentrated oil of wintergreen contains about five grams of methyl salicylate, which is equivalent to maybe seven and a half grams of aspirin. The use of topical salicylates is not uncommon, and he was probably using more than the directed amount," I say.

"So, he was absorbing salicylates through the skin. Wow. The skin does have the largest surface area of any organ in the body, so I guess it makes sense," says Kelley. "Good catch, Doc."

*   *   *

My lecture is coming up tomorrow. Like JP said, I need to be prepared for the inevitable. Will Rose sit in the seats close to the podium, or is she one of those students that teeter on the auditorium's topmost section? Will I be obvious if I scrutinize all the students as they walk in? Will my hesitation give me away? I can feel my foot tapping on the floor in typewriter fashion.

Another knock at the door. It's been so hard to get things accomplished this week with all the interruptions. Lisa has gone overboard, setting up meetings to try and fill the void. I'm sure this is another one of her queries on what comes next.

"Yes, come in," I say gently, fully prepared to let Lisa have her way and review her list with me of all things that must happen in the next two weeks.

"Um, Dr. Robinson. I'm sorry to bother you, but your assistant said it would be okay if I just said hello and set up another time to meet with you. I've loved your lectures, and you're the reason I want to go into pathology. Dr. Kelley has been so helpful and…"

254

I look up from my writing, not hearing the rest of her speech. It takes every ounce of strength in me to keep myself bound behind my desk because every impulse in my body says leap forward and embrace what's before me. I see her now. Beautiful long dark hair, emerald-green eyes, and a certain kindness in her voice. My heart is exposed. I can feel it in my chest, choking on the blood rushing in.

"Yes, hello. I have a minute. You are one of our medical students?" I start slowly, tiptoeing as if I were walking on rice paper.

"Oh, sorry. My name is Rose Moreau, and I'm a first-year medical student. Could I ask your assistant to set up an appointment with you for a later time?" she asks.

I'm mesmerized. I can't take my eyes off of this young woman. My baby. And then her phone rings to break the spell.

"Oh, excuse me, Dr. Robinson. I need to take this call. It's from overseas," she says and stands up abruptly, heading toward my office door.

But before she crosses the threshold, I hear a gasp. A sharp pain has just pierced Rose's being. I feel it. My instinct cannot be shut down.

"Rose, what is it? Are you all right?" I ask, trembling at our interaction.

Rose turns around and looks at me. Our eyes meet, and I can see disquiet behind her gaze. Is it sadness, is it…?

"It's my mother," Rose blurts out, tears welling up and clinging to the edge. "She's awake," Rose adds, the tears now ignoring the boundaries and spilling forth without hesitation. Rose's face is wet with emotion.

I move in and take this stranger, yet not a stranger, in my arms to comfort her. Yes, her mother is awake. With every bone in my body.

ABOUT THE AUTHOR

BJ Magnani (Dr. Barbarajean Magnani, PhD, MD, FCAP) is the author of the Dr. Lily Robinson Novels: *The Queen of All Poisons* (Encircle Publications, 2019), and *The Power of Poison* (Encircle Publications, 2021), book two in the series. *Lily Robinson and the Art of Secret Poisoning*, the original collection of short stories featuring the femme fatale doctor, will be re-released by Encircle Publications in 2021.

Dr. Magnani is internationally recognized for her expertise in clinical chemistry and toxicology, has been named a "Top Doctor" in Boston magazine, and was named one of the Top 100 Most Influential Laboratory Medicine Professionals in the World by The Pathologist. She is currently Professor of Anatomic and Clinical Pathology (and Professor of Medicine) at Tufts University School of Medicine, Boston, MA, and serves as the Chair of the College of American Pathologists (CAP) Toxicology Committee. Follow BJ Magnani on Facebook.

Questions for
Book Clubs and Reading Groups

How would you describe the protagonist, Lily Robinson?

Do you feel she has a compelling voice?

How do you feel about Lily's conflict between her Hippocratic Oath and the oath to her country?

Do you agree with Lily's mantra that "the good of the many outweighs the good of the one"?

What characters did you identify with? Or like?

What plot twists were unexpected?

What emotions did the antagonists (Markovic and Stone) evoke in you?

The Power of Poison contains some "Easter Eggs."
Consider the following:

Alexis' flat number is 303

Stone's hotel room number is 12-258

Stone's hospital room number 256

Markovic's flat number while in South Korea is 224

Mr. Chen's hospital room number is 152

What is the significance of each of these numbers?

See the next page for the answer.

Each of the numbers represents the Molecular Weight (MW) of a drug or toxin associated with the character. The MW is the sum of the atomic weight values of atoms in a molecule (for example, the number of atoms of carbon, hydrogen, nitrogen, or oxygen multiplied by each of the individual atomic weights that make up one compound.)

Here are the MWs of some of the drugs and compounds (expressed as g/mol) used in *The Power of Poison:*

Cocaine	303.35
Cicutoxin	258.35
Lamotrigine	256.09
Methyl salicylate	152.15
Novichok A-234	224.22

For Additional Reading on Toxicology and Poisons:

Magnani, BJ
Lily Robinson and the Art of Secret Poisoning
nVision Press, 2011, New York, NY, 135 pages

Magnani BJ, Kwong T, McMillin G and Wu A, Editors
Clinical Toxicology Testing: A Guide for Laboratory Professionals
(Second Edition)
CAP Press, Northfield, IL, 2020, 376 pages

Kwong TC, Magnani BJ, Rosano TG, Shaw LM, Editors
The Clinical Toxicology Laboratory: Contemporary Practice of Poisoning Evaluation. (Second Edition)
AACC Press, Washington D.C., 2013, 525 pages

Magnani, BJ and Woolf, A.
"Cardiotoxic Plants" in
Critical Care Toxicology, Diagnosis and Management of the Critically Poisoned Patient
Brent J, Burkhart K, Dargan P, Hatten B, Megargane B, and Palmer R. Eds.(Second Edition) Springer International Publishing, 2017
Pages 2187-2203

George, David
Poisons, An Introduction for Forensic Investigators
CRC Press, Boca Raton, FL, 2018, 385 pages

If you enjoyed reading this book,
please consider writing your honest review
and sharing it with other readers.

Many of our Authors are happy to participate in
Book Club and Reader Group discussions.
For more information, contact us at info@encirclepub.com.

Thank you,
Encircle Publications

For news about more exciting new fiction, join us at:

Facebook: www.facebook.com/encirclepub

Twitter: twitter.com/encirclepub

Instagram: www.instagram.com/encirclepublications

Sign up for Encircle Publications newsletter and specials:
eepurl.com/cs8taP

CPSIA information can be obtained
at www.ICGtesting.com
Printed in the USA
LVHW021028160321
681669LV00008BA/137